To. Glen
The bestest
all. But me [signature]

RACK AND RUIN

Email:
Destroyagear @ hotmail.com

RACK AND RUIN
ISBN 978-1-4637623-9-1

For bulk order prices or any other inquiries, please visit www.rackandruinbook.com

RACK AND RUIN

GLENN R. SUGGITT

A NOVEL

For all the men and women who served in Iraq, it was my pleasure to know and work with you. For all my friends and loved ones who helped me with editing and made this book a labor of fun.

Thank you.

CHAPTER 1

Market Day

There were few places on the globe more dangerous than a crowded market square in Samarra, Iraq and it was not a particularly nice summer day to be out and about with the temperatures reaching 135 Fahrenheit. Dakar thought it was a far cry from the coolness of his summers in the mountains of Idaho. Early evening brought some respite; it had cooled a few degrees as the sun rapidly fell towards the west. Dakar and Mick, the other member of his team, both worked for a private security company making sure no harm came to Tariq al-Hashimi, provincial governor of Samarra, a Sunni and an honest, sincere man—a rare commodity in this country.

Dakar stood under an awning not far from Tariq and Mick. His job was to keep an eye on the crowd. He was grateful for the shade and the cold water he had brought with him. The cooler was stacked with water bottles and ice. They both needed to drink lots of water: at least four or five one-liter bottles a day. To do otherwise meant heat stroke and being out of the game for days—or worse yet, being sent home. Dakar looked over to Mick, who shadowed Tariq closely.

Mick was a squat, middle aged, ex-SAS Scot, who could be mistaken for a small armored vehicle. He had an acid wit and was a very good soldier, more suited to combat than babysitting, as he called the security work he and Dakar did. Mick looked miserable, as sweat poured off his face in the direct sun. Dakar yelled at him, "Sure is cool here in the shade."

Mick answered, in his typical cheerful manner, "Fuck you, Dakar."

Tariq moved among the crowd easily and received, as always, a warm welcome from his own Sunni tribesmen and women. Dakar, nonetheless, kept a close watch; the open air market provided an excellent opportunity for an assassin to strike. It was Tariq's most vulnerable time. The market was crowded with people making last-minute deals and packing up, as the day ended. The heat of the day gave the market a slightly rotten smell, as the fruit and vegetables deteriorated.

The edge of Dakar's nostrils burned ever so slightly when he sucked in the oven hot air. He was thankful for his sunglasses, which not only protected his eyes from the glare, but also from the wind that would otherwise make his eyelids feel like they were being bombarded by a blast furnace. Soon the mosques would be calling the faithful to prayers over a multitude of loud speakers everywhere. There were lots of mosques and lots of true believers, a deadly combination for violence.

Dakar watched the milling people closely as Tariq worked the crowd, shook hands, embraced friends and joked with everyone. Dakar sensed a wrongness in the air. Something was amiss and that something caught Dak's eye. Just at the edge of his vision, the movement pattern was off and there was a slight change in the din. Glancing casually to his left, he picked out a middle-aged, frail man dressed in ragged, loose fitting clothing moving slowly but deliberately towards Tariq. The haunted, frightened look in his eyes was not right. Engrossed in his progress through the crowd, the man had not noticed Dak glance in his direction. Dakar was careful not to give away his obvious interest in the man by looking his way. He watched him out of the corner of his eye. The frail looking man stared for a moment to his left and Dakar caught who he was looking at. A younger, bearded man nodded almost imperceptibly back at him.

The frail looking man was perhaps fifty feet away and made deliberate progress through the square towards Tariq. Dakar flicked the safety off his rifle and waited. As the man hit the thirty foot mark, Dak raised his rifle and fired a single shot straight through the head of the man, who crumpled straight to the ground. Dakar then swung his rifle over and shot the second man, who stood frozen for a second in his tracks by the sound of the sudden gunshot, before dropping to the ground himself, after the bullet passed through his brain.

General pandemonium, screaming and a rush away from the gunshots ensued as people scrambled for safety, fearing, as was usually the case, a suicide bomber. A woman screamed from behind the frail looking man. She had been sprayed with brains and blood, and her black chador, face and veil were covered from the shot as it passed through the man's head. However, she was unharmed, as was her son, who held desperately onto her hand, looking terrified and bewildered by what had happened.

Mick reacted instinctively to take the governor to the ground.

Dakar scanned the crowd to see if there were other threats and noticing none, yelled to Mick, "GO, GO, GO!!"

Mick pulled Tariq up and hustled him off to the waiting armored SUV and out of the market to safety.

Dakar strode the few steps to the first body. He had to know, had to see for himself, whether he had killed innocent men or saved Tariq's life, as well as his own and many others. He opened the garments of the first man he had shot. There it was—a suicide vest. A nasty little thing, undoubtedly packed with explosives and nails and bits of metal, made to shred them all to bits if the bomber had flicked the tiny switch clutched in his right hand. A crude weapon, but very effective. Dakar went to the second man and found in his hand a small transmitter. He guessed it was a backup to detonate the bomb should the first man fail to press the switch when the time came.

Many in the crowd gasped at the sight of the exposed bomb, and stared in disbelief and relief. Turning they murmured and gestured to others around them. Dakar's eyes locked with an Iraqi man in the crowd, who nodded ever so slightly in a gesture of gratitude. Dakar felt relieved that his instincts had been correct. At least today he wouldn't be another murdering American. The Iraqi police hurried over, clearing the crowd out of the market far away from the bodies.

Dakar headed to the other SUV and back to Patrol Base Olsen, where Mick was now en route with Tariq. Dak called in the incident, so Explosive Ordinance Disposal could diffuse the bomb.

Throughout the entire incident, Dakar's emotional and physiological state never changed. These past few years, danger, either real or imagined, affected him little. In fact, he became calmer, more focused, intuitive, and in his own way, more deadly at his job.

During his time in the army and a previous stint in Iraq, Dakar's intuition had become frightening, almost psychic on occasion. He was nowhere near the fittest soldier in his squad or the best marksman. Today's shots were more luck than skill, although from short distances they were easy: two shots, two kills. Some might have missed, even at that close range, with so much on the line, and ninety-nine out of a hundred would not have taken the shots on such a vague feeling of unease. But in the past six years, Dak had learned to trust his instinct and it hadn't let him down yet.

You would also be hard-pressed to find a more easygoing guy than Dakar Raymond Anderson. His mother had given him the name Dakar because she thought it sounded exotic, just before she had left for parts unknown. She'd OD'd a few years later in a Los Angeles crack house. After high school, Dak had followed in his dad's footsteps, becoming an electrician and a union member like his father. He joined the army at twenty-five and served four years. Dakar was not a big man; standing barely five-foot, six-inches tall and weighing in at one hundred and forty-two pounds, his physique could best be described as muscularly lean. He looked completely average, other than his green eyes that seemed to penetrate everything he looked at.

The military had given him something to do, to keep busy at, and it had kept him relatively fit. Dakar's coolness, innate intelligence and relaxed demeanor made him a sergeant quickly. His commanding officer wanted him to join the ROTC program and become an officer. By that time, Dakar had already decided he was getting out of the army. Dakar's two tours in Iraq had been uneventful. His squad trusted him and obeyed his commands without question, and there was little they would not do for him—or he for them.

Fortunately, no one had died or even been wounded in his squad, although they had been in several life-threatening situations. An IED (improvised explosive device) could have killed many in his squad, but his intuition had told him to back off, not to go down that street, so they didn't. The insurgents had set the IED off anyway, but his squad was too far away to be affected. Dakar had handled another insurgent ambush by having an airstrike hit the building the insurgents were holed up in, reducing it to a pile of rubble. Dakar and his squad had managed to stay safe and complete all their missions, unlike other so-called elite units, who managed to end up in firefights and suffer casualties.

After that, Dakar had decided that it was time to move on, so he had tried civilian life. But he wasn't making the kind of money he could in Iraq, and Dakar missed being there, so when Alliance Security International had an opening, he took it. Life on the base as a civilian military contractor with ASI was easier in some respects than his time in the military in Iraq. He was not subject to military orders or discipline, and had a good relationship with the base commander, Captain Michael Murphy, whom he called Murph, but only in private. He had done some favors for Murph.

They had shared a bottle of cheap Turkish liquor one night and swapped war stories. Murph liked Dakar and he liked Murph because of the respect he showed his men. It was against the rules to consume alcohol and the penalties were severe, but everything was against the rules in Iraq.

Strictly speaking, Dakar shouldn't have shot the men in the market today. There had been no clear indication of imminent harm or danger. But he'd recognized the determined, deadly look in the man's eyes from another suicide bomber he'd dealt with during his first deployment to Iraq. That one had detonated his bomb too early and too far away to hurt anyone. From the sadness in that would-be bomber's eyes, he suspected the man didn't have the heart to kill anyone but himself. Dakar thought that regardless of age, race, ethnic background or nationality, most men could not kill mindlessly. There had to be a compelling personal reason. Dakar knew from experience, it was harder still to commit suicide. The will to live was such a powerful instinct.

Dakar waved at Specialist Sanchez, the sentry at the gate, and the Humvee blocking the gate drove out of the way, allowing him into the compound. On the way back to the base, Dakar had used the satellite phone to call Holly, at the ops center in Newark, and give ASI a heads-up on what had happened. They were grateful that Tariq was OK, and of course wanted Dakar's written report pronto. He would fudge it a bit and say he had glimpsed tell-tale wires and explosives when the man's jacket had slipped open while he made his way across the market. Couldn't have them thinking he'd killed the guy on a hunch, could he?

He swung out of the front seat and bellowed at Murph, "Hey, Captain! You missed all the fun."

"I heard," Murph answered. "And you can keep all that fun for yourself." He smiled. "You okay?"

"Yeah, I'm fine, Captain," Dakar said. Murph knew he was, because he was Dakar. Their relationship was more than just one bottle of whiskey—Dakar helped Murph whenever he could. He spoke a little Arabic, and had aided with insights and information about the whereabouts of guns and munitions. Once he had noticed subtle inconsistencies about a house in the north end of Samarra when they drove by it one day. He saw tension in the face of the man exiting the door, and the house looked staged as it was in its use and appearance. Murph sent a squad to raid the home and found a cache of weapons. It looked good for Murph to find the weapons and Dakar couldn't care less about who got the credit.

An old Iraqi casino building now served as HQ and dwellings for the one hundred and thirty-four men and women on base. Besides the main casino building, where Dak had a room, Patrol Base Olsen had a collection of portable containerized housing units—and ramshackle plywood huts constructed by Air Force construction crews. All the rooms were air conditioned, and the whole base was powered by large electrical generators fuelled by the diesel fuel that supplied the vehicles, aircraft and generators in Iraq. Patrol Base Olsen, located on the banks of the Tigris River near the edge of

Samarra, had several portable latrine and shower units and even three or four small, spin-dry washers for laundry.

Dakar strode to the Tactical Operations Center and knocked on the door. He would never enter the TOC uninvited. First Sergeant Laskins, a small nervous man who sweated profusely even in the air conditioning, opened the door.

"Hey Dak," Laskins greeted him. "I heard. Deakins and I will meet you here in an hour for a debriefing. You probably need some grub and a little time."

"Thanks. I should hit the DFAC line and get something to eat before it closes," Dakar said. One truly great thing about PB Olsen was the food, which was outstanding. Unlike the overcooked, bland food served at other bases, the cook here took pride in what he served and preparation was everything.

Dakar took the few steps from the TOC door to the dining facility, and as he opened the door he could see Tariq and Mick sitting down eating. Tariq was visibly shaken. Dakar walked to him, put his hand on his shoulder, and said, *"Insha' Allah"*—if it is the will of Allah. Dakar understood exactly what that meant in its entirety and practiced an acceptance of life as it came.

Tariq rose and embraced him, kissing him on both cheeks, and whispered in his ear, "Thank you, my friend." Most men would have been offended or uncomfortable at the thought of another man hugging or kissing them, but Dakar accepted it as an expression of the high regard the two men had for each other, which manifested itself in a gesture of friendship and gratitude.

It was Italian night and Dakar got a plate of tasty looking spaghetti and meatballs, covered it in parmesan cheese, and then joined them. "That was as close as we've ever had it, Tariq," he said, sitting down.

"How could you have known? What tipped you off? What if you had missed?" Tariq asked, in a flurry.

"Don't know for sure—he just didn't look right. And I guess we all get one lucky shot in our lives." Dakar continued, "Officially, I saw wires and the hint of explosives."

"One, you shot twice and both died! If this casino were still open, I would bring you as a lucky—how you call it?—charm, Mr. Dakar."

"Don't count on me being on a lucky streak every day, Tariq."

"You have been for me, Dakar—you are my lucky charm."

Dinner was over, and Dak wandered back to his room for a rest before the interrogation, which the army liked to call a debriefing. He passed Simmons in the hall: beautiful, shapely, sexy, smiling Sergeant Alicia Simmons who turned him on by who she was and how she used that body of hers. "Hi, Dak. Glad you made it back alive. Want some company later?" she said, after making sure no one was listening.

That was Simmons, direct and to the point, and yes, thank you, he could use some company at 22:00. The assignations were always in his room. Simmons shared her room with another woman. Here was another rule he was breaking: having a relationship with someone in the military. Perhaps people knew. He didn't care. No one asked; they didn't broadcast the fact and would deny the affair, if asked. A sort of weird twist to the US military policy of "don't ask, don't tell," he thought. Hey, that was funny. He would use that in a joke somehow. Ten feet later was his door and he flopped onto the bed, suddenly tired. Perhaps it did affect him; the killing and death had made him tired afterwards. He pulled back the blanket to crawl under the covers and found his bed had been short sheeted, no doubt by Simmons who seemed to revel in tormenting him with her practical jokes. With twenty-five minutes to go before he had to meet Laskins and Deakins, the CIA mole—or was that mouse?—he flicked on the TV and CNN came to life.

"The president today assured the nation that we are on the road to recovery in spite of another downturn in the stock market, which he referred to as a market correction," the talking head drawled. What else was new? The economic downturn was still playing itself out. Everyone hoped that the worst was over. A power nap of fifteen or twenty minutes helped him focus, and he left for the debriefing, clear-headed and ready to lie his little ass off.

At 22:00, Simmons walked into his room and his arms. She asked him, "Did you enjoy my surprise?" and then giggled afterwards.

"I'll wipe that smirk off your face, Simmons!!" Dakar countered. He loved kissing her and she was an extraordinary lover. He loved the taste of her. How she felt wrapped around him when he was inside her and especially her multiple orgasms that seemed to go on forever. They lay, as the cliché goes, wrapped up in each other's arms till a little after 23:00 and then she was gone. There was never any discussion or thought about love or anything long-term; nothing except the here and now. Simmons would go home to her husband and son, and he would move on to another place and another woman, wanting only the promise of what was now.

Dakar had turned the TV on again, after Simmons had left his room, and the economy was in the news. This time it was a story about some small place in Kentucky, where a bank had run out of cash in the bank machine one weekend. Rumors of the bank's shaky condition had started and on Monday when the bank opened, the good folks of Bowling Green were lined up in front of the doors to get their money out before it went under. The police were called to disperse the crowd and it had gotten ugly with several of the townsfolk threatening to get their guns and return to the bank to get the money owed them.

CHAPTER 2

Teddy Goes to Washington

A llan Theodore Braxton worked in the US Congressional Budget Office as an economic analyst; a fortunate state of affairs for him, after graduating from university with a Masters in Economics and Mathematics. Actually, he was an actuary and quite good at his job. As an avid supporter and hard worker in the campaign that elected President Haines, he had earned the job. Teddy was a bear of a man, six-foot, four-inches in height, two hundred and forty-five pounds and not an inch of fat on him. People were intimidated in his presence in spite of his odd constant chuckling as he spoke. His red curly hair drooped to and fro over his ears like a hat that was two sizes too big for him, his size thirteen shoes were always out of style. His face and body were covered in freckles both large and small. His stature and look were so unlikely for a man of his intelligence.

His job was to run the numbers, the projections on the economy for a multitude of scenarios and conditions using data supplied to him from many government departments and pollsters. The most recent numbers were not looking good. The longer the recession lasted, the greater the chance of a larger breakdown, perhaps even a catastrophic collapse of the economy. In addition the more unstable the economic situation became, the greater the degree of error his results had. His work was classified and only for the eyes of the innermost circle of the administration.

The latest meeting of the cabinet had been frightening in its mood of desperation; the administration was clearly worried about the direction and ferocity of the economic crisis that still gripped the United States and by extension the rest of the world. The economic stimulus package given to major banks and financial institutions was well beyond the capacity of the federal government to fund or repay the huge fourteen trillion dollar debt the country had accumulated. The worst part was the fixes didn't seem to be working. Much of the American economy rested on confidence and Americans had little confidence in the fix. The government was reacting swiftly to each individual incident of economic instability or crisis—such as the recent run on that small bank in Kentucky—and had elaborate plans in place for even more disastrous economic conditions. Thoughtful Republicans and Democrats were both worried, with good reason. Teddy had been summoned to the office of the director for a meeting and not now, but RIGHT NOW!

He sauntered into the director's office ten minutes later and was ushered in.

"What the fuck is this?" Director Corson raged, waving a sheaf of papers at him.

"We can't take this shit to the president. You need to change this and now," he bellowed, stabbing his finger into Teddy's chest forcefully.

Teddy was a great worker and loyal to the core, but he did not react well to intimidation, especially given his size. He batted the director's hand away and told him pointedly, "Keep your fucking hands off me and don't yell at me. I don't do it to you, so don't do it to me!"

When he was in one of his moods, Director Corson was not accustomed to being spoken back to and stood stunned for a moment before muttering, "Have a seat, Teddy."

His mood suddenly somber, he said, "Teddy, the president isn't going to like this negative shit. For Christ's sake, can't you change these numbers? Surely you must have made a mistake."

"I've checked and rechecked the raw data, the formulas, and this is as good as it gets. In fact it could be worse, even more pessimistic or some might say, more realistic, if the trends continue the way they are and there's no indication they won't," Teddy replied.

Corson remained silent for some time and then looked Teddy straight in the eye and declared, "Well, I'm not taking this to the president and he has come to rely on your little reports and guesses. In fact, he wants to meet you. It seems your crystal ball has been uncannily accurate in the last year or so. Today at the White House, 4:00 PM, son."

He noticed a small smile on Director Corson's face as he closed the door behind him and heard the director mumble to himself, "Man's got some balls. Smart as a whip and what's better, no Washington bullshit about him."

That left Teddy four hours to prepare. No use pretending he wasn't apprehensive. His hands were shaking as he left the director's office. First thing he would do was call his best friend in the whole wide world, Dakar, and tell him he was going to meet the president. They had grown up together and remained tight ever since they were eleven years old. Almost completely different in their appearance, lifestyles and jobs, their friendship was still one of the most important things in his life, and he was entirely loyal to his friend of all these years. Dakar's father had been a father to him also. He was grateful for the way Dakar's dad treated him and made him part of his family. Teddy's father was a garden variety alcoholic, whose only concern was the next drink, with no time or kindness in his soul for him or any of his siblings. He died an alcoholic's death, when Teddy was twelve. He died drunk; he died alone, at the end of a rope in their garage. His mother was barely able to feed and clothe the family after that. Teddy clung to the memory of the man who treated him as one of his own and his death had been almost as severe a blow to him as Dakar. And when Dakar had entered his darkness it was Teddy who stood with him, listened, hugged him when he cried and stayed with his friend when he needed him.

Teddy was grateful Dakar had given him the money for his university tuition from his father's meager estate and appreciated that Dak had introduced him to Rosie, his fiancée. Dakar knew they would like each other and he was right. This fall they would marry, have 3.78 children and live happily ever after if he had his way. He was as crazy about Rosie as she was about him.

He dialed Dak's satellite phone number, realizing too late that it was almost midnight in Iraq. *Oh well,* he thought, *the son of a bitch shouldn't be in bed that early.*

Dakar picked up the phone. "Only you would call me at midnight, Teddy. What happened? Did you knock her up?"

"No buddy, that would be really good news. However, yours truly is going to meet the president this afternoon by special request," Teddy replied.

"Only you would think knocking up your girlfriend is good news. How did you get by the security check? Will you be handcuffed when you see the president? You will frighten the shit out of the poor man, you big gorilla," Dakar said and laughed.

"Look, I've got to get ready. Just called to make sure you hadn't been blown to bits yet. And you need your beauty sleep, unless you're in the process of banging that sergeant. Hey, haven't you made enough money? Time for you to come home, don't you think?" Teddy remarked.

"Just six months more and I'll have my three hundred grand and more, which is lots for me," Dakar ventured.

"Why not just come home now? You have lots of money. Rosie and I miss you," Teddy asked.

"Think I'll stay, Teddy, but thanks for missing me. Talk soon." Dakar hung up the satellite phone. It was hooked up to the external antenna, and he got exceptional reception and clarity when it was connected that way. That was a little odd of Teddy to be pressing him to come home. Dak rolled over and was back in la-la land in a few moments. He slept like the dead, fell asleep easily. Like many soldiers he could sleep anywhere.

Teddy spent the next hour or so in his office, preparing his report and the supporting documentation, and going over in his mind the type of questions he might be asked this afternoon at the White House. Feeling vaguely satisfied that he was as prepared as he could be, he set off an hour early just to make sure he wasn't late. The Secret Service searched both him and his attaché case, and he was ushered into the briefing room. All the president's chief advisors and confidants would be there. Some had arrived before him and were busy gabbing near the table where the coffee was.

Debby and Richard introduced themselves. Debby asked him, "What would your Tarot cards tell you about me, Teddy?" It was her way of paying him a compliment for his incredibly insightful predictions.

He joked in reply, "I can tell right now, you are living outside the limits of your pay grade. Those shoes must have cost you a week's pay."

They laughed together at the quip and within minutes the room filled up. President Haines entered and they sat down. President Haines was a Republican who'd barely squeaked into office a year ago. When he spoke during the election campaign his promises lacked substance. His "Get America Moving" platform had done nothing to help the economic situation. Political pundits had branded his first year in office as weak and lacking in direction. His public profile could use a boost; his numbers were down. The president looked older in person and a bit haggard. His thinning hair and glasses lent him a bemused, grandfatherly air.

There was little in the way of formalities; it was all business and Teddy was first up. Get up, give his spiel, answer the questions and then he would be escorted out. The heavyweights would then decide on the issues that faced the nation.

The president's questions were direct. "You see marginal improvement in the economy for three years, and a sixty-three percent to seventy-two percent chance it is going to get worse overall, Teddy?"

"Yes, Mr. President, the numbers say exactly that, given no changes to the status quo or in general societal conditions or government intervention," was Teddy's short reply.

"How are you able to be so precise with your predictions, Teddy? The proverbial crystal ball? I don't mind telling you many of us are impressed with your previous reports."

"In brief, sir, I have developed a formula or calculation, originally through trial and error, that is able to factor in societal reactions to various economic stimulus and general economic conditions in the country. The Formula cannot predict the actions of individuals or even specific socio-economic groups or segments in our country, and it is a work in progress. Put even more simply I've incorporated mass psychology into economics, by taking it out of the realm of subjectivity and using strictly objective evidence," Teddy said in response.

"Now that is fascinating, Mr. Braxton. Thanks for your input," President Haines said.

With that Teddy was ushered out of the room unsure of what impression he had made on the president and his staff. He trekked back to his office, where he stashed his papers in the safe and listened to a lone voice message that said a Colonel Bernice Guay from Homeland Security, whoever she was, would be by to speak to him at 9:00 AM tomorrow morning.

He was home by 5:45 PM having sex with Rosie on the couch. Having sex usually occurred whenever they had a few spare moments. Tonight he spent a good fifteen minutes licking her pussy while she straddled his face. Hearing her moans and the writhing of her body when she had an orgasm made him rock hard. She moved down his body and impaled herself on his long, thick member. He marveled at how she did that. Rosie was only four-foot, eleven-inches tall and weighed one hundred and two pounds. But she did it and with gusto, riding him like a bull until she was satisfied again. Then she draped herself over the arm of the couch for Teddy to enter her from behind and fill her up. They lay exhausted on the couch for ten minutes before moving on to more mundane pursuits.

Rosie was one of the best things that had happened to Teddy since his father died. Dakar was right; they had an instant attraction to one another. Dakar had met Rosie on an Internet dating site. They shared some common interests in their love of the outdoors. She wanted a serious relationship; he didn't and preferred blonds, women taller than he was and definitely not a nurse. Finally, he e-mailed her and suggested, "Have I got a guy for you!" and that was how Teddy met Rosie, an old fashioned, Internet dating site referral romance.

There would be four kids in short order, they had agreed, but not until after they were married, provided the birth control worked its magic. They ate leftovers for supper that he reheated in the microwave, and settled into a relaxing night on the couch, watching movies and talking till after the late news, before jumping into bed. By dawn, they had made love three more times and it was time to get ready for work. He kissed her many times before going out the door. He could not seem to kiss her enough. Very often their sex or conversations dissolved into laughter, sometimes hysterical, but not last night; last night was all lust.

Colonel what's-her-name was there waiting for him when he arrived to work at ten minutes to 9:00. The colonel closed the door to Teddy's office and sat down. He couldn't help noticing she was a big, chunky bitch with closely cropped hair, hard looking, fifty something and of undetermined sexual orientation. She didn't make any small talk, other than to introduce herself.

"Hi, Teddy, I am the deputy secretary of Homeland Security and just retired from the Marine Corps. My name is Colonel Bernice Guay," she said.

"If I understood you correctly yesterday, you can predict people's behavior to certain stimuli with some accuracy," Colonel continued. The colonel was obviously at the meeting yesterday, but he could not remember her. There were more than a few women in the room.

"No, not people's behavior, rather how the economy will perform based not on individual or even large identifiable groups, only on the population as a whole, and with a range of error that grows incrementally larger the more unstable the economy, and by extension, social upheaval, increases."

"We believe your work may have some important applications for other government departments, and need the information you have on this system or formula, as you called it," the colonel said.

"I wrote a thesis for my Master's degree and it describes in detail the process I used to develop the inputs I needed in the formula I now use. You're welcome to it. I have a copy kicking around at home or there is a copy available from Gonzaga University in Spokane."

"No, Teddy, we want it all, including everything you are working on and notes, etc., that you used in developing this theory. We also want you to work with our people to develop other applications for your work."

"I assume you have or will get my boss to OK this or you wouldn't be asking for the material. I'll assemble the information you need and have it ready for you tomorrow morning at 9:00 AM, Colonel, after I clear it with my superiors."

"Thanks, Teddy. Tomorrow morning some of our staff members will be here to pick up the materials. As of today, as of right now, your work is classified, Ultra Top Secret. Please talk to no one about this." With that, she was out of the chair and out the door.

Teddy sat for a moment, baffled by this latest development and thinking, *What the fuck could they want with my thesis?* His thesis proposal had only been accepted after some hard arguments to the panel reviewing it. One panel member had called it entirely subjective and a flight of fantasy. It was only because his advisor had pointed out to them that all new radical theory and discovery was at one time or another called a flight of fantasy that they should grant some leeway to his research. They had accepted the proposal. Teddy had to admit that at the time the research supporting his hypothesis was mighty thin. It was only in the last few years of refining and honing the formula that it was bearing fruit. And what the fuck was Ultra Top Secret? His work was only level two and the president was looking at it! Oh well, way above his pay grade, today would be spent photocopying his files and making a pile for tomorrow. And who were our people? Whoever they were, he would find out soon enough.

Nothing like spending the day photocopying to make a guy horny and hungry, and the evening featured more fucking and feasting with the young and beautiful Rosie. He was deliriously happy and much of their talk centered around plans: plans for a house and holidays and what the mix would be vis-à-vis boys and girls. A consensus was reached at gender parity, as if they would get to choose.

At 9:00 AM the next morning, two men and two women arrived and hauled away the four banker's boxes of materials and some thumb drives that Teddy had assembled the day before. They said little, other than to introduce themselves and make small talk about the weather and such. Then it was back to the grind for Teddy. What had come to mind were his most recent guesses or, more correctly, his calculations regarding the psychological part of his equations. Within the confines of a normal socio-economic model they were very accurate. Such work could earn him a doctorate if published, he was sure. That was no longer going to happen if Bernice and her bosses had their way.

"Ultra Top Secret, my ass," he swore under his breath.

He heard nothing from the colonel or her minions for a month, and watched the economic situation get worse, with more home foreclosures, and an increased jobless rate nationwide. Some areas were harder hit than others, especially Michigan with all the car plant closures. You could pick up a home in Flint for a song. Teddy was living an uneventful life, which is exactly the way Teddy liked it.

The colonel called and wanted him to meet with some of her subject matter experts about his work. He met with the other actuaries and mathematicians. They were astounded that he had been able to take such an esoteric concept and meld it with actuarial science. He explained in detail how he had made educated guesses originally at the value the numbers should be, and then through trial and error narrowed his calculations to an error factor of between four percent and nine percent. His results all had to do with economic performance in the future such as growth in the GDP, housing starts, unemployment and manufacturing. Most recently all these areas showed decline. They were not particularly pleased with the trial and error method, but accepting his word, promised to get back to him in a few weeks, as they investigated and applied his theoretical formulas.

The stock market had rebounded slightly during the spring and now had dropped in the summer. September was typically the time that the market rallied, but Teddy didn't think that was going to happen—at least not this year.

CHAPTER 3

Party at Olsen

Dakar had started his military career disjointed, detached, and experiencing the tail end of a profound depression. At the time, he was emotionally lost, devastated by loss: the loss of Jenn, the only woman he had ever loved and the death of his father, who had been literally everything to Dakar, having raised Dak as a single parent. His dad was struck down by a heart attack at the young age of forty-nine while hunting elk with Dakar on a gorgeous fall day.

Jenn left him four months after his father died, explaining that she no longer had the same feelings for him. He had watched helplessly as she slowly drifted away. He could not confide in her about the growing darkness in his soul and became increasingly irritable, sullen and withdrawn. First came the "We need to take a break" speech. He was too in love and emotionally unstable to see that for what it was—the beginning of the end. Then came the day a month later when she told him she was leaving, in clear, concise terms, using non-emotive language, so as not to evoke an overly emotional response. It was all very clinically correct and to be expected from a counselor. Jenn worked at an alcohol and drug rehab center in Spokane. Emotional detachment was part and parcel of her job. But it hadn't always been that way with Dakar. At one time he shared a deep spiritual and emotional bond with Jenn that was difficult to put into words. The loss was so profound that at times Dakar felt as if part of his body or soul were missing.

After she left, Dakar waited for months for a call from her to say she wanted to see him again. It never came. Even though he loved her still and his heart ached as only a lover's heart can whenever he thought of her, he would never bother her or intrude on her life. He had written to her a year after they had split, and she had e-mailed back and explained that she was in love and to be married soon. All he could do was pray for her health and happiness, which he did for a few years.

Even if he did hook up with her again, there was little chance she would recognize the new Dakar, nor want to be with him, or perhaps even he with her; he had changed so much. The profound depression he had experienced had made him a different man. Now he lived strictly for the moment and had no real long-term goals. His senses and intuition had become acute, and he enjoyed and savored life's experiences as they presented themselves. With this newfound outlook on life came a peace and serenity he cherished, a calmness of spirit and mind. He spent much of his downtime by himself and was comfortable being alone. The pain of separation and loss had diminished as the years passed. He neither feared death nor sought it out. He was past caring about his own life or death. He could never be called cold or indifferent—he had empathy and compassion for many. It was part of living in the moment or living at all.

It had taken another year or more for the depression to subside. Divulging the depression to his superiors was out of the question. He knew it meant forced drugging or incarceration in a mental institution, perhaps even discharge, and certainly a label and little if any advancement in his career. Dakar didn't want to take any drugs for the depression and become addicted like others. He noticed that those of his fellow soldiers on anti-depressants and other drugs were all a bit off, not as quick mentally, or alive emotionally—in many ways robbed of their souls.

The heat of summer turned into the coolness of fall and the cold of winter at Patrol Base Olsen. Things had changed a lot in Iraq in that short period of time. He noticed the highway was busier with traffic and not just the frequent military convoys that roared up and down the highway at all hours. Now there were lots of other trucks bringing goods into Iraq from Turkey, and he suspected a general upturn in the Iraqi economy. In an effort to reduce the visible presence of the US in Iraq the convoys had been ordered to travel at night. US patrols in the cities were reduced, and the Iraqi Army and Iraqi Police were now on duty in all Iraqi cities.

In the glorious spring, Iraq changed. The base bloomed with flowers in the rain. There was a spectacular butterfly migration. Millions upon millions of them all headed north streaming through the base for three solid days. They looked like monarchs with their orange and black wings. Sometimes so much rain fell, the whole base became a quagmire of thick, sticky clay and when dry it produced a dust that was finer than talcum powder and it got in everywhere.

Dakar was still guarding and escorting Tariq everywhere he went that fall. It had been quiet since the bomber last summer. Dakar's bank account was looking very fine and all of it was stashed in an account in the Caymans. With that type of cash he could live very well for years. Many of his compatriots had been laid off. He was kept because Tariq insisted on having Dakar. Both he and Tariq knew it was only a matter of some months before he would be gone. Tariq was not looking forward to the prospect of being guarded by the Iraqi Police.

Dakar had met Tariq's wife and two young daughters one day in Samarra. She had prepared a great lunch at his home. His wife professed her gratitude for saving her husband's life and he was welcomed as just another member of the family. It was as close to family as Dakar had in many years, since the death of his father.

At 05:00 a faint glow on the eastern horizon was all that permeated the morning and Dakar was one of the few people awake at Patrol Base Olsen. To start his day out right, he headed for the gym as part of a regular routine first thing in the morning. In the darkness, he made his way out of the main building towards the portable gym facility across the roadway. Dakar rounded one set of T-walls (tall massive concrete barriers with a large base) that were supposed to supply some protection against indirect rocket and mortar fire. As he reached for the door to the gym, a large flash and bang erupted to his left. Then two more explosions came within seconds of each other and the guard post tower eighty feet to his left collapsed into a shambles of tin and sand bags, throwing clouds of dust and debris in the air. The guard vanished from sight in the debris.

At first, his instinct was to run to the bunker about fifteen feet away and seek shelter until the incoming stopped. Choking on the dust and confused he realized the explosions were not caused by incoming and must have been from RPGs (rocket propelled grenades) fired from short range at the tower. The distinctive sound of AK-47 fire filled the air—lots of it. It was answered by first one, then two M-16s, both firing short bursts. He heard the telltale whistle of rocket fins from indirect fire, which was followed by an explosion to the rear near the mechanic's shop. Dakar slammed one of the two clips he had with him into his rifle. He ran to the T-wall and peered down the narrow roadway to the main gate, sixty yards away. The enemy had overrun the sentry manning the Humvee and poured through the entrance. The living quarters and ops center were eighty yards away and the enemy raced there to start their killing spree.

Flicking the safety off his rifle, he started firing at the leaders of the group, cutting down three of them before they turned their attention to his position, and sent a hail of bullets his way forcing him behind cover with his head down. He aimed for the body on full auto. This was no time for head shots. One of the insurgents Dakar shot was wounded and he could hear the boy crying in pain and see him clutching his stomach.

Barely thirty seconds had elapsed from the time of the initial blast and the only other sound came from one M-16 about sixty yards to his right. Thin odds against so many attackers, as they pressed on in a desperate bid to reach more cover and wreak havoc on the still groggy inhabitants. Dak dropped to the prone position and again started firing bursts at the leaders of the group. The enemy had thought this attack out well and behind the initial fifteen or so rushing past the Humvee were three insurgents armed with RPGs. One of them with his ball cap on backwards was clearly going to use his on Dakar. He managed to shoot the man just as he fired and the round soared twenty feet over his head. He would not last long if help did not arrive soon. By the time he got back to trying to pick off the lead insurgents, a dozen or more had made it to next cover, some jersey barriers about thirty yards away. Only he and the sentry at the TOC stood in their way of taking out the command center.

Out on the road, Dak could make out three large white panel vans pulling away on the main road. He estimated the attacking force to be between forty and fifty men, all yelling, *"Allahu Akbar"* (Allah is Great) in Arabic. Another loud explosion occurred to his right and the sound of the other M-16 was silenced. This wasn't going well and Dakar was going to have to change positions to intercept the dozen enemy headed for the TOC. The soldiers inside would be busy ordering in air support and reinforcements at the moment, and would be unaware of the close proximity of the fighters, made up of many young men and boys and a few older men. All were dressed in long pants and shirts; some had white shirts and head scarves.

Instinctively, he rose and ran twenty feet to a generator that would give him a better vantage point, and allow him to cover the open area between the jersey barriers where the insurgents were rising to press forward and the front T-wall barrier leading to the TOC. His move left his backside completely wide open for the insurgents to rush up to the spot he had just vacated, shoot his ass off and then advance to still more living areas up the slight rise.

His situation couldn't be helped and he shot the rest of his clip into the two front men rising to rush the TOC. The deafening sound of all the weapons, explosions and the dust made it confusing. He went down behind the generator as the return fire started ricocheting off the generator and whistling by his ear. Dakar coughed from all the dust in the air as his last clip went in, and he poked his head up again to fire another ten or twelve rounds into the ragtag group who were now up en mass to charge the TOC. Four more insurgents dropped to the ground, including a few young boys before he was out of ammo for the rifle. None of the insurgents looked like soldiers. He imagined the Third Reich army near the end of the war must have looked the same as this group. He drew his sidearm and turned around too late, noticing a single insurgent less than thirty feet away raise his AK-47 to shoot him. A short burst from an M-16 cut him down from somewhere behind him.

Then the sweet sound of multiple M-16s and a 50 caliber greeted Dakar's ears. The smell of gunpowder filled his nose to the exclusion of all other scents. A deafening hail of fire from first three or four, and then countless more opened up on the lead group and the remaining insurgents still rushing across the first open area.

Still more rifle fire and the enemy was being slaughtered from all sides including his vulnerable area behind him as soldiers, some not yet dressed, pressed forward moving from cover to cover and firing all the time. Another RPG round exploded near the generator and one of the fuel tanks below caught fire. The good thing about diesel was it didn't explode very easily or Dak's ass would have been barbecued. Speaking of asses, he recognized the ass on that soldier. It was Simmons clad only in a T-shirt and skivvies, firing on full auto into the rapidly developing carnage, near the Humvee.

She dropped in beside him and asked him, "How the fuck are you?"

Deadpanning, he said to her, "Thanks for saving me from an untimely end. I see you're dressed for action, but not now, honey. I'm busy. I could use a clip, however."

"OK, later, baby," as she threw one over and Dakar joined in the firefight that ensued. The insurgents were now outnumbered and the battle heavily weighed against them. The fifty was cutting them to pieces, shredding the Humvee to bits and the men behind it. It was then he noticed blood. Hell, it was his blood, soaking his leg and he noted a wound on his thigh that had started bleeding.

Simmons noticed too and said pointedly, "We're going to get that looked at NOW." For a woman who wasn't supposed to give a shit, she was starting to act like she did. Truth is he cared about her too, but it wasn't that kind of love: more a friends with benefits type of thing.

"Jesus, Simmons, it's just a graze. I'll be OK for a bit."

The gunfire subsidized. Only a handful of insurgents who were undercover remained and in short order they surrendered. Within five minutes, two Kiowa helicopters arrived and several minutes later a pair of Apaches helicopters circled overhead providing cover for the base. The Kiowas swung away over the city searching for the panel vans that had been used in the attack. A pair of F-16s roared by low and fast in a show of strength moments later, and a convoy of relief troops was dispatched from C-2c, eight miles north. Several soldiers extinguished the fire from the fuel tank using fire extinguishers.

One of the junior officers and several soldiers had control of six prisoners. The men were kneeling on the ground with their hands on their heads. One of the soldiers left to get some restraints to bind their wrists. The officer in charge, Lieutenant Gradin, shook badly, and yelled at the prisoners, "You fucking murdering bastards. I am going to kill all you motherfucking murderers," Gradin said, as he raised his rifle to shoot.

"Hey, Lieutenant, that's enough!" Dakar yelled at him. Dakar had done some terrible things in his life, but never murder.

On Dakar's first tour, some of the other "elite" units had done exactly that, dragged men from their homes and shot them in the street and bragged about it afterwards. It was hard to be angry at insurgents for the atrocities they were committing against US troops when our troops were doing the same thing. He wasn't going to allow Gradin to do that.

"Stay out of this, civilian. This is an army matter and one of these hajis is armed and trying to kill us," Gradin shot back.

Without hesitation Dakar leveled his weapon at Gradin and said in a calm cool voice, "Pull that trigger and I will kill you where you stand."

Gradin glanced up at Dakar, paused and not liking the look in Dakar's eyes, lowered his rifle and ordered the other slack-jawed and nervous soldier who stood frozen at the unfolding drama, to "Take this man into custody."

Still bewildered, the soldier hesitated, then swung his rifle over to point at Gradin, ordering him to "Drop the weapon, sir."

Faced with two weapons pointing at him, Gradin dropped his rifle to the ground, as he sputtered and mumbled to himself about the "murdering bastards." Another half dozen soldiers arrived to see what the commotion was about and the soon-to-be-sent-home-in-disgrace Gradin was led away.

Dakar, who was now starting to bleed heavily, was led by Simmons to the surgery. A medic dressed his slight wound. The surgeon was busy elsewhere working on the badly wounded. Another bunch with not so serious injuries and one other like Dakar who only had superficial wounds were being treated by a few medics.

Murph lost a toe during the ruckus and was just getting it attended to, busy as he was securing the base and putting out fires both literally and figuratively. He sat next to Dakar giving orders in the infirmary, while the medic patched him up. There was little chance the insurgents would launch another attack, but then again this one had been totally unexpected. There had not been a direct attack of this size on a US base in some years, until now. One thing Dakar had learned in his time here was not to underestimate the enemy. Every time the US came up with a solution for some particular type of attack the insurgents discovered a way or method to overcome it.

Shaped explosive charges were the response to the US introduction of more heavily armored vehicles like the MRAP and up-armored Humvees. In Samarra particularly, they used an old, Russian-made grenade called an RKG that contained a shaped charge, was thrown by hand and had a drogue chute pop out the back end that kept the grenade oriented at ninety degrees to the armor. They were used with some effect on MRAPS and the insurgents had become quite accurate throwing them, even hitting the small windows of the MRAPS with the grenades. There were a host of questions to be answered about failures in intelligence and how they were logistically able to mount such a sophisticated assault. But for right now that would have to wait.

Finally Murph said, "Saw you duking it out with the enemy. Lucky for us you are an early riser, Dakar, and were there at the right spot. You seem to have a talent for being where the action is."

"Not too lucky. I did catch one or at least a small part of one, but I'm better off than some of the others. I see you were literally toe to toe and lost one to prove it, Captain," Dakar teased.

"Only you would make fun of a wounded man!" Murph said, half chuckling at the pun through the pain. "Looks like five dead, thirteen wounded, including three pretty seriously. I heard about Gradin. Fuck, Dak, you never know about a guy for sure until he's in the fire. The asshole never fired a shot and he was all fucked up like that. Thanks, Dak."

"You're welcome anytime, Captain," Dakar responded.

With that, Murph turned to Simmons and said, "Better get some clothes on, Sergeant. You done good today."

Simmons replied somewhat embarrassed, "Yes, sir." She had forgotten the state of her undress and left to put on more suitable attire.

"You can call me Murph for the rest of the day, Dakar. You'll probably get a medal for what you did today and you deserve it."

"No, thanks on the medal part... ahhhh... Captain Murph, sir," Dakar said. He was still not able to use Murph's nickname in public. He thought it disrespectful.

"Outta my hands and not my decision to make, Dak," Murph told him.

Another thing not to look forward to, Dakar hobbled out of the surgery to survey the damage to the base with his own eyes and take a few pictures now that the shooting was over.

CHAPTER 4

New Beginnings

Dak was exhausted physically and emotionally. During the battle, he was calm and collected, but later he felt the effects of the bloody melee. He flopped on the bed and woke to the sat phone ringing beside his bed twenty minutes later. Holly called from ASI headquarters wanting to know what had happened. All she heard was that there was an incident at PB Olsen. "Dakar, are you OK? We heard there was some sort of attack at your base."

Dakar was brief.. There had been an incident at PB Olsen. "I'm fine, other than a small scratch. I'll let you know what happened when I'm permitted to."

"Take care of yourself. We're all glad you are all right," Holly said as she hung up. She understood the rules of the game and ASI would have to be content with knowledge that he was okay for the time being.

Within seconds, he fell asleep again for another two hours and was famished when he arose. Heading for the chow hall, he passed the interior door to the TOC and could hear the excited chatter within. Whatever was cooking in the DFAC smelled wonderful and into the dining hall he went. Thirty soldiers and Mick were inside; all looked his way when he entered. Dakar heaped his plate full of bacon and sausages, and Rob, the cook, made him one of his famous omelets with extra eggs, with everything of course. Sitting down beside Mick he barely paused and said, "Hello," before the fork was shoveling the grub into his mouth.

Mick, like Dak, was a man of few words. He said, "Why do you always insist on being the hero? That can be a dangerous occupation after a while. A sensible man like me would be asleep at five in the morning!" He laughed afterwards.

"I wish I could stop being in the middle of the shit storm when it occurs, but it just seems to happen that way. I must be the chosen one," Dakar said.

"Next you will be telling us you are the second coming!" Mick teased.

The TV was tuned to CNN and everyone was half listening for any mention of the attack on the news that should come soon. The government would suppress the news for as long as they could, but did not want under any circumstances to be scooped by some other source lest the spin they wanted to give the attack suddenly become the truth as told by someone else. The news this morning was, however, more doom and gloom about the economy.

The news anchor said, "More bad news out of New York today as First Federated Bank of America has filed for Chapter 11 bankruptcy protection. Senior executives at the bank are being criticized by consumer groups for the lavish bonuses the CEO and board members of the bank paid themselves and stock options they cashed in shortly before filing for bankruptcy. Consumer groups across the nation called on the federal government to make them pay the money back to depositors and face criminal prosecution."

Mick had turned forty-five yesterday. The birthday boy looked towards Dakar and said, "This morning I told ASI I am demobbing (quitting). Going to live someplace warm and wet. I have my eye on a little beach house in the Dominican Republic and a small bar."

"I'm going to drink cervezas while I tell tales about my war exploits to my patrons and enjoy the beautiful girls," he said. Mick continued and said he would wait until his replacement came in. It was the right thing to do. The company had treated him well and his paycheck had always been in his account on time every month. There was no sense in burning any bridges behind him. Mick saw the writing on the wall. The president was pulling some troops out of Iraq and the gig was just about up. Dakar was sorry to see him go. Mick always had his back. He was a seasoned warrior, not a cowboy: quiet, thoughtful, and funny, a near perfect partner for Dakar.

"You know, Mick, I think you have the right idea. Time to call it a day," Dakar said. He would have liked a few months more, but... maybe he should get out of the country before some prick decided he should get a medal, which he would turn down flat. He didn't do medals. That was for heroes, and God save us from heroes and true believers.

Dakar couldn't say he hadn't thought about it in the last few months and had been online looking at sailboats. There was one that he fancied in Tel Aviv. The economy had driven the prices down to the point that many were half the cost they were a few years ago. It was all outfitted and ready to go—a Decker, eight years old, forty-five feet long, diesel auxiliary, solar cells and a wind generator to charge the batteries. The ad said the boat seldom had the sails up.

Dakar telephoned the marina where it was moored. The manager of the marina said, "Yeah, I know the boat. It's in excellent condition. The man who owns it now doesn't do much sailing. He uses it primarily as a place to bang his girlfriend. When he does take it out, he prefers to putt around the inner harbor and marina, showing off to his yacht club buddies rather than attempt any real sailing."

Of course, he would need another opinion or, better yet, a look at it before slapping down the cash. Cash was a great motivator in this economy. He had sailed on a Decker before and it was a sweet boat: stable, well constructed and quite capable of a comfortable trans-Atlantic voyage. It would be a great way to end his tour here—to sail back, perhaps even stopping in the Dominican. If Mick was there Dakar would buy him a beer and perhaps Mick could hook him up with a girl for the duration of his visit. Tomorrow he would call ASI and let them know. He stopped in Murph's office. Murph's eyes had bags under them and he rubbed them frequently to ward off the tiredness.

"Have you thought about a power nap, Captain? I had one and it was great," Dak suggested.

"Wish I could. Every officer in theatre above captain is calling me wanting a blow by blow, and a couple of generals in Washington. I should have put them through to you; once again you were right where the action was. What the hell is it with you? Depraved childhood, small penis, self-esteem issues?

"In any event, I'm glad you were there, Dak. My report is, as I said, going to recommend a commendation for you. Things would have been a lot worse had you not been on the line. Thank you again, my friend," the captain replied.

"Please don't do that, Captain. You know how I am about medals. Tell you what, a Starbucks Grande when we get back stateside and we'll call it even. Besides, I'm dragging up tomorrow. I've had enough action to last me a lifetime."

"You're right about that, Dakar. Most soldiers never see the amount of combat you have, I understand." He rose and shook his hand and continued, "We will miss you here, but your name and what you did is going in the report. It has to."

Normally, Dakar wouldn't visit Simmons in her quarters. Both thought it wasn't good to advertise the relationship they had. But today was different and he wanted to make sure she was OK and to tell her he was leaving shortly. He strolled the thirty yards to her quarters and knocked, calling out, "Simmons." She came to the door and asked him in.

"How are you doing? Everything all right?" Dakar asked.

"I'm always OK when you're around, Dakar," Alicia said, tears forming in her eyes.

He told her straight up what was happening. Alicia hugged him, and said him she was happy for him and then started to softly weep. Dakar sensed she wept because they were both safe after this morning's action, not because he was leaving.

She had duty in a few hours and asked him," Can we be together now?"

"I'd like that, Alicia." It was the first time he had used her first name. He kissed her and left for his quarters. She dressed to follow him in a few minutes.

For the few hours they had together, they made love in a dozen different ways, their lovemaking full of passion, tenderness and lots of kissing and cuddling. The whole episode in contrast to the raw animal nature of their usual sexual trysts. She left his room with fifteen minutes to go, to straighten up in time for her duty.

Alicia passed the captain in the hallway, as she left Dak's room and she saluted him.

"Nice job today, Simmons. You were outstanding, Staff Sergeant," Murph said.

She could barely sputter a "Thank you, sir," as she continued down the hallway. *Wahoo,* she thought, *damn Staff Sergeant.* An E-6. The extra pay would be welcome. The promotion would have to be approved, but the chances were excellent given the circumstances.

The next morning Dakar picked up the sat phone and asked to speak with Aaron Morrow, his boss, and he gave him the good news. He let him know he would stay for the month or so it would take to get the replacements in for Mick and himself, and provide a transition period of a week or so.

"I'm grateful for the job you've done for ASI and you're welcome back anytime, provided there is still a war zone to go to," Aaron said. That was a joke; there was always a war zone to go to. "We need some guys in Afghanistan. Your job will be here when you are ready," he added.

Aaron suspected the work was ending soon in Iraq. He also knew that for men like Dakar it was hard to leave the action. Perhaps in six months or a year the phone would ring, and it would be Dakar looking for a job and he would hire him. Dak was the calmest man in battle he had ever known and he loved the action. Dakar was the best they had, hands down. The word was out detailing Dakar's role during the insurgent attack and Aaron said when they finished up the call, "Dak, outstanding work in helping repulse the attack. You make us all look good."

Dakar watched the morning news in his room. The attack on PB Olsen was the lead story. "Units of the 25th Infantry Division, 3rd Brigade, 2nd Battalion, 35th Infantry Regiment "Cacti" had repulsed an attack by what was believed to be the largest al-Quaida group ever in Iraq. An estimated forty-six terrorists had assaulted the base, the Pentagon spokesman said.

"Fucking what!" Dak said out loud. "Al-Quaida!!!"

The attack had been by Iraqi insurgents, men who thought their country should not be occupied by America. It was obvious to anyone in the fight that the attackers were not al-Quaida. Almost all members of al-Quaida were from outside Iraq. Most of them had been driven out or killed by '08 after there were pitch battles in the streets of Samarra between Sunni tribal leaders and al-Quaida, which was trying to take over the insurgency. Wisely the US had backed the Sunni tribal leaders and formed the Sons of Iraq. What followed were three years of relative peace in Samarra. Obviously that was over now, and the Sons were becoming targets for collaborating with the occupying Americans.

Dakar left his room and headed for the MWR and the Internet. He went online and looked at the Decker again. A Decker could be sailed alone. It would be hard work and having some help and a steady piece of ass on board would be nice. But how to find a first mate was the question. He wished it were Jenn. They had sailed together often on Lake Coeur d'Alene, spending days sailing and camping at remote locations on the lake. He didn't think of her as often as he had, but he missed Jenn at times terribly. He craved her touch so much that one night, as he lay in bed before falling asleep, he ran his own hand gently over his face imaging it were Jenn touching him as she so often did.

Dakar could always advertise online, on one of the many dating websites, but there were risks and he preferred to meet the woman first before spending some months with her on a forty-five foot boat. Just because a woman was good-looking didn't mean she wasn't nuts, or didn't like to babble endlessly or worse yet couldn't actually sail. Alicia was great, but her practical jokes were starting to wear a little thin on him. Online once again, he looked up the number of a boat repair facility in Tel Aviv that specialized in sailboats. He called the owner and asked him to look her over and let him know his opinion of the Decker.

"I'll pay you for your troubles, Simon," Dakar assured him.

"I know this boat. It is a very good price, in very good condition. I will go this afternoon to the marina and look very closely for you," Simon said.

"OK, Simon, I'll call tomorrow and you can let me know what's what."

"What's what? I do not understand, my friend," Simon queried.

"Nothing, just if it is OK or not." He hung up, went online again and checked his bank balance. It was enough to do what he pleased for quite a few years on a sailboat all over the Caribbean or wherever his heart took him. Tomorrow if everything checked out, he was going to buy that boat.

He lay back on the bed and flicked the remote from station to station, hoping to catch a movie to occupy his time. CNN news was on and the Olsen story once again dominated. This time President Haines was telling the American people that the war on terror was not over. That al-Quaida "could and would strike again and again at the heart of the American people, if we are not vigilant." He thought to himself, *Fuck, someone is handling the president nicely with that line of bullshit.*

Most of the soldiers who served in Iraq were under no illusions. There were no weapons of mass destruction, no al-Quaida, no nothing, except the Iraqi people who, for the most part, did not want them here and wanted desperately to return to a normal way of life. American soldiers were loyal and served because their country asked them to. This latest insult was too much for Dakar to swallow and now that he was a free man, maybe there was something he could do about it.

The day after the communications blackout was lifted, Dak called Teddy to ask him to get the contact information for Adrienne Assad, a CNN journalist, whom he noticed had a no-nonsense style and accurately reported events in the first Gulf War. He always read her written articles and enjoyed her perspective about many issues in the Middle East.

Dak e-mailed her and she called him back on the sat phone within the hour. She was excited to hear about his part in the battle and that he had some photographs of the scene afterwards. She called back shortly with an offer of thirty thousand for two interviews: first one by webcam and a short video segment he would record himself while he was in Iraq and then a sit-down interview when he returned to the US.

Dakar said, "Fifty thousand would be better and half upfront. The rest after the first interview airs." Adrienne agreed to the revised demand. He might have gotten more, but perhaps not without an agent or some other sort of nonsense. Hell, that kind of money would pay for his new sailboat.

He'd bought the Decker when Simon had given it a clean bill of health. In fact, Simon told him he wished he had the money to get such a boat at that price. Dakar loved a bargain and asked him to make sure the boat would be ready when he got to Tel Aviv in a month or so. The papers were all signed via electronic means and she was his. Dakar would have to head to Bagdad four days before he planned to demob. First a military air flight from C2c to Speicher, and then another to Bagdad where he would catch a commercial flight to Amman, Jordan and then drive to Israel and Tel Aviv. Dakar also phoned Adrienne Assad and told her he was sailing back to the US from Tel Aviv and would be another few months getting there. Adrienne was concerned about keeping the story alive and topical, so asked if she could meet him in Tel Aviv on a prearranged date. That sounded good to Dakar: getting it over sooner rather than later and also giving him some options of whether he wanted to return directly to the US or head for the Caribbean.

CHAPTER 5

Into the Fire

Teddy's life had taken a number of interesting twists and turns. Not with Rosie, thank God. Everything was as it should be; hopelessly in love and enjoying every minute of it. The twists had come from Colonel Bernice Guay. She was now demanding more and more of his time. At first, it was only an hour or so on the phone with her actuarial and mathematical minions, and then some half days at an office in a drab, no-name building in Washington. Bernice was constantly reminding him not to discuss his work with anyone else and he had signed more secrecy documents that threatened him with lengthy jail time should he breach confidentiality.

Teddy took some pleasure in giving Dakar the contact information for Adrienne Assad after Dakar told him of his plan to blow the lid off the nature of the attack on PB Olsen. Within a few days, the story should break on CNN and the questions would start.

Teddy doubted the president was aware of what really happened at the base.

At the moment, he was busy explaining to the minions the impossibility of using his work to predict anything other than cold, hard, economic data. There were too many variables when trying to apply his psychological equation with anything other than economics, and the margins of error made the answers meaningless. They, however, seemed intent on developing a way to predict the overall emotional and social behaviors of people in near anarchistic social conditions. Teddy was making no headway when he argued with them and headed home.

On the way home Teddy picked up his cell phone and called Dakar to ask him about his new purchase. "A Decker. What a great buy, Dak!" was his comment.

Teddy was excited his friend was coming home and with a new sailboat that he and Rosie could also use. Dakar and Teddy had spent many days on the waters of Lake Coeur d'Alene, sailing a little sixteen footer and then a twenty foot sailboat up and down the lake everywhere and in all kinds of weather. Later they spent some months crewing for a friend's dad in the Caribbean on a Decker. Almost all their time together was spent outdoors in the mountains or on the water. They fished for trout in creeks and lakes that were many miles off the beaten path. They hiked high alpine meadows covered in wild flowers and spent many a night camped beside a mountain stream. Both understood and loved the wilderness—the bite of a cool breeze on the face felt wonderful and the feeling of belonging that being in the wilderness brought them. Different in many respects, and yet soul mates and brothers in so many other ways. It would be good to see his brother again.

Dak said, "See you in a few months, Teddy, and yes I expect you and Rosie to use the Decker whenever you want."

When he hung up, his mind wandered back to the minions and their mindless quest for the impossible. All this fuss had made him think long and hard about his work in economics in the last month. He was starting to ponder expanding his horizons and trying the formula out on increasingly difficult economic conditions to see where the boundary lay between meaningful and meaningless results. But not tonight. Tonight was a Rosie night; every night was a Rosie night. He wished Dakar could find a "Rosie," but he knew that might never happen. His friend differed in that way. He was a loner who, like as not, would not become emotionally involved with another woman. Still, Dakar was happy living in the moment and there was a lesson in that for Teddy.

Back at the office, Teddy commenced running his projections using the monstrous computers in the US Congressional Budget Office. He started by changing the number in the psych part of the equation and leaving the economic indicators constant. Then he tried it the other way around. There was absolutely nothing to be learned from his little exercise as he suspected, other than the fact all of it ended in a maelstrom of unfathomable numbers. Oh well, it was comforting to know he was correct in telling the minions they were chasing their tail in trying to predict the future.

The weather in Washington was nasty for the fall; tropical storms and hurricanes seemed to be driving torrential rains in, as one front after another hit the area in rapid succession. He and Rosie had become accustomed to walking in the many parks of Washington, exploring each, one by one, enjoying the fresh air and historical city. Breaking his reverie and paying attention to where he was, he looked out the car window on the drive home and noticed that today was an exception. It looked pretty clear and a good day for a walk.

Teddy and Rosie headed out to Bartholdi Park. It was great to be out for the hour, the fresh air doing wonders for their souls. Bartholdi Park was not very big, but had a lovely fountain and its clean wide sidewalks and immaculate gardens, some of which were still in bloom, provided a burst of color against the otherwise gray overcast of the last few weeks. They felt alive after a few circuits of the perimeter and the promenade around the gardens. Not many people out today, a handful, including another couple obviously as wrapped up in the day as they were. They piled into his Honda CRV and headed back to the apartment. It was an older model, four cylinder, manual transmission. He had always driven standards, which were relatively good on gas.

Rosie and he had been saving for the down payment on a house. A new car could wait. The requirements were much harder now after the collapse of the subprime mortgage market and they would need every penny saved to buy a home somewhere in the Washington area. Of course it had to have four bedrooms at a minimum; the kids would need room to grow, and a big kitchen to entertain in. Teddy and Rosie were not living room types of people. Rosie had taken over the financial management in the family. Teddy was no good with money, often spending it as soon as he had it in his pocket. This was odd for a man who worked in the US Congressional Budget Office. Teddy knew he wasn't good with money and was happy with the cash Rosie handed him every week for spending money.

He swung the car into the underground parking lot and as Rosie headed upstairs to start supper, he went to the lobby to get the mail. Not that they got much mail, other than bills and junk mail. Glancing casually out the front window he noticed a couple getting out of a car parked across the street. It looked like the same couple from the park. He wondered if they lived in the same building. Bartholdi Park was a good forty minutes from where they lived; he guessed they liked walking, too.

Back in their apartment, it became very clear to Teddy that the fresh air had made his Rosie very, very horny and he had just the cure for that ailment. Dinner could wait a bit. He had her on the kitchen table, first having her lay on it and then bent over the table itself. Before supper he turned the TV on to the local ABC affiliate, as Rosie prepared supper. *Jeopardy* would soon be on, and he and Rosie liked to watch. They would compete by seeing who could shout the answer out first and then pass comments on the various contestants' skill or lack thereof. Neither was in the same league as Ken Jennings. Teddy supposed putting their names in as contestants would be required first before their dream of a chance to play one day for the big money could come true. In truth Rosie was much better than he was at getting the answers. He would settle for his fifteen minutes of fame on the *The Price is Right*, if he had to.

The sports report was on and Teddy had no interest in that as it droned on, with only a few minutes to go. Rosie and he would da-da-daaa-dah-du-du-du... along with the theme song for *Jeopardy* when it began. Just as Buck "what's his name" was describing why the Redskins were not going to make the playoffs, a banner appeared rolling across the bottom of the screen. It said, "Large explosion reported near the Port of Newark in New Jersey. Stand by for the ABC National News Desk."

Teddy hoped the story was about an accident and that there would not be the usual speculation about it being a terrorist attack. The markets and investor confidence were already shaken and they would bail from the markets, if even a whiff of instability reared its ugly head.

The station cut straight away from the sports caster to Zane Smith, a national news caster. He spoke in a cold level tone. "It appears a large explosion has taken place at the container unloading facility, at the Port of Newark, on the Hudson River in New Jersey. Preliminary reports are that the explosion has caused at least two deaths and extensive damage to nearby containers. The facilities loading and unloading equipment appear to have suffered little damage. We go now to Sarah Rankin from our ABC affiliate who is on the scene and has this report."

"Hi Zane, I'm here outside the main gate at the Port of Newark on Corbin Street. Right now we know a container inside the facility that was being moved by one of the giant lift trucks exploded as it was lifted from its resting place. Sources tell us that the driver and his loading assistant were both killed and there was extensive damage to other containers in a large radius from the blast center. The blast caused a fireball to rise over two hundred feet into the air. All we can see now is black and gray smoke rising from the area. The blast happened at about 6:15 PM, some forty minutes ago. Other than that police aren't giving us much information. The police bomb squad was seen entering the facility fifteen minutes ago and we should have more information shortly as to the nature and perhaps the cause of this explosion. Just a minute, Zane. As you can see there is a police officer approaching us now from inside the facility. He looks..."

The camera focused on an excited cop, as he rushed straight to Sarah and the gathering crowd. He yelled, "Everyone, get the hell out of here now. Clear the area. The bomb had radioactivity in it. Get as far away from here as possible."

The camera panned back to Sarah and her suddenly ashen face; she looked straight into the camera and said, "We may have a dirty bomb here, Zane; we're packing up the equipment and headed for a safer location."

"I understand, Sarah. Get yourselves to safety." Peering at the camera, he uttered directly, "It now appears a radioactive, dirty bomb has been detonated at the Port of Newark container handling facility in New Jersey. Police just ordered our crew and all the people at the terminal gates to vacate the area because of the radiation hazard. This facility is located directly across the Hudson River from downtown New York. We don't know what effect the bomb will have on the city of New York."

Teddy was flabbergasted and looked at Rosie in disbelief. As the evening wore on a police spokesman, the secretary of Homeland Security and a scientist from the nuclear regulatory agency, came on to assure the good people of New Jersey and New York. He said, "There is no great danger to your health. The levels of radioactivity that have been detected are low in most areas. The radioactive element used was plutonium and has been detected in a downwind area from the blast site."

The secretary of Homeland Security also said that it was now "virtually certain there had been another terrorist attack against the American people." In the first few hours many people panicked hearing only the word "radioactive" come from the police officer's mouths, and massive traffic jams ensued with people trying to flee the cloud of radioactivity. The partly cloudy evening was evidence to many people that a cloud of nuclear radioactive death was coming their way. There had even some violence as frantic motorists drove on the shoulders of turnpikes and interstates, screaming at each other.

By 7:00 AM the next morning, people still clogged the roads trying to leave the area and the governors of New Jersey and New York ordered all the major highways leaving the area closed, and urged people to go home and remain calm. In a pre-emptive bid to stop financial panic, the SEC ordered the stock markets and commodity exchanges closed until Monday. It was now Thursday morning and the administration hoped that four days would help cool off what was sure to be rising anxiety in the minds of investors. The president was scheduled to address the nation at 6:00 PM tonight.

From a purely technical point of view, this latest development should make for some interesting results when Teddy plugged the new numbers into the equation and ran the results, so he left for the office half an hour early the next morning, forgoing his usual second round of morning sex with Rosie, who told him in no uncertain terms he was skating dangerously close to sexual abuse by leaving her wanting.

CHAPTER 6

Unraveling

T eddy wasn't the only one in the office this early. Lots of people had arrived early. The phones were busy and e-mails flew here and there. Plans were floated for the inevitable intervention the government and financial institutions would have to make in the economy. He could well imagine the discussions taking place higher up on the food chain. Not his problem and soon enough they would want to know the probable outcome of last night's events. He had to remind them constantly it wasn't the event that was the problem; it was people's reaction to it and this latest attack would be damn difficult to quantify.

He set out using a wider range of possible psychological reactions to the event and ran a varying number of scenarios. Inside the hour the results were back. If the administration didn't like his previous results they sure weren't going to like what he was seeing now.

The phone rang and it was Director Corson. He was blunt. "What have you got for me, Teddy?"

"I'll have something in your inbox in about twenty minutes, but I can tell you now, if you thought I was giving you bad news before, you're in for a shock," Teddy explained.

"Fuck, I'm going to have to nominate you as the Gloom and Doom Poster Boy, if this continues," Corson said.

"As long as you don't shoot the messenger, I'll take any recognition you give me." With that, the phone went dead in Teddy's hand.

Teddy knew his report would help shape the nature and magnitude of the administration's response. His analysis showed that even if they pulled out all stops and there was massive government intervention, there was only a forty percent chance of the fix being mildly successful. But what the hell did being unsuccessful mean? It suddenly dawned on him that the results from last night and today, which appeared to be meaningless jumbles of numbers and indices under certain conditions, were not meaningless at all. They indicated economic collapse of the system, in the manner it now functioned. A chill ran up his spine when he hastily plugged the new results into the template of previous reports and wrote his two paragraph summary. After a couple of quick rereads for content and grammatical errors, he hit the send button. Leaning back in the chair, the realization that there was a significant chance life as he knew it was about to change came as a shock. He was so focused on minutiae and sometimes he missed the big picture.

Within ten minutes the director was back on the phone. "Under no circumstances are you to talk about the report with anyone in any way, and Colonel Guay requests your immediate attendance at the project office."

The next few days and the weekend were spent at the special office, which Rosie was not happy about and neither was he, but not reporting for work was out of the question. He had to admit the minions were making progress, but he still felt their results would never be of value using so many psychological variants in the equations. It looked like they had narrowed the maximum error, by fudging the formula slightly. It still wasn't reasonable to think they could make this work. Teddy suspected they were attempting to predict the reaction from the general public to certain events such as the one that occurred on Thursday. The biggest problem he saw with their work was there was no definable result even if they knew there was a seventy percent chance of a certain reaction. What was that reaction? They seemed to have no idea what that "the reaction" might be.

The colonel showed up late Sunday and told him, "A team has been assigned to you for security reasons."

Teddy's mind mulled over the new information. What security reasons? This explained the couple he had noticed at the park and then again back at the apartment. He supposed if it panned out, foreign governments might be interested in his work. But they could access what he did easily enough through his Master's thesis, which was available in the public domain.

Teddy wondered whether his apartment was bugged. If it was, his sexual antics with Rosie might make interesting viewing. He hoped it wasn't going to show up on some Internet porn site like "kinkyactuaries.com." There was a whole unexplored area for additional part-time income for him and Rosie. He would have to talk to her about that. At least they would have a good laugh over the thought, after searching the apartment for bugs. Today's surveillance equipment was so tiny he doubted they would find anything.

Sunday night, Teddy called Dakar from a friend's cell phone, paranoia about the security team leading him to think his phones might be tapped.

Dakar answered, "Hey, Teddy? What's the story?", referring obviously to the events on Thursday.

Teddy was plainspoken. "Dakar, come home now. There is no telling where this thing will end up."

"I thought with all your contacts in Washington you'd have some sort of scoop on what happened."

"I only know what I see on the news, Dak, but there are some very worried people in Washington." Teddy wondered if he was going too far already, but he thought his comments obscure enough not to arise the suspicions of anyone listening. He repeated again, "Dakar, come home, come home. I can't say any more." The satellite phone conversation was monitored, he knew, but he thought not by the same people who were watching him.

"Yeah, I am coming home, but I can't right now. What do you think of my new boat? Do you and Rosie want to join me in the Caribbean for a few weeks?" Talk centered on how the boat handled, and Dakar had forwarded pictures of his pride and joy. Teddy wasn't envious, just excited for his friend and truthfully looking forward to taking her for a spin, which was no problem with Dakar; their friendship was so close that whatever one owned was by extension the other's to use whenever he wanted. Lately most of the stuff had been Dakar's. He was so filthy rich compared to Teddy.

"I'll be out of Iraq in a month and home in another couple of months, just like I said, Teddy. Miss you guys," Dakar said as he disconnected. Teddy's plea to Dakar had been uncharacteristic of his friend and he took what he said very seriously. Our Teddy was not the dramatic type. He would not be so adamant without good reason.

On Monday, the NY Stock Exchange opened again and the Dow promptly nosedived to new depths below eight thousand. The Feds, Federal Reserve Bank and most of the major financial institutions all intervened, and had barely been able to slow the collapse near the end of the trading day. The markets were closed for trading for another two days and traders became resigned to desperate times ahead in the financial sector.

In Jersey, amateur prospectors and conspiracy nuts had their Geiger counters out measuring radioactive levels in the downwind path the radioactive particles from the Newark bomb had taken. The Geiger counters would "go crazy," but not with levels that were an immediate health risk. Long term exposure might cause some problems and increases in some types of cancer were likely. Funny thing about radioactivity; the very mention of it sent panic rushing through the veins of otherwise very normal people.

All the major TV networks and most of the radio stations felt they should practice responsible journalism and parroted the government story, not wishing to spread panic among the population. A few stations aired stories about the possible long term effects of prolonged exposure to plutonium and were labeled as scare-mongers and nay–saying, unpatriotic paranoids.

The main interstate highways heading south and west out of the two states were still plugged with traffic, trying to escape the radioactivity. The bulk of the radioactivity had spread to the north in a nearly V-shaped plume as far north as Goshen, before the concentrations levels became immeasurable. Most urban areas were completely unaffected by the radioactivity, but that was of little interest to a great many terrified residents of the city. Comparisons with the nuclear disaster in Japan after the tsunami abounded.

The governors again asked everyone to go home and wait a few days till the situation stabilized. Police set up road blocks diverting people back to their homes. Many tried to circumvent the major highways by navigating the back roads, only to be turned around at police road blocks. The police only allowed local residents through to their homes. Commerce ground down because many people could not make it into work. One man was killed trying to shoot his way through a police road block, his family watching in horror from their car when police gunned him down. Authorities were lucky more were not killed or injured in that incident. Over two hundred arrests were made for charges that ranged from mischief to looting.

The Federal Emergency Management Agency (FEMA) was appointed to oversee the situation, and came up with a plan to bring life back to normal in New Jersey and New York. It had to be done and done quickly. Panic could and would spread if the situation continued.

The plan espoused protecting the public from exposure to the radiation and the best way they said was to have everyone stay indoors. FEMA assured the public that levels in affected areas had already fallen considerably and most areas were not affected at all. For the next forty-eight hours the only traffic allowed in and out of the twenty-five mile radius were commercial vehicles. Trucks carrying goods, service vehicles, etc., would be allowed, and private vehicles could only operate within the containment area. FEMA stressed that to insure unfettered access for emergency vehicles and the clean-up crews at the Port Authority this was necessary. FEMA's problem was making sure people would buy it and that some semblance of normality would emerge after a few days.

Teddy, meanwhile, was back at work producing reports at a furious pace. The director now expected a new report every two days instead of the previous weekly briefing he had been producing. The government needed to keep its eye on the pulse of the economy and who could have been better for the job than their soothsayer, Teddy? His predictions had become an integral part of that process. On Thursday when the ban on travel was lifted, things largely returned to normal in Jersey, if only because it was the only thing people knew— routine. Some thousands still fled the city for safer locations, but mostly people went back to their jobs and life as they knew it. Some rationalized, what was a little radiation, with so many other toxic chemicals and pollutants in the area? They were used to living surrounded by a toxic soup of unknown lethality. Teddy was able to quantify this return to normal economic activity and plug the new number into the equation; the results looked better than his report on Wednesday. He was happy to send it the director's way.

CHAPTER 7

Goodbyes

Dakar's interview about the attack on Olsen aired the previous day. He received more than a few phone calls about it and more than one threatening the job he had already quit. There was some reaction on the Thursday both in support and denial of his allegations, and his account of what had really happened. The story was already washed away by the bombing. That was OK. He was already twenty-five thousand richer for his efforts. It was now part of the record as to what really happened at PB Olsen that morning.

Aaron had called to give him a blast and tell him ASI was threatened with having their contract terminated if they couldn't shut Dakar up. He couldn't tell them to fuck off. The players had the power to terminate the contract. So he lied, and told them he had fired Dakar this morning for breaking the terms and conditions of his contract, and was getting him out of there as soon as possible, which would be thirty days, but they didn't know that. Aaron begged him to lay low and keep quiet for the next month. Dakar agreed because that was exactly the plan. His next interview with Adrienne wasn't until he arrived in Tel Aviv.

Dakar had less than four weeks left until he was done. His role in protecting Tariq was decreasing all the time. Tariq was sorry to see him go, but understood it had to end sometime. He had tried to keep Dak, but the US was pulling out of most of the visible roles in providing security within the country. Tariq had been assigned an IP (Iraqi Police) security team. Dakar had met them both and they were now working together, Dakar training them in the job of being bodyguards. Both Iraqi men were young, inexperienced, somewhat idealistic, but were willing to learn. Their advantage over Dakar was knowledge of the culture and language, a big plus over what Dakar could offer in those areas. The official date for the termination of the contract and for the IP to assume sole responsibility was three months away.

The new guys coming in to replace Dak and Mick would not get much work before it was over. He heard they'd been here for a while; their contract had ended in Baghdad and they were simply riding out the job as long as they could, which was something he had thought of doing, but the situation had changed. Rumor was Olsen was closing in a few months. Teddy's plea to get the hell out, and the sailboat waiting for him in the Mediterranean, had driven away any lingering doubts about staying. Maybe he would consider a few months touring Greece, Turkey and Italy with the sailboat. He thought he had made the right decision and it felt right. Dakar always followed his intuition.

Simmons was with him every evening for at least an hour or so, their relationship the worst kept secret at PB Olsen. Still, they were discreet and professional in public at all times. He was going to miss that girl when she was gone. Not only was she a wonderful lover, but she had grown to be a close friend. There were few people who got that close to Dakar. She came on Wednesday night at 21:00 as usual. Not bothering to knock, she slipped into the room locking the door behind her. Dakar lay on the bed, with a raging hard on, begging for attention. She was out of her gear in a few seconds and he could see she was wet from where he lay on the bed. It was obvious she had been possessed by some sort of sex devil. She had her way with him, ordering him not to move and thrashing atop him wildly while she rode him to orgasm.

"Simmons, you were horny tonight," Dakar said inquisitively, after the festivities had ended for the evening.

"Oh, yeah! But you did your part tonight, Dakar. We'll be rotating out of here soon, Dak, and my stop loss is almost over." Stop loss was used to prevent soldiers from leaving the forces when their service contract had been fulfilled. The administration said it was needed in this time of war. Many soldiers were bitter over being forced to continue to serve, but went along because they had no choice in the matter.

"We will be returning home and I know you are done soon. Any chance for you and I to be together back home?"

Oh, oh, Dakar thought, *this isn't supposed to happen.* Dakar did love her, but not the same way he loved Jenn. He turned to her, looked straight at her and said, "Alicia, I love you as a friend, but I can't love you the way I loved and still love Jenn. I don't ever think I can or will get into another long term relationship with a woman. I'm sorry if you were hoping for something else."

Tears formed in her eyes. She looked at him and said, "I know part of the reason I have such strong feelings for you is where we are and what has happened to us over the past nine months. I had to ask.

My heart is so much yours right now. My husband, Dwight, is such a good man and a wonderful father to Dwayne. I know I can be happy with them when I get home, but I had to ask."

"Some of the reasons I admire you so much, Alicia, is the type of woman you are, full of the joy of life, sensual and you have an inherent sense of natural justice. I'm always going to want to keep in touch with you, even if it is just the occasional e-mail. I think our personalities are so compatible, it made us very close and it's the reason why our physical connection is so incredible."

Alicia exited awkwardly; she knew in her heart there had not been much chance for her and Dakar from the start. But she had to ask and was happy knowing that he cared.

Dakar was scheduled for duty today watching Tariq and training the two new guys. Mick was leaving tomorrow provided he could get a mil-air flight. A Chinook made its rounds every night and sometimes you could reserve a seat. Olsen was also a helicopter refueling base and often had Blackhawks, Apaches, Kiowas and Chinooks in for fuel. If a Blackhawk came in tomorrow he could always hitch a ride with them if they had room. The condition was Mick had to be ready to go in fifteen minutes, so he packed his bags in anticipation of getting a seat on an incoming Blackhawk. Long sleeve shirt, protective glasses, and of course, his personal protective equipment, were mandatory to fly mil-air. It might not happen at all tomorrow. There were so many dust storms. They frequently grounded all but essential missions. The dust was incredibly hard on the helicopter engines.

Dakar and Mick met in the DFAC for breakfast a little late this morning, after 8:00 AM. Mick sat down and Dak could tell from the look in his eyes he was relieved to be done.

"You're headed home first, Mick?" Dak asked.

"Yep, gotta get that bitch out of my house, and make sure she hasn't pawned or stolen half the furniture before I get back. That's why I haven't let her know I'm coming. She was one expensive piece of ass, Dakar. The worst of it is she isn't even that good in the sack anymore. She used to fuck me silly every morning and getting a blow job was as easy as unzipping my fly. When I left, blow jobs were few and far between, and she was pissed off if I woke her in the morning for some action," Mick commented on Cynthia, his current live-in. "God, that woman is going through two thousand pounds a month of my money and she doesn't have to pay for the rent or utilities. Now my mates tell me she's screwing some wanker from Glasgow. If she stays another three months she could have some claim on my house. As it stands now she has no right to stay. She hasn't contributed a shilling to the rent or upkeep of the house, and it will be easy to throw her out. Hell, I'll even give her a ride to the other bastard's house if she wants. I wonder how he will like her after a few months."

Mick's thick Scottish baroque made the whole thing sound slightly comical, and Dakar couldn't help but laugh out loud and comment, "That'll teach you for having a live-in. You probably weren't getting much because she was giving it to the other bastard. Too tired to fuck you, after giving it up to him!"

"Well, no more of that bullshit. I'll keep the place, but close it up and have one of my mates look in on it. In a few weeks I'll head to the Dominican and look for the perfect bar to buy. Sosua is where I'll likely be, mate, if you're sailing my way. The ladies, I hear, are lovely and the beer just divine. It's also possible to get a bottle of Guinness and some Red Label. Not sure where I'll live. Maybe buy a villa or condo."

"Well, good luck getting her out, my friend, and I'll see you before you go tomorrow." Dak's ride left in thirty minutes and he would have to suit up before leaving. His driver would be ready to go and this morning they were travelling in a convoy of MRAPs (Mine Resistant Ambush Protected) trucks that had thick armor sloped on the bottom to deflect blasts. The newer ones had auxiliary or deflective metal mounted on the outside skin about ten to twelve inches off the main armor, to protect against an IED with a shaped charge. The steel was thin, just enough to set the IED off before it reached the heavier armor underneath and burnt a hole through it.

Before going to his room to change, he headed to the MWR (Morale, Welfare and Recreation) hall to check his e-mail at the Internet terminals. When his home page popped up, he noticed the lead story was about the problems that the bombing was causing in the financial markets and the banking communities. In some parts of the United States, mostly conservative, middle-class neighborhoods, there were the beginnings of a run on the banks. Long line-ups and angry folk queued up in front of these institutions for hours, until the banks finally closed for the day. It was localized, and tied to existing rumors or stories about banks that were already on shaky financial ground. Banks in Arizona, Florida and Michigan were particular targets in that they had already suffered badly from a drastic decline in the housing market with lots of foreclosures. At least five other states were affected. The Federal Reserve had to step in and was shipping large amounts of cash to the banks to restore confidence in the banking system. The federal government was now looking at having to take over the ones in the worst shape, once again forced into the banking business. Glancing at his watch, Dak realized he only had ten minutes to show time, which meant he had to leave now, even though he had not checked his e-mail. He had been too engrossed in reading the story.

The rhythm and flow of daily life in Iraq were vibrant and approaching normal, after so many years of war. It was good for Iraq to have a semblance of normalcy in so many communities. The war had upset much of the country: so many people affected by the destruction, and worse yet, the loss of a stable government, electricity, water and any chance at a peaceful life.

All had their lives altered forever. He shared sweet black tea with an Iraqi citrus farmer, Mohammed Aziz, in the small bazaar (shop) he operated at PB Olsen, selling cigarettes, DVDs and Iraqi "souvenirs." Mohammed spoke with passion about the citrus farm he had, growing large juicy oranges and grapefruit—good oranges, the best in the area. People would come to his farm especially because of the great quality, and he could get a good price because they were so big and plump. When the war came, the electricity was cut off, and so were the irrigation pumps that supplied his orchard with water and the trees died. He and a neighbor had hand dug a well thirty feet and had water, but the water was too alkaline. The trees were dead and so ended Mohammed's simple life as a citrus farmer. Now he worked every day in the small store and had not seen his family for six months. His two sons were in high school and needed money for their education. His sister's husband had been killed by the insurgents for being a translator, and now he had her and her children to support also.

He hopped into the Tahoe with a few minutes to spare and they were out the gate en route to Tariq's house. In the other MRAPs, soldiers, members of the provincial reconstruction team and US advisors were going to inspect a new power station that was due to open in a few days. Electricity had been a huge problem in Iraq after the initial fighting. Power stations everywhere were knocked out. Electricity was available on a limited basis and only for a few hours a day. The new power plant would provide power twenty-four hours a day to Samarra and the surrounding area.

Today's trip was uneventful, just the way Dakar liked it. In the Tahoe, on the way over, Tariq and he talked about the economic turmoil and Dakar's impending departure.

"Do you think these puppies," referring to the new IP security team, "will keep me as safe, Dakar?" Tariq teased.

"Maybe. Just make sure the life insurance policy is paid up," Dakar quipped.

"Ha ha! Always the funny one, my friend, and for me, the lucky one. I think my life is not so safe now. The bastards kill more of us every day with their bombs," Tariq observed. "My family and I wish you well on your boat and perhaps one day we will visit you in America. Although from what I hear now on the news, you might be safer in Iraq."

"You might be right, my friend," Dakar joked. "You are always welcome in my home. You have made me welcome in yours."

"Let me know if there is anything I can do for you before you go. I have 'friends in high places in Baghdad,'" Tariq offered. Tariq was one of a handful of Sunni politicians who had the respect of Shiite and Kurdish politicians. The prime minister, a Shia, was a personal friend of Tariq's.

Dakar got back to base a little after 14:00 and noticed more activity than usual around the TOC and the open door of the captain's office. As he walked back to his room to get rid of his gear, Murph waved to him to come in, dismissing the soldier inside and asking him to have a seat.

"What up, Captain?" Dakar could sense something was going on.

"We have been ordered to close this base in forty-five days and are being redeployed stateside. Dakar, I know you'll be gone by then, but I thought I'd pass the news along. The Iraqi government will be assuming control of this property. I think they are turning it back to some sort of private use."

"You guys will probably beat me back to the States by the time I sail home. Congrats, Captain. I know you're looking forward to seeing your family again."

"Yeah, I miss Mary Lou and the kids. I'm about done here in any event. By the way, you won't be getting any medal after the interview with that woman from CNN. Confidentially, what happened here needed to be exposed to the American public and for fifty thousand, I'd post porno videos of my wife and I on the Internet, except no one would watch them, I'm sure."

Time for an afternoon nap. He wished Simmons would join him in the morning also; he loved having sex immediately after opening his eyes.

CHAPTER 8

Hell in a Hand Basket

Teddy took in the news of the last few days with a growing feeling of uncertainty, for the country and Rosie and himself. The last ten days had been remarkable in their unpredictability. The Dow rose and dove like a yo-yo, sometimes six hundred points in a single day. Currency traders were kicking the hell out of the American dollar, and foreign governments, notably some of the Arab states, had stepped in buying billions of US currency to prop up the now sagging dollar. In addition to the continuing run on some of the weaker banks which had slowed a little, some people had started hoarding food. Huge food retailers like Costco and Sam's Club had run out of the large quantities of such basic staples as rice and flour and beans, as consumers flooded the stores to stock up on non-perishables.

Teddy's predictions seemed to be without relevance. Director Corson called first thing in the morning to ask Teddy why this was. Teddy pulled no punches in his assessment. The greater the instability in the economy, the greater the margin of error. Until things calmed down a bit, the numbers would be off. It was as simple as that. He had no sooner hung up the phone, when the colonel called and asked that he report to the center ASAP. They had to have a workable formula now and he was needed to get that done. Teddy didn't enjoy being this popular with the establishment, and yearned for a more sedate and unnoticeable job. He supposed that because he was an actuary, it was second nature to want this—secure more in the world of numbers than the politics of Washington and its intrigues.

He made his way directly to the third floor of the Homeland Security office. Over the next four hours, he painstaking explained, once again, to his fellow mathematicians and actuaries the nature and fallibility of his work. This time he was able to show them his last two economic reports and how wrong they had been. It began to dawn on them that perhaps he was correct. It certainly looked that way. Instability breeds error. No matter how much the colonel badgered them to get results, there were none. Perhaps, just perhaps, in the future, when and if things calmed down they would be able to predict in the broadest of terms reactions to some issues or events of national significance, but that was still a long way off.

Exhausted Teddy drove home early, not bothering to return to the office. It was almost 3:30, and he would barely get back there and it would be past quitting time. He called in to retrieve his non-existent phone messages. By 5:00 PM, he was soundly asleep on the couch when Rosie strolled in the door. He didn't even notice when she unzipped his pants and barely opened one eye when she had his now soft dick in her mouth. It wasn't soft for long and she gave wonderful blowjobs. After ten minutes of hard work, she slurped down the last of her reward, rose from her knees, kissed his cheek and told him to nap a bit longer and she would prepare supper.

Teddy drifted back to sleep, comfortable and sated. He wondered if she would still suck his cock after they were married. He hoped so. He thought she would. She was so submissive sexually that she would do anything to keep him happy and perform any sexual act Teddy wanted. *Could it get any better than that?* he wondered.

Teddy's slept soundly that night. At the office the next morning, Tony, the guy occupying the office next to him, came rushing in the door at 11:30, telling him there had been an explosion in LA and to come to the staff room to see the TV report. "Fuck!" he said out loud. That was all the country needed: another act of terrorism. This might put them over the top. He hoped it wasn't so. He walked in and there it was—the helicopter circling overhead, zooming in on a plume of black smoke rising from a yard full of containers in LA. The chopper had been on morning traffic duty over the city when the explosion happened and was first on the scene. The fire trucks were rushing to the scene and visible six blocks away, sirens blaring and lights flashing. A small fire was burning at the base of the smoke plume that had already risen to eight hundred feet. The KABC traffic reporter was busy describing the scene and making sure the chopper pilot didn't take them anywhere near the smoke plume. He suspected the plume might be radioactive. He was sure many people viewing the scene were also thinking the same thing.

His report was broken up… "We can see many of the containers adjacent to the explosion area have been thrown about like a jumble of children's building blocks. We could hear and feel the explosion in the helicopter over a mile away. There was a terrific boom and the helicopter shuddered a few moments later, as the shock wave hit us."

Teddy knew the footage was a huge scoop for the reporter and the station. Sooner, rather than later, the helicopter would be ordered to back away from the scene by air traffic control. For the time being the reporter was getting as much footage as possible. Workers were running away from the scene of the fire, headed for what looked like the main building at the site. Teddy was unsure of what the facility was, but there were lots of transport trucks and trailers, and several rail lines ran into the place.

Teddy was well aware of the similarities between the previous bombing on the East Coast and he knew most people would be able to plainly see that. He stood for another hour with his co-workers watching the TV and noted the absence of any mention of radioactivity from the scene. There were many vaguely worded statements such as, "No mention yet of whether we are dealing with another radiological incident."

The story that the plume was radioactive was first broken on an Internet news site four hours after the initial report. Radiation had been detected by many amateurs using Geiger counters. The members of the mainstream media had all been asked by Homeland Security and FEMA to delay release of the radioactive nature of the bomb. There was also a short personal plea by President Haines to withhold the information from the general public until measures could be put in place to control public hysteria and keep the peace. All the major networks agreed. At the six hour mark, the news became more widespread. E-mails, word of mouth, and some local independent TV and radio stations carried the story about the radioactivity in the plume of smoke. Line-ups at gas stations and grocery stores, and growing volumes of rush-hour traffic proportions heading out of the LA area, were evident by mid-afternoon. By 4:30 Pacific time, the cat was fully out of the bag and the national TV stations were now carrying the story along with messages by the governor of California, the president, FEMA and Homeland Security, all pleading with the public to remain calm, stay indoors, not to travel and hoard food or money. The stations also carried the story of their decision not to let people know immediately about the radiation hazard because of the request of the authorities. Their excuse was that they were being responsible corporate citizens. On the orders of the governor, the interstate highways were all closed in LA.

For those people living in a ten mile radius around the blast, the black cloud was clearly visible against the rare smog-free and clear LA skyline. Panic had already set in, in this area, and people fled in their cars helter-skelter, as fast as they could. Unsure of the direction the cloud was drifting and with the thought always in their minds of the invisible radiation blanketing them and their loved ones, family-laden cars headed for the interstate highways.

Being stopped by the police at all the on-ramps to the interstate highways and told to return home did not sit well with many of them, but most did as they were ordered. At the Warner Ave. on-ramp to I-405, a group of motorists, cars loaded with family members, decided they were not returning to their irradiated homes and were leaving via the interstate highway. Six armed citizens approached the two cops guarding the entrance to the freeway and demanded they move aside. The police officers drew their weapons and ordered them to back off. Who fired first wasn't determined. One cop was killed, the other seriously wounded. One of the motorists died in the ensuing shootout. The others jumped into their cars abandoning the dead and wounded, frantically driving away from the blast, unaware of the snarled traffic three miles farther down the road.

Similar isolated incidents of violence, looting and panic spread throughout the city. Not all areas were affected. Some were almost normal. It was serious enough that by 10:00 PM, the governor had declared a state of emergency and immediate curfew. By 6: 00 AM the next morning, the National Guard had been called in. Across the city, murder, rape, looting, random killings and shootings of police officers continued. The police were becoming overwhelmed by the level of violence and disruptions. Otherwise law abiding citizens were shooting and killing, or being shot. The first night, over two hundred people were killed or wounded in the violence.

The next day ATMs in LA had long line-ups as people started stocking up on cash. Many grocery stores closed their doors to the general public; even corner stores were now being shuttered. The drift away from normalcy added to the sense of unease the majority of people felt. It caused greater numbers of them to sleep with their guns and act irrationally. Acts of violence from fear, fear of the radiation, fear of not having food, fear of their neighbors or whatever, led to more killing.

By noon the next day, the National Guard started patrolling the streets in the most affected areas, and violent or threatening acts were met with military force. By nightfall, another four hundred and forty-five members of the pubic had been shot and killed, and three soldiers slightly wounded. The level of violence dropped in most of the city the next day.

Teddy watched in horror at the drama as it unfolded on the West Coast. It turned out to be only one of many national problems that were starting to develop across the United States. Almost all the regular flow of commerce and business had slowly started again after the previous week's bombing on the East Coast. The last bombing had thrown a large monkey wrench into the gears of the economy that Teddy didn't think could be fixed. The stock and commodity exchanges, including money markets, were all closed for a week.

An emergency meeting of the finance ministers and leaders of the G-8 was scheduled in two days in Washington, and a week from that representatives of the G-20 were assembling in Zurich. Money markets in Europe and Asia had a run on the US dollar, having lost ten percent of its value in three hours, that no amount of government and bank intervention could stem and the money markets were promptly closed. International stock markets were reacting in a similar fashion and US companies trading on foreign exchanges, or companies with significant American holdings, all experienced sharp drops in value and trading was halted in those stocks. Investors started bailing on all stocks liquidating their portfolios in favor of precious metals or Swiss francs across the globe. This brought about the closure of all stock trading worldwide.

All of the financial meltdown happened so quickly, it caught everyone by surprise. Governments and leaders around the world were appealing to investors and the public in general not to make a bad situation even worse. Not to give the terrorists the victory they wanted. A number of Islamic extremist groups were claiming credit, but US intelligence services had a good lead that the latest attacks had been home-grown; the container on the East Coast had been shipped from within the country bound for Panama, and supposedly contained household goods. Teddy's mind raced through possible scenarios. Most had very bad endings. For the first time he was starting to become concerned for his and Rosie's safety.

CHAPTER 9

Indecision

Dakar could not believe what he was hearing and seeing on the television. He was stuck eight thousand miles away from home as the world unraveled and he said out loud, "Motherfucker!" The media continued to wail the bad news from across the globe. In Hong Kong the stock market was closed and wealthy Chinese were now trying to convert as much of their wealth as they could into precious metals, gold, silver, platinum, and palladium which were all in short supply. The difficult part for them was the precious metal exchanges were also closed. That meant taking physical possession of their metals was impossible and there just wasn't that much for sale. Anyone holding those metals was keeping them, partly to insure their own financial survival and partly because they knew there would be further dramatic increases in their value, increasing their profits dramatically.

Dakar's and Mick's replacements, Ryan and Alan, another Scot, had arrived in the past few days. Dakar spent the day acquainting them with what was happening regarding Tariq's guard duty and their roles in training the IP team now in charge of Tariq's security.

"Sorry, doesn't look like you will get more than a few months out of these guys," Dak observed.

Alan summed it up for both of them. "A few months translates into forty thousand more for me than I have now, and with so many of the guys pulling the plug, maybe there will be other short-term gigs after this one."

Dakar knew his logic was sound. It was a scenario he had thought of also. Ryan was the youngster at twenty-eight and Alan would be thirty-nine in a few days. Mick had e-mailed him from Scotland, having rid his house of vermin, as he called Cynthia. He was packing up and getting ready to fly to the Dominican Republic tomorrow. Both Mick and he had bought gold as a hedge against the future in the past year. Mick had purchased his via the Internet and took delivery when he returned to Scotland. Dakar bought some that way for pickup when he returned to the US, five thousand, in quarter and half ounce gold Maple Leafs. It was easy enough to find someone in Samarra to buy bullion from and he purchased another five thousand in small bits and chunks, and a few one ounce bars, in total a little over four ounces. The gold was hidden inside his air conditioning unit behind a panel that could only be removed with a screwdriver. He hoped it didn't break down and get replaced while he wasn't there one day.

Time dragged; he was really getting bored at PB Olsen and he hated being bored. Alicia took the edge off and he was going to miss her when they parted. She had begun to speak of the plans her husband, Dwight, and she were making to purchase a home and perhaps have another child when she returned from Iraq. Dakar was happy to know her thoughts were elsewhere. He had nothing to offer

Alicia in the long run. Over the next two days, the Internet and TV news continued to give increasing gloomy news from around the globe. There were no stocks being traded legally anywhere. The US government had placed daily limits on the amount anyone could take out in cash from their bank accounts and then reduced it even further when the hemorrhaging of cash from banks continued unabated.

Air travel had initially been brisk because people flew home to be with their families. Now flights were empty as few people flew anywhere to do anything. US airlines cancelled over eighty percent of their worldwide and domestic flights. Special charter flights were now required to shuttle the non-military personnel out of Iraq stateside. The regularly scheduled flight he hoped to take from Baghdad to Amman, Jordan, had been cancelled and the travel agency had not credited his credit card with the refund. How he was going to get to Tel Aviv was not clear and would require some thought on his part.

Dakar hadn't heard about British airlines, but he thought many of them would also have cancelled flights. Mick might be swimming to the Dominican or already there if he was lucky. Airlines, manufacturers, retail outlets, fast food joints, and many private sector jobs were lost either temporarily or permanently as businesses shut their doors in more and more cities and towns across the United States. He worried from time to time about Jenn; he hoped she was okay, happy, healthy and most importantly, safe.

The story that started to emerge was a shock to many who thought it was a clear case of al-Qaida or some other Islamic extremist group responsible for the bombings. It came to light that the bombings were perpetrated not by foreign based groups, but by a violent segment of the "Patriotic Community," in particular a small cadre of white supremacists from Wisconsin. The media speculated from comments on the group's website that they were attempting to foment a revolution that would spark a race war and return, as they saw it, "A truly white democracy based on adherence to God's laws and the Constitution. In all, the group had a few dozen members, but only ten were considered hardcore: the rest being hangers-on and weekend racists, at best. Of the ten, only four could not be located and a nationwide hunt was now on for the three men and one woman. The who and why of it were no help in stemming the economic disaster now unfolding. Tracking down the guilty parties would take time and time was running out.

Simon called Dakar, from his boat repair shop in Tel Aviv, to tell him his boat was ready to go. The fuel tanks were full, the fresh water tanks disinfected and flushed, and would be again just prior to his arrival and then filled, which would only take a few hours. Dakar could use a break and thought a few days at one of the luxury hotels that lined the waterfront in Tel Aviv would be nice. He made arrangements with a private air charter firm from Jordan to fly him from Baghdad to Amman. It was a two thousand dollar flight, but he had few options. There were no one-way car rentals available from Baghdad and travel by land might be too risky.

There were ten days to go before he left and Dakar had little contact with Tariq. Almost all the duties had been taken over by Ryan and Alan. He wasn't sure why he was still there; he was just putting in time. For the company it was billable time and for Dakar every day meant another seven hundred and eighty six dollars in his pocket. He supposed he should think of it as another seven thousand, eight hundred and sixty dollars to make in the next ten days. He kept a diary of how much money he made every day and a cumulative total. To date the total was over three hundred and ten grand—not too shabby for a kid from the sticks in Idaho.

The situation in the US had not stabilized at all. In twenty-two states the National Guard had been mobilized to maintain order. In many major cities, food riots and demonstrations by the unemployed and disaffected were a daily occurrence. In the previous six days, eight hundred and fifty-four Americans had died in the violence. The panic and unrest had spread to Europe and those countries with a history of political unrest now had their streets filled with protesters. Worldwide commerce was grinding to a halt at the international, national and even neighborhood levels, as people lost confidence in their currencies or stores ran out of consumer goods and food.

Interestingly, the poorest economies were not as affected as the heavily industrialized nations. Having most of their populations engaged in the business of growing food and supplying their countrymen with basic services had helped the poorest countries. These locally-based economies were not totally crippled by the world situation. Life was as it had been for some hundreds of years in villages, towns and small cities. Being poor, they were accustomed to making do with what they had, accepting that today some goods were not available at the store and perhaps would be tomorrow. In the consumer-based economies of the West, much of the panic in the population was not based on the fact that people were hungry, but rather that they could no longer get everything they wanted at the supermarkets or in the quantities they wanted. It was all too much for some people and drove them to do insane things for which they were arrested or killed.

Dakar was concerned about his friend Teddy; he called to ask how he was doing. Rosie answered in her usual chipper tone.

"Dak, it's good to hear your voice. Hope you will soon be the hell out of Iraq! Although what you are coming home to might not be that great. Teddy's just coming out of the shower now," she said as she handed the phone to Teddy.

Dak barely had time to say, "Good talking to you, Rosie" before Teddy was running down all that was happening in the US. Teddy had heard that the major news networks had been subject to censorship in the past few days on an official basis. Teddy kept a watch on the "news" not only through the major news outlets, but also several alternate Internet websites. It was plain to see things were much worse than what was presented on the news. Whole sections of LA, Detroit, Baltimore, Chicago, Phoenix, New York, Philly, Miami, Houston and even the DC area were lawless. Police dared not enter and the troops were being fired on with increasing regularity. Other cities had sporadic incidents of violence and the National Guard in many states was stretched to the limit.

Several of the North Western states disliked what they perceived as the high handed tactics the federal government was advocating for the maintenance of order. Teddy heard a rumor that martial law was about to be declared across the US. Potential troublemakers and radicals were to be rounded up and detained until the situation calmed down. The websites quoted governors in Washington, Idaho, Wyoming and Montana as saying they would refuse to obey any order that suspended Constitutional rights. All of those states, although not enjoying business as normal, were a lot quieter than a wide band across the southern US and many on the Eastern seaboard.

Dak took all of this in with concern for Teddy. "I'm starting to think you should get out of the city, Teddy. Take Rosie and head back to Idaho. You can always stay in the cabin. I'm worried about you, my friend."

"That's a strange one. A month ago I was asking you to leave Iraq and now you're asking me to leave Washington. I don't know whether I would be allowed to quit my job or leave. The federal government has ordered all employees to report to work regardless of their job classification and we've been assured our paychecks will keep coming."

"Get out while the getting is good, Teddy. Next thing you know they'll be closing the highways. You already have gas and food rationing of a sort. You may not get another opportunity in a few weeks or even days the way things are going."

"I know, Dak. I've been thinking about that. It's a hard thing to do, to abandon our future. I can't help hoping that things will settle down and be back to normal in a few weeks or days. My own reports tell me that is not so, and who knows what the economy or the world will look like in a year? Rosie has been at the hospital for four years and is hoping to get the supervisor's job which is coming up in a few weeks. I guess we will stick it out for a bit and then make a dash for it, if things get really bad."

"You may not get that chance, Teddy. Keep in touch," Dakar said.

CHAPTER 10

Big Changes

Teddy didn't have to wait long for the rumors of marital law to become reality. One evening, two days later, the president "spoke to the nation."

The president's words and mood were somber. "In this time of national tragedy, of great suffering and sacrifice of Americans everywhere, I am asking you to help in keeping this country whole and alive. We can no longer maintain law and order in many of our cities…" He continued by describing the acts of the home-grown terrorists as "playing into the hands of America's enemies by creating havoc and economic difficulties around the world."

"Therefore, so that we can maintain order in the cities and towns of America, I am declaring a state of national emergency and invoking martial law. All National Guard units are now under the control of the federal government. We will keep control and order in our country. All those who seek to destabilize this great country through violence have become enemies of the United States and will be treated as such. We cannot and will not allow these individuals and small groups of extremists and criminals to tear down our nation and the democratic ideals we cherish."

The move to martial law stunned the population as a whole and especially the Christian Right, which looked upon this as another act foretelling the apocalypse and the coming of the Anti-Christ. The Patriotic Community ratcheted up the rhetoric by proclaiming their right to bear arms and how they would fight to their last breath to keep their guns. The government would have "to pry their guns from their cold, dead hands" was their rallying cry and other such nonsensical clichés.

Most people were too dazed to do anything other than accept what happened: afraid to speak up lest their whole way of life or family's wellbeing be jeopardized. Teddy was in this group of people. Rosie was very busy at work, the hospitals were filling up with the genuinely ill or wounded in the fighting and those suffering a multitude of stress related problems. Doctors wrote mountains of prescriptions for anti-depressants, anti-anxiety drugs and other sedatives.

Television was now full of experts explaining how the economy was going to bounce back shortly in a slow and steady upward climb. Still other health experts urged people to see their family physicians if they were having trouble coping with these temporary changes in their lives. They assured everyone there were treatments to help with the anxiety and stress. Others offered practical advice on topics ranging from the impact on the fashion industry to growing your own garden, which resulted in a rush on the seed supply across the country.

From lists prepared by the FBI, Homeland Security and the police began rounding up all those they thought of as troublemakers and holding them in special facilities without criminal charge or legal recourse. The lists had been assembled over many years and contained the names of outspoken opponents to the government or those with viewpoints of an inflammatory nature. Leftists of all sorts and members of the Patriotic Community were detained. The government was conscious of the need to maintain political allies and the Christian Right was one of those groups. Pastors who preached resistance received a visit from the local authorities, advising them to tone down the rhetoric or face arrest.

In an attempt to placate the Christian Right, President Haines offered to make their church members and other patriotic Americans special officers, with the powers of the police and under the command of the local military authority. They were asked to help in the rebuilding of America, and to prevent radical elements from hijacking the democratic system and seizing control of the country. The fact the country was already under martial law seemed lost on them; they were all too ready to be part of the good guys. The Presidential Patriotic Force was born and a hundred thousand Americans asked to join the first day. A million within three days.

Teddy was sick to his stomach about the rapidness with which the country was disintegrating and now he was stuck. He was unable to leave his job, as was Rosie. Their work was declared essential. Travel was restricted to essential commercial traffic and authorized individuals. When he and Rosie shopped they were limited in quantity as to what and how much they could buy. The administration limited cash withdrawals from personal bank accounts. People subsisted on what little cash and funds they had in their existing bank accounts. All financial transactions were in shambles and no plan had been announced yet as to how the whole mess was to be handled. Travel by car was restricted to and from work only and not allowed in the city core. He and Rosie walked the six blocks to the supermarket from their apartment. The poor and indigent were fed by large kitchens located throughout the cities.

The chaos in the US was not the case throughout the world. Canada, although severely impacted by their giant neighbor to the south, was relatively peaceful, being a nation whose people valued peace, order and good government above all else. The Japanese and Indians likewise didn't have large problems with violence. Their economies were in chaos, though.

Teddy had taken to consulting the Internet news sites exclusively. The news took a turn for the worse. The four northwest governors of Washington, Idaho, Wyoming, and Montana had been joined by two others, Colorado and Arizona, in resisting federal control of the National Guard and local governments. California was ungovernable, and the National Guard could not maintain law and order. It was purely academic as to whether California would join the coalition. It was impossible given the turmoil in the state. The governor, a Republican, was also a staunch ally of President Haines. Some people were hinting at taking control of the situation themselves. Oregon was wavering in its support for the declaration of martial law, and mutterings were heard from the Dakotas, and three or four other western states. The governor of Montana, John Maier, made a public statement urging people to resist marital law and if necessary to use force to maintain the protection of the Constitution in his state.

The next day, the president made a grievous error and ordered the director of the FBI to arrest the governor as an enemy of the United States. Ten FBI agents attempted to gain access to the State Capitol building; an armed standoff ensued between the state police and the FBI. An overzealous FBI agent fired on a state trooper, killing him, and the troopers returned fire at the men who had killed their fellow officer. Reason prevailed after a few minutes and the FBI withdrew, but the damage was done. Those states that were wavering in their support for the Western Coalition, as it had been named, were now solidly entrenched behind it, afraid that they too would have their senior state officials or governors arrested and imprisoned, or worse. The other western states that had been sympathetic were now leaning heavily in their support for the Western Coalition. Frantic phone calls and personal pleas from respected politicians in Washington were falling on deaf ears; the attempted arrest showed them that actions spoke louder than words.

It was now unlikely that the National Guard in many of the Coalition states would obey any direct orders from Washington that involved military action against the citizens of their state. Discretion became the better part of valor in Washington and to ease tensions the orders given were to stand down, not to provoke or encourage any action that would precipitate an armed military conflict. Not since the civil war had armed rebellion become so imminent.

The president, Joint Chiefs and his advisors met long into the night throwing around various scenarios in their minds, some ridiculous in their extremity. The secretary of state, Kevin Beck, urged the president to launch a preemptive strike against Montana by sending in Special Forces to arrest Governor Maier. He felt a show of force would put an end to all the nonsense talk coming out of the west.

Lincoln Lancaster, the secretary of Homeland Security, counseled the president to deal with the problem at a later date. In the end, the president decided that keeping the country intact was the number one priority. The decision was made to pull all the troops in Iraq and Afghanistan out and bring them home to keep the peace. The backdrop to this decision was a possible civil war, something no one

GLENN R. SUGGITT

wanted, but which everyone knew was possible. They reviewed the status and security of all nuclear weapons in the states affected, and beefed up security at all nuclear weapons' sites or transferred the weapons to larger more secure military bases.

The regular forces were not a problem. They still obeyed orders from Washington without question. The National Guard was another story. In Montana, the National Guard was now the de-facto state army and was supplemented by a State Defense Force, a militia made up of many veterans and other patriotic citizens. It had grown to over forty thousand in two days. The State Capitol building was an armed fortress. The Montana local media called upon Governor Maier to arrest the FBI agent who had killed the state trooper and put her on trial for murder. The governor declined and in an address to the people of Montana urged them to remain vigilant in their defense of freedom and American values, but not to become violent. The president was relieved, but could not regain the trust of Maier. The best he could do was to thank him by phone, personally, for helping to relieve tensions.

The rest of the world was a mixed bag. Military coups had taken place in many smaller nations in Latin America, Africa and Asia that had fragile democracies. Greece had a military coup and the European Union was threatening them with loss of membership. For Greece, the choice other than military rule was dictatorship of the left; the democratic process was in shambles. The prime minister of Greece had been assassinated and there was a hopeless deadlock in the Hellenic Parliament. Athens had become a seething cauldron of political demonstrations and violence. The communists were sure they could seize power and the military felt it had to act, and quickly, to avoid a communist takeover.

Much of Europe had significant unrest, but not to the extent of what was happening in America. France was hard hit: Germany, England, the Scandinavian countries less so. Italy was starting to see widespread demonstrations in their cities and the Communist Party was making big gains in its already large membership.

Teddy no longer trusted any of the mainstream media outlets at all and the government was talking about shutting down the Internet. Those in positions of power felt the decision to shut down the internet would foment unrest and the decision to disable it was put in abeyance. A campaign of disinformation was already working for many sensitive issues like the huge number of arrests and detentions of so-called troublemakers. Like good propagandists everywhere they made it hard to tell the truth from lies and they used lots of both—a mixture of disinformation, the truth, "expert opinions" and patriotic double-speak, to alter public opinion. All live broadcasts were now prohibited, and censors manned the control booths of all TV and radio stations in the eastern and southern states. Teddy made his mind up to go home, to take Rosie and head to Idaho.

He called Dakar on his sat phone to tell him, speaking in vagaries, ever mindful of the ears sure to be listening. "Dak, I think Rosie and I will head home shortly. Not sure how that is going to happen. What about you?"

Dak answered, "Well, I am sticking with my original plan with a few twists for the current situation. Want me to come and pick you up?"

Teddy wasn't exactly sure what that meant or how he planned to do it. One thing was for sure, Dakar and he were an awesome team and their chances of making it back to Idaho together were much better than if he attempted the journey by himself. He answered, "Let me explore some other possibilities and get back to you about your generous offer. I'll talk it over with Rosie and let you know."

"Let me know soon, Teddy, so I can change my plans if need be. Miss you, buddy. Stay safe," Dakar answered, as he hung up.

CHAPTER 11

The Plan

After Dakar hung up the phone his mind started wrestling with the problem of how to get to Tel Aviv. Air travel around the globe was now suspended on all commercial levels other than authorized government flights and there sure as hell wouldn't be one from Baghdad to Amman, Jordan, anytime in the near future. His charter flight option was dead. He wondered if there were any mil-air flights to Israel. He doubted that also.

Dak left his room to hook up with the new guys in the DFAC for supper. Soldiers were scurrying everywhere: all of them, from the self-absorbed looks on their faces, on some sort of mission. Curious, Dakar went to Murph's office to find out what was going on. The door lay open and when Dakar approached, he could hear Murph giving orders to a sergeant to get the comm. equipment into the container and get it ready to go. There were several others waiting for

Murph's direction and Dakar turned to go, not wanting to disturb him if he was busy. He would return later when things calmed down.

Murph called to him, "Dak, hold up a minute. You need to hear this. We have been ordered home in two weeks."

"You mean they're shutting this base down that quickly?" Dakar questioned.

"No, Dak, everyone in Iraq is going home in two weeks. All forty-six thousand of us are to assemble at the nearest military air base for airlift to the States. A small contingent of marines is to hold the bulk of our heavy equipment in Basra for shipment by sea and air home. All other bases are to be turned over to the Iraqis, including the four super bases we were supposed to keep. Anything that can be loaded on a plane is going home with us. All civilian contractors in Iraq have had their contracts terminated and are to assemble in Basra for the airlift home. Come back later and I'll give you the rest of the details." Murph then turned to the next soldier in line giving him orders for the types of materials and equipment that were to be turned over to the Iraqis and what was to be destroyed.

This latest development would require more creative thinking on his part, but for now he had better break the news to Alan and Ryan, and get something to eat. He strode into the DFAC, headed to the chow line and sat down with them at the far end of a line of tables. The tables were filled with soldiers talking animatedly about the current state of affairs. There was a lot of speculation about why they were being recalled. Some still didn't know about the explosive situation in the northwest of the country and the lawless nature of large pockets in America.

"Well, guys, looks like you aren't going to get any more time in. We've all been fired," Dakar deadpanned.

"We heard, Dakar. At this rate we'll be lucky to get paid or have access to our money, for that matter. The fucking bastards!!" Alan lamented.

"Apparently they are airlifting us out of Basra sometime in the near future. I'll phone ASI and ask them how they are handling our transport and get back to you," Dakar said.

Ryan was noticeably upset and asked what was going to happen to them. The fear of uncertainty visible in his eyes, the fear, he said, of being abandoned in Iraq.

Dakar assured him they would get all the contractors out using civilian passenger jets, he imagined. The people who worked at the bases were from many different countries: Kenya, the Balkans, South Africa and Britain. There was a legion of poorly paid subcontract workers, mainly from the India, Sri Lanka, Nepal and the Philippines and all of them would require flights home. They were treated little better than ancient feudal serfs, receiving as little as two hundred and fifty dollars a month or less and having to pay bribes to get the jobs in the first place. He was sure the companies that hired these poor souls would not pay for them to go home or make any arrangements to get them home. He would hate to be in their shoes. He guessed there would be blood spilled over the issue and it would probably be the blood of the subcontract workers. It would require many hundreds of flights to get everyone home.

Finishing supper, he headed back to his room and called ASI. Holly answered and her usually happy voice was troubled. "Dakar, from what I've been told, it is as you heard. Everyone is to go to Basra and be airlifted from there. I'm sorry I don't have any other details for you. I know that makes it tough for you to get that new sailboat. In fact, they may shut down ASI in a few days or weeks. No one knows how or when we are getting paid or if we are at all. It's such a mess. We keep getting assured that everything is OK, but who knows for sure?"

"Thanks, Holly. Good luck. Let me talk to Aaron," Dakar asked.

"Hold on, Dak. I'll transfer the call," Holly said.

"Dakar, looks like the party is really over for good," Aaron flatly stated. "I'm not sure what is going on my friend. I keep hearing from my bosses that Washington says they're going to take care of us, but I wonder what that means. The sat phones will stay operational, I am assured, but exact details about the Basra airlift are sketchy. I don't know what to do with the equipment. The three of you can take the armored SUVs in a military convoy when one leaves for Basra."

Dakar didn't like the uncertain nature of his hypothetical ride home; he knew Basra was not big enough to handle the massive influx of tens of thousands of soldiers and civilians at one time. Shit would definitely happen there and not much of it nice. The idea to drive to Jordan and then Israel had come to mind suddenly, and he blurted out his request without thinking it through. This was vintage Dakar, following his intuition.

He asked, "Aaron, I'd like to use one of the Tahoes to drive to Israel through Jordan. The highways are still open. I could also use my weapons and a few other incidentals."

There was a short pause and Aaron said, "Of course you can. I don't have the authority to tell you that, but at this point who really gives a damn? Go ahead, Dakar, take what you want. Alan and Ryan can take the other Tahoe to Basra. I'll call Alan tomorrow when I have more details on the Basra airlift. Good luck, Dakar. I hope we will get a chance to get together again when all the craziness stops. In the meantime, God help us all, in the next few weeks."

There were a hell of a lot of questions to be answered, but for now "The Plan" was to drive. Perhaps he should dub this Plan A.

You never know what might happen; by tomorrow he could be working on Plan C.

Any concern he had about getting to Tel Aviv had vanished, after he had voiced his request. His mind churned with questions. Would the SUV's dual fuel tanks hold enough fuel for the entire trip? Would he be free to travel in Iraq? Did he need permission from the Iraqi authorities? Was the border still open between Iraq and Jordan, and Jordan and Israel?

He hunted down Alan and Ryan, passing on what he had learned and his plan to strike out north across the desert to Jordan.

Alan was not impressed. "You stupid fuck. Why don't you just put a sign on the SUV saying shoot me and take all my stuff? Dakar, this is not one of your smarter ideas."

Sober second thought was not part of Dakar's nature either and he simply said, "It will be fine. I'll fall in with the next convoy to Tikrit and then it's a leisurely drive across the desert to the air base at al Asad from Tikrit. Another four hours puts me at the border. Hell, in 24 hours I'll be sipping a cold one in Amman while you assholes are still packing up your gear."

"In your dreams, young fella. What do you want done with what will be left of you? Cremated? Hold on, you will probably get your ass barbecued, so no need to do that," Alan continued.

"I am not giving up my boat and there's no way to get from Basra to Tel Aviv. Besides I might have to give a friend of mine a lift!!" Dak said, adamant about his plan.

"It's been a slice, Dakar. Good luck. You'll need it," Alan said, shaking his head as he turned and left with Ryan. Dakar would see both before he left and the bullshit talk was just Alan's way of telling him to be careful. Everyone was wishing him good luck and he would need it.

Laying out his plan rapidly in his mind, he realized he would need some sort of permission from the military to travel in Iraq. He returned to Murph's office to fill him in on what he had decided. After knocking on Murph's door to announce his presence, Murph waved him in.

"Captain, I've cooked up a plan to drive to Jordan in one of the SUVs and I'm thinking I'll need some sort of transit pass," said Dakar pointedly.

"What! You are one scary individual, Dakar, to try that. The good news and bad news are you won't need any pass or authority from the US military to travel the Iraqi roads. The roads are entirely under Iraqi control, and have been for a year and a half. Maybe Tariq can help you with some sort of Iraqi pass or letter. The Iraqis are supposed to allow free passage for all American military and civilian contractor convoys. I think I can arrange for some help for you, though. Which road are you going to use? The main highway runs out of Baghdad, but Baghdad is a cluster fuck right now and it might be difficult to get through."

"I was thinking north to Tikrit and then across the desert road to al Asad, cross the Euphrates there and then rejoin the main road to Jordan."

"Let me get some intel on the road and see if I can get you some help on the way, Dakar. Come and see me tomorrow."

Murph's suggestion about Tariq was something Dakar had been mulling over, and he returned to his room, picked up his cell phone and called him. He outlined his plan to Tariq.

Tariq was to the point. "I will contact my friend in Baghdad and also draft a letter directing all Iraqi government agencies to give their full cooperation and support to you, Dakar. It is the least I can do, my friend. I owe you my life many times. Call me tomorrow afternoon and I will have some answer for you. May Allah bless you and travel with you, Dakar."

Dakar made one more call, but on the sat phone this time, to Simon in Tel Aviv to let him know about his plan to drive and check again on his boat. Simon assured him it was ready to go and that Israel was stable, comparatively speaking to the US and that he heard Jordan was not bad either. On impulse he asked Simon if he could get some gold or silver for him to take with him on the boat. He might need more ready cash in the form of gold. People would be crazy for gold. His account in the Caymans was still active and a lot of the world's capital had fled to such offshore places. The rich were hedging their bets. The US dollar was weak in off-market trading, down almost a third in comparison to the Euro and more compared to the Canadian dollar.

"Let me see… there are small amounts of gold being smuggled into Israel from Arab states. The price is very high, too much, almost ten thousand dollars an ounce," Simon answered.

"All right, try and get me ten ounces in small coins or bullion, even gold jewelry is fine. I can still wire transfer money to you from the Caymans. Also ask around about the border crossings to Iraq from Jordan, and between Israel and Jordan," Dakar said.

"You call tomorrow, Dakar, in the afternoon," Simon said, as he disconnected. The next thing Dakar did was head for the storage container where the MREs (Meals Ready to Eat) were stored and get a whack of them in a large duffel bag. His favorite was the pasta, and he got half a dozen of them and another dozen assorted. He drove the big Tahoe over to the skid of water bottles and threw eight packages of twelve one-liter bottles in the back. All of the food and water were easily six to ten times more than he calculated he might need, but better to have too much than too little. The armored SUV would easily take the extra weight. He went to the fueling station and filled up. He would hate to pay for the fuel. The big six-liter diesel burned a lot of fuel. The basics were covered, and he went to find Alicia and tell her about Plan A. She was coming over tonight at the usual time. He would phone Teddy tomorrow. Tonight he'd mull over his details, and what he might encounter on his road trip and his voyage through the Mediterranean and across the Atlantic.

That night, Alicia arrived at the appointed time and left before the witching hour. God, it was going to be hard to leave her behind. She was such a great lover. He supposed the sex was great because of the person she was and of the feelings they had for each other, her sudden intense feelings being a bit more than either had bargained for. The shared experience of combat and the daily danger added spice and fury to their lovemaking.

CHAPTER 12

Teddy's Choice

T eddy and Rosie talked that night, snuggled up on the couch, about their alternatives. Rosie felt she would be deserting all her patients if she left her job. She worried about what would happen to them if they were caught leaving their jobs and the capital. Teddy knew they would not get far before they were stopped, asked for ID and then arrested and then what would happen after that, he didn't know. Teddy had a private pilot's license, but no plane and the single engine aircraft he was capable of flying would not have the range to fly to Idaho without a few stops for fuel, which was impossible. In the end he and Rosie decided to throw their lot in with Dakar and plan their escape with him.

"I'll call Dakar in the morning on your cell phone and ask him to pick us up when he gets here," Teddy said with a sigh. He was dreading more weeks working for the bitch.

Teddy felt so helpless in face of the enormous problems that faced the nation. There was nothing wrong with the infrastructure, industries or the will of the American people to work. It was the system per se that was broken. Confidence, as in his formula, as part of his economic equation was broken. Until control could be restored on the streets and confidence restored in the hearts of Americans, things were going to get worse. He wondered how that could be done. Greater minds than his were wrestling with these questions at that very moment, he was sure.

Rosie lay in his arms that night crying softly for a few moments and holding him tighter than usual. It was late at night before they both dozed off into a fitful sleep after some incredibly tender lovemaking. Teddy and Rosie walked arm in arm to work in the morning. Rosie's work was close, less than a mile, and when they parted he kissed her and told her he loved her, as he did every day. Teddy had a mile hike to a central transportation hub and then a short commute in a van six miles into the center of Washington. The drab gray skies were an apt background for their mood and the mood of the country.

On his hike to the van Teddy used Rosie's cell phone to call Dakar. Dakar answered on the first ring and Teddy started right in. "Hi, Buddy, we've decided to take you up on your offer of a lift home. Let me know when you're close to Washington. Rosie and I will be ready to go when you get here."

Dakar updated Teddy on his plan to drive to Tel Aviv. "It's going to take me a few months to sail home, plus the trip from Tel Aviv to Gibraltar. I'm going to leave in a couple of days for Tel Aviv. It should be a smooth trip, and take two or three days, if things go well. I'll call you from Tel Aviv in four or five days, Teddy."

"Sounds good, Dak. Be careful. I'm not looking forward to working for that grumpy bitch, Colonel Bernice Guay, for any longer than I have to," Teddy lamented.

"You have Rosie to take your mind off her, Teddy. I'm worried about you, as well. Be careful yourself. No telling what will happen," Dakar said as he hung up.

Teddy had been assigned on a temporary basis to the care and control of Colonel Bernice Guay, who had become increasing irritated at the lack of progress in finding the miraculous formula that would predict the future and allow the government to control the reactions and emotions of its citizens. His new office was at the Homeland Security building working on an equation everyone now knew was pointless. In order to assuage the feeling of uselessness that he and most of his coworkers were feeling he decided to change his perspective and do it the other way around. What would it take to make people trust an economic model? What would the economic conditions have to be for people to get that confidence? The colonel showed up just before noon to check on their progress. He hoped she wouldn't be giving one of her "the nation is depending on you" speeches.

Teddy broached the idea to her. "Colonel, what if we reversed our approach to this whole question and were able to construct a model detailing what it would take to restore confidence in the economy? The approach we are using now is a dead end. Nothing is coming out of our work." His coworkers were nodding their heads in agreement and generally reinforcing a conclusion most had already reached themselves. As for Teddy's new idea, why not? There was nothing else that looked promising.

"I'm not sure that will help us or how. Perhaps you can explain it to me in your office," the colonel demanded.

Teddy wasn't sure why the woman had to be so abrasive all the time, her demeanor more like a pit bull than a team player. It was obvious in her years as a military officer she was used to being obeyed without question. She looked like a pit bull, too. Her jowls drooped slightly and she never wore makeup of any kind. She was not accustomed to wearing civilian clothes. The clothes she wore were expensive, but she looked so uncomfortable in them. They hung on her like wet laundry on a line. She sported a small pin on her blouse of two crossed rifles, whatever that meant. Her hair was colored a shade of mousy brown to match her beady brown eyes. They walked into his office and she closed the door.

"Give me a rundown on what you propose to do," she asked flatly.

"To tell you the truth I have only been mulling this around in my mind for a few hours, but anything has got to be better than what we have been doing," Teddy replied.

"Fine, let me know tomorrow what you propose, your work plan and what the timelines are, so I can take it up the chain of command. Oh and by the way, Teddy, this 'Bitch' says you had better not abandon your job and your country, and leave Washington." She paused to let the statement sink in and continued. "If you so much as think about leaving again, I'll have you detained at a secure facility and you won't be banging that cute piece of ass you have any time soon." Again she stopped, and then looking Teddy straight in the eye and with venom in her voice said, "Do you fucking understand?"

Teddy was shocked beyond belief. The paranoia he felt about being bugged was real. The cursory sweep he and Rosie had conducted of the apartment had turned up nothing. He thought the couple watching them was for his security, not to spy on him and Rosie. It was now apparent his phones were all being monitored, too.

He wanted to reach across the table and slap her arrogant face, but restrained himself and took a deep breath. He sat speechless for a moment, his lips tightly pursed in anger.

"DO YOU FUCKING UNDERSTAND!!!" she screamed.

"YESSS!" he angrily replied.

"Okay, Teddy. Now we are clear. Do your job, stay put and everything will be fine. Talk to you tomorrow," she said when she turned to leave.

Teddy spent the rest of the day feeling angry and betrayed by his country. He would love to bitch slap the dyke for the way she threatened him. He wasn't sure how, but he and Rosie were definitely going to get the fuck out of Washington and home to Idaho somehow.

There was a way he might be able to talk to Dakar and that was to phone him on his personal cell phone from a phone that did not belong to either Rosie or him. As long as Dak had his Iraqi cell phone with him, he just had to catch him with it on. Rachel, a colleague and an actuary like him, was a likely person to ask. She was always flirting with him, even though she knew he was engaged to Rosie. She had a very pretty face, but carried about forty pounds too much weight.

He approached Rachel during lunch and asked to use her cell phone later for a long distance call to a friend in Europe, explaining that he had left his phone at home and insisted she accept forty dollars for the use of it. It would be some weeks before she would see the charge on her account. The international country code would be confusing to her, and she would probably not look up which country if he kept the call brief and below the forty dollars he had given her.

The rest of the afternoon he spent brainstorming with his colleagues about his hair-brained idea. There were lots of negative comments and this new approach, they agreed, was not likely to give them anything useable.

About 3:00 PM, when everyone was taking a break, he went outside to use Rachel's cell phone for the call to Dakar.

The phone rang five times before Dakar finally answered. Teddy spilled his guts quickly. "Dakar, I have to be brief. Rosie and I are under surveillance and The Bitch is aware we are planning to leave. I've been threatened with a detention center, if I talk to you. I won't be able to call you on the sat phone again. I am going to try to get a throw-away cell phone, and call or text you in a few days with a new contact number. If not, still come and get us, and we'll figure out a way to contact you when you get close to the States."

Dakar was likewise brief. "Whatever you do, don't get thrown in jail, Teddy. I can't get you out of that sort of a mess. Chill for a month or two. We will limit contact to essential information. Perhaps using new e-mail accounts might work if the Internet stays up, although leaving a written record might not be a good idea. My plan is to sail to the Canaries, and then catch the trade winds to the Caribbean and work my way up the coast to you."

There was no need to say anything else; Teddy knew that Dakar was coming for them without a doubt. And Dakar knew that whoever had threatened Teddy had made a grave mistake; the affable Teddy became a dangerous man when those he cared about were threatened. In high school, Dakar's slight stature had drawn the attention of school bullies. Teddy had frightened him and the bullies with his savage reaction. He had no more problems with bullies in school. Teddy was the wrong guy to piss off—the type of man tough guys intuitively avoided.

Teddy went back into the building. For the next few hours, his group tossed around all sorts of different angles and ideas. A consensus was reached that they needed the input of a good psychologist if they were to have any chance at making the new scheme work.

He had the basis of his old formula which he could use to develop fixed psychological parameters that indicated a stable state of mind for the bulk of the American public. The question was, what sort of economic model would do that, how long would it take to achieve and would the changes need to be radical?

On their walk to the supermarket that night he filled Rosie in on everything that had happened, including the threats that the colonel had made. He held back nothing of what had transpired, even what Dakar and he had discussed. Rosie was strong emotionally and would need to know the whole story if anything did happen to him. Their partnership had always been based on this type of sharing. They agreed upon the need for secrecy and to keep absolutely quiet at all times even when they were out of the apartment. They decided to try and make their lives as normal as possible for the next few months, concluding they were powerless over the present situation and may as well carry on as such. That was easier said than done when your home was bugged with surveillance gear.

CHAPTER 13

Almost Hitting the Road

For the first time, in a long time, after Alicia left his room that night, Dakar lay awake going over in his mind what he needed to do. As was the case from time to time, his mind wandered to thoughts of Jenn and the dull ache of loss that always came with those memories. Tonight, he remembered their Sunday morning ritual of breakfast in bed, and on one occasion an accident that left the sheets covered in syrup and half-eaten pancakes. There was nothing else to do but laugh, and they did until it turned into tears. Perhaps she would be waiting for him again in his dreams tonight and with that he fell asleep.

He was up early as usual, off to the gym and back in his room, fed and ready to go. His plan was to wait until tomorrow morning to leave, provided there was a convoy to COB Speicher in Tikrit. He would risk a solo drive to C2c-FOB Brassfield-Mora, eight miles up the road, if need be, and hook up with one there. There was more chance of catching a convoy at C2c, a refueling stop for the trucks coming in and out of Turkey.

At 07:00, he walked by Murph's office and Murph waved him in.

"Dak, I asked upstairs for something special for you, a letter getting you fuel and supplies wherever you go in Iraq. The officious little pricks in Baghdad thought I was crazy, but our commanding officer, Lieutenant General Imhoff, thinks differently. She knows what you did here. She also saw your interview with Adrienne Assad on CNN. No one is saying it publicly, but off the record we all know what's happening in Iraq is not right. The Washington spin doctors had it coming to them when you set the record straight. I for one am grateful we are headed home. It still escapes me why we came here in the first place. Going stateside is what's worrying everyone right now. I'm not sure what to believe anymore. I hear conflicting reports every day about the situation there. Your letter will be here sometime tomorrow."

"I had planned to leave tomorrow, but I'll wait for the letter. Damn decent of her to do that for me," Dak said. That sort of pass was worth waiting for.

"I might be able to get you a mil-air flight to al Asad air base, but that would still not get you to the border. You could hitch a ride with the commercial Iraqi trucks going to Jordan, but riding with strangers can be dangerous, little boy," Murph said, as he laughed.

"Thanks, Captain, and you're right. It would be risky getting a ride with some Iraqi trucker. Plus I am not all that sure what the border situation is like. Nothing would be worse than being stuck at the Jordan-Iraq border with no place to go," Dakar replied.

"Which reminds me, I received some intel on the roads and border crossing. The road from al Asad to the border is open all the way and the border crossing is wide open, but with significant delays of up to twenty hours at the border itself. The road across the desert from Tikrit to al Asad is another matter. Intel says it is open and not reporting any problems, but they suspect that some of the IA soldiers guarding the checkpoints might not be all that reliable. Their loyalties are suspect. It is part of the reason they were sent out to guard the checkpoints in the desert in the first place. They might deny you passage, rob you or kill you for no reason, if they see you're traveling alone. We have nothing going on out there. Be very, very careful on that road. The roads in and out of Baghdad are still too risky. There are many closures, IEDs and attacks on convoys. Now that we're pulling out, it is bound to get worse. The insurgents see more targets of opportunity."

"Thanks, Captain, I will also need some good maps, if I am going to be travelling the hinterlands of Iraq. Any chance you can help me with that?" Dakar asked.

"Sorry, Dakar, that would get my nuts in a wringer, for sure. You could download maps from the Internet. They are excellent in quality and I sometimes wonder if they might be better than the maps they give us. Feel free to use the printer in the office. If you zoom in on the sections you want and keep an overall larger scale map that should do the trick," Murph suggested.

"Thanks, that's a great idea. It will give me something to do today," Dakar said, when he turned and left Murph's office.

Alicia had become particularly enthusiastic in her lovemaking in the last few days, if that was possible, when she learned of his imminent departure. What had been a strictly nightly affair had evolved, in the last few days, to whenever they had a few spare moments. He walked down the corridor, as Alicia eyed him hungrily from the other end and dragged him into his room, grabbed the collar on his shirt and kissed him passionately as the door closed

112

behind them. There were no other formalities other than the quick passionate kiss. He pulled down her pants and panties, bent her over his desk and entered her. He was rock hard and in a single stroke buried himself all the way inside her. As she whined and whimpered he was sure the noise could be heard clearly in the hall. He thought he heard a snicker as someone walked by the room. Alicia's ass was definitely her best asset. He loved to feel it and look at the full roundness of her hind quarter.

Alicia paused before she left to tell Dakar, "Dwight has his eye on a small house we might buy, and we have decided to try for another baby for sure when I get return. I don't want to jeopardize that when I get back. Could you do me a favor and not e-mail or contact me? I wouldn't want Dwight to find out about us." He was relieved to hear that. Simmons would be moving on.

Meanwhile, she left his sperm inside her to drip for the next few hours, a wonderful reminder of the morning quickie. Alicia thought she might have to return for a refill this afternoon.

Dakar explained his need for a one day delay in leaving and Simmons was plainly delighted at the prospect of another twenty-four hours with him. He would look for a hot woman in Israel or enlist a first mate for his sailboat before leaving Tel Aviv. He had forgotten to ask Simon if he knew of anyone who had some sailing skills and might be interested in a trip to America. That would be bizarre. Who would want to go to the States given the anarchy in the country?

The rest of the morning he downloaded and printed out excellent topographical maps that Murph suggested he use. He hooked up with Alan and Ryan for lunch. Once again the cook had prepared a treat for everyone, barbecued hamburgers, with all the fixings and they were delicious. One of the things he would miss at PB Olsen was the food.

The route was one hundred and fifty-eight miles to the border from Tikrit. The SUV should have lots of fuel, and even at a leisurely average speed of thirty miles an hour he should be there in six or seven hours. If need be he could stay the night in al Asad. At most he would be two days to Amman and then another day to Tel Aviv, if there was a lot of bullshit at the Jordanian-Israeli border and that was a given.

A little after 13:00 Tariq called to say his driver was delivering the papers to the front gate of the base for him within the hour. "My friend, it pains me to see you go." Again he joked, "Perhaps you might want to consider living in Iraq. It sounds safer than the US right now."

"You are probably right, Tariq," Dakar laughed. "But with my hunger for girlfriends I would be in trouble with your police in no time."

Tariq burst into laughter at that. "Yes, Dakar, you had better go. Even I cannot save you from yourself. My wife, Salina, and my children say goodbye also and may Allah bless you." He hung up the phone with the sound of his laughter still ringing in Dakar's ears.

True to his word, the papers arrived at the front gate within thirty minutes. He opened the envelope and pulled our four single sheets. All were in Arabic; it looked like two were generic Iraqi documents of some sort. One was a personal letter signed by Tariq and the other was signed by someone he didn't know.

The Iraqis he met were almost all on the base and employed in one capacity or another as interpreters, suppliers or support for the fledgling Iraqi government: their lives worth little in the general population of Iraq. Many who lived outside the base, and were found out, were assassinated on a regular basis. The Iraqi people looked at the US troops with a mixture of emotions: relief for the limited stability and security from the constant violence that had befallen the country, and resentment or hatred for being invaders and occupiers.

He took the letters to Hasan, one of the interpreters stationed on the base. Hasan looked them over and then said to Dakar, "You do have powerful friends. No one gets a letter from the president of Iraq, demanding that you get free passage and assistance, without question, from all those who read this letter. The letter from Tariq is good, too, although outside this province not so much alone. With the president's letter, you have two people, the president and a provincial governor, speaking for you. The other two papers are standard Iraqi travel documents. One, a letter of authorization from the ministry of the interior, grants you the right to travel; the other says you can go anywhere in Iraq. Allah, be merciful on the ones who cause you any problems with these letters, Dakar!"

"Thanks, Hasan. What are your plans? Going home?" Dakar asked.

"Yes, home to my wife and family in Baghdad, praying that no one finds out I was working for the US government for four years. I have good money from this job, enough to open a good size store in my neighborhood," Hasan answered.

Dakar nodded and tucked the papers into his shirt, thinking to himself that he was well armed for his journey across the desert. He wondered how many former translators would be dead within a year of the troop pullout. Or how long the country would take to fragment into warring sects and years of bloodshed before another dictator emerged to exert iron control over the population. He knew it wasn't his problem and he could not do anything about it. It was a shame that men of good will, like Tariq, might not prevail in Iraq.

He started back to his room and as he crossed the small road, Alicia appeared from around the corner. Noticing no one else around, she stuck out her tush and slapped it, and put two fingers into her mouth to suck on. Dakar chuckled at how brazen she had become in the last week, and simply bobbed his head up and down slightly. Dakar liked brazen. This time they spent about twenty minutes naked and wildly enjoying one another.

"You will have to get another girlfriend quickly, Dakar. I can't see you going without sex for more than a few days!!" Alicia stated.

"Yeah, I would offer you a ride home and being on the run with a deserter seems at first exciting, but even I know you don't enjoy the sex that much," he answered, as he peered into the hallway to make sure the coast was clear before she left.

He made his final call of the day to Simon in Tel Aviv. "Hi, Simon, how did you make out with the gold?"

"Not so good, Dakar. I can get only five ounces from someone I trust. It is five one ounce Krugerrands, so I know this is good. I do not trust many. Our country has a great many criminals, like most others. My commission for the sale is ten percent or five thousand, and I will guarantee the gold is here when you arrive. I tell you this upfront, so you know I don't cheat you. But we must do this today. The gold is gone very quickly now," Simon said.

"Okay, I will wire the money within the hour and your commission. Do you know of anyone who would like to crew with me on the boat back to America? I need someone experienced to help me. I can do it by myself, but I prefer some help, preferably a young woman, Simon," Dakar quipped.

"You are not paying commission. I give you gold first. This is not necessary. You horny bastard, you cannot ask for a woman. Only God gives this to you. I will ask at the marina, put a paper up and a small ad in the Tel Aviv newspaper for a few days. When will you be here? I must have this information for the person," Simon continued.

"Should be four days at maximum, but tell them we will leave within one week, say next Friday. This will give me some extra time in Tel Aviv. I prefer to pay your commission now. It is easier for me than to try again for another wire transfer," Dakar answered. On impulse he also said, "I will send five thousand extra. Please take it out in cash for me."

"As you wish. It will all be here when you come. Do you want dollars or Euros or both? It is good. If you go soon, you should miss the hurricanes by the time you hit the Atlantic. The season should be over," Simon answered.

"Half and half, Simon. Thank you for your help. I will call in a day or two." Dakar said as he disconnected.

Dakar headed for the MWR and the Internet to transfer the sixty thousand to Simon's account. He had done everything he wanted to date and for a man he had not met, he trusted him. He returned to his room, took out his Leatherman multi-tool and removed the cover on the air conditioner where his gold stash was hidden and pocketed it.

CHAPTER 14

Teddy's Folly

The stress of their situation was starting to show a little on Rosie and Teddy. Rosie snapped at Teddy for his stupidity in supposing they weren't being listened to. Rosie finally admitted to Teddy, she was as guilty as he was in thinking it was impossible that their own government would do such a thing. They had nothing but time now, time to think and time to stew. Waiting and doing nothing was a hard thing to deal with.

The United States was, by far, the country with the worst problems in the world, given the violence and disorder in the streets. As the economic conditions worsened in the US, so did the rest of the world. Much of Europe was stable, but paralyzed economically with no clear idea of what to do next. The heads of the EU were meeting to plot a course of action. Travel was still restricted and although the ban on air travel was lifted to some areas, few people went anywhere other than to return to their homes. The flights were more repatriation mercy flights and no one expected many airlines to survive this economic disaster.

The news that the nation had started to stabilize a little could not be taken at face value. One of the more popular Internet news sites Teddy had frequented was now looking strikingly similar to the mainstream media in content. He reasoned it showed that the site had been co-opted or compromised by the powers that be. His news sources now gravitated to sites located outside the United States or from within the loose boundaries of the Western Coalition States.

Peace was not restored in vast areas in many major cities and pockets of rural America that historically mistrusted the federal government. President Haines assembled a coalition of his own: the Evangelical Christian Right had by and large endorsed Haines's "Saving America Plan." Haines said, "It was a broad group of patriotic Americans ready to put the needs of the country ahead of their own." The president stressed that "not only was it in the best interest of Americans to cooperate in restoring order, it was their duty." He pointed to the wonderful job Governor Drayton had done in making Texas safe again for ordinary Americans. He had also negotiated an uneasy truce with the Western Coalition states. He stated that he would consider removing martial law in the states that were not in chaos and a bipartisan congressional committee was now studying the proposal. He also agreed that federal authorities would back off exerting control over state and municipal facilities, and government operations. Everyone said calmer heads needed to prevail.

Texas had reached a semblance of order, through a huge number of killings. It was reported that law enforcement officials and elements of the National Guard had killed one hundred and eighty looters and rioters over the past week in Houston and Dallas. The "looters" killed included a twelve year old girl and the dead "rioters" included eight members of the American Civil Liberties Union peacefully demonstrating the imposition of martial law. In addition, several Patriotic Communities that had set up illegal roadblocks and fired on federal authorities were neutralized. The Presidential Patriot Force, as the president had dubbed them, from several local churches had participated in restoring calm. Governor Dayton thanked them all and asked everyone to pray for America. Some eight hundred suspected looters, saboteurs and troublemakers were also rounded up and detained at special federal facilities.

Europeans thought the violence problems in the US were entirely due to a gun happy culture and shoot 'em up mentality. To some extent this was true, as Americans shot each other over the slightest incident or excuse, but the truth was most of the shootings and killings were now being done by the authorities or by government authorized vigilantes. The Christian Right in partnership with other extreme rightists believed the name "The Presidential Patriot Force" reflected their commitment to the country and their neighbors. The Tea Party held public Unite America rallies, which started with everyone pledging the oath of allegiance. Speakers urged them on to greater acts of selfless patriotism. President Haines never missed an opportunity to thank his new allies in their common fight against the enemies of America.

In Washington, in closed meetings with his advisors, President Haines planned to use the returning troops from Iraq and Afghanistan to enforce federal power in the wayward states. He was sure the National Guard in those states would waver when faced with the overwhelming military superiority of a large number of combat hardened troops and direct orders from the office of the president to stand down. A few combat ready divisions in Montana would do the trick. It would never come to armed conflict, Haines concluded, provided the threat of sufficient military force and political pressure was used. If need be, an example could be made in one of the states and the rest would fall into line.

On the home front, by 10:00 AM the next morning, Teddy had cobbled together some basic ideas on how his work group proposed to proceed and what the results might be if they succeeded. There was no way to accurately assess the end product. He would need a few weeks before he could report any concrete results to Colonel Bitch.

The Bitch, who showed up slightly before lunch, headed straight for Teddy's office, plunked herself down in a chair and queried, "What do you have for me?"

"Just the broadest of outlines about the direction of the project, Colonel," he replied, using the coldest voice and tone he could imagine.

She took the three page outline from him, quickly scanned it and said, "This will do for now. Does the team know how to proceed?" she asked.

"Yes, they are fully in the loop and are working the numbers now," Teddy said.

"Good, then they won't be requiring your guidance anymore, will they?" she said. Two men in proverbial dark suits appeared from nowhere. "You didn't really think I wouldn't find out about your call to your friend, did you? The instructions were simple, Teddy, and you did not follow them."

The men entered the office, told Teddy to stand up and he was handcuffed. They stood rigidly beside Teddy, until Colonel Bitch told them to wait outside for a moment. She commented salaciously, "Don't worry, Teddy. I will drop by your place tonight and let Rosie know about your predicament. Who knows? With you locked up and with the right sort of incentive, Rosie might even be persuaded to play for the other team. She's such a delicate and pretty little thing, isn't she? And I have always had a thing for petite nurses. They look so sexy in those cute little uniforms." She nodded slightly and the men came back and took him away.

The coldness and hatred that ran down Teddy's spine was not difficult to measure; you only had to look into his eyes. His coworkers were shocked when Teddy was hustled handcuffed through the office and they stared at him incredulously. He noticed Rachel was not looking at him, apparently engrossed in some work on her computer.

He was taken downstairs and into one of the numerous black SUVs with tinted dark windows that seemed to be everywhere in Washington these days and they drove off into the city. They drove the semi-deserted streets that had little traffic, in a generally southwest direction on another gloomy cold day, much like Teddy's mood and life right now. Black and gray clouds hung low over the capital. An hour or so and many miles later they entered a gated facility in a wooded area with guards and a chain link fence topped with concertina wire all round. The SUV drove straight into the first warehouse. There were armed military guards everywhere and Teddy was taken to a desk with a large sign marked Intake. The sound of a single gunshot echoed in the distance.

Intake did not consist of much, other than to exchange his handcuffs for a set of leg restraints made of some sort of plastic material. Apparently, they had expected him. The brief interview consisted of them asking his name and address, which he was sure they already had. He was strip searched and then escorted through a door into a vast open area of bunks filled with men all similarly shackled by plastic leg restraints. He was shown a cot to use. There were five portable johns and a few open troughs which he took to be washing up areas. Every prisoner had a blanket for his cot and a toothbrush handy. All in all, about one hundred men occupied the space, which looked filled to capacity. When they had driven in, he had noticed at least six buildings of similar size.

He slumped onto the cot. Scanning the room, he observed most of the men milling about in small groups talking: some smoking, some not, others by themselves reading and a few weeping on their cots. The man next to him appeared to be in his late forties and was reading. Teddy leaned over and said, "Hi, my name's Teddy," and extended his hand.

The man looked him over quickly, shook his hand and said, "Jim. Welcome to your new home away from home and one hundred of your new best buddies. Sorry to see you here. Let me give you a quick rundown, lest you run afoul of the rules. This is a federal detention center the president has set up using his executive powers under martial law. If you try to escape you will be executed. They are conducting trials and executing people now for other types of 'crimes,' too. I guess you can't really call them trials. They are tribunals. It takes about an hour to find you guilty and they execute you immediately with a single gunshot to the back of the head."

"What, they can't do that!!" Teddy exclaimed.

Jim continued, "Tell that to the eighty-six men they've executed here since the center opened a few weeks ago. We keep track of the number of shots. Your cot was occupied by one of them up until an hour and a half ago. Tommy's crime was being a union steward for the railway. He got too mouthy in the coffee room one day, and suggested his brothers and sisters should stop the trains from running for a few days in protest against the imposition of martial law. When his union brethren did so, they called it treason and shot Tommy. Poor bastard had a big family, too. Four kids and a wife at home. That family is missing a father and husband now. You can be shot for nearly anything here, if they put their minds to it. Don't give them a reason to shoot you, Teddy."

Teddy suppressed the urge to cry; he felt helpless. He wished he were home in Idaho with Rosie up at the cabin in the mountains away from this insanity.

"Don't talk foolishness to anyone here either. Men will rat on you for a chance to get out of here. My family doesn't know where I am or if I am alive or dead. We can't make any calls or talk to anyone on the outside, and they don't tell you jack shit about why they are holding you," Jim warned him.

Teddy did not understand why he hadn't heard about these places on the news, why people weren't outraged, standing up and demanding it to stop. He realized they didn't know. You can't be angry about something you aren't aware of and with the censorship, those who did know or suspect were never given the chance to tell others. So simple—even the rare outbursts of the truth via whatever media or method could be handled in such a manner as to paint the information as ridiculous and untrue. A half-truth worked well in most cases. Yes, people were being detained and held, but only those who advocated violence, or participated in the riots and knowingly encouraged unlawful behavior: those who wanted to tear America down. There had been a number of deaths, it was true—a little over four thousand three hundred nationwide almost all were rioters or looters. In the national state of emergency, what choice did the authorities have other than to use lethal force? Sooner or later, the truth would come out, but when and what would the truth be, when told by others, Teddy didn't know. Certainly it was nothing like what was happening here and now. For now, playing along was the only feasible thing for him to do. For what The Bitch had said and done, he vowed she would receive a beating when the opportunity presented itself. If not right away, there would come a time and place…

CHAPTER 15

Onward and Upward

During his last night at PB Olsen, Dakar spent the better part of four hours with Alicia. She did not return to her quarters until well after midnight. There were no tears this time, just kisses, long embraces, hugs and of course, making love many times. There was so much work to do before the company left in a week for Anaconda that it didn't matter to anyone who she was sleeping with. Some of the other female soldiers were a bit jealous of the silly grin she wore most of the time.

This morning there was no trip to the gym. Dakar got up at 04:30 as usual. The sun hadn't risen yet. He piled his gear into the SUV, several of the extra weapons, including a grenade launcher and sniper rifle with a bipod. He went through his checklist methodically: water, food, guns, ammo, his kit and gear, fuel, passport, travel documents, cash and gold. The temperature in the mornings was wonderful, sixty degrees, until the sun rose and the temperature rocketed upwards. November was not as hot during the day as the summer, but hot enough. At night the temperature plummeted to the fifties on some nights and in the winter would drop below freezing on occasion. By 05:30 he was loaded up and ready to go. He still had half an hour to go before the chow hall opened for breakfast, and he spent the time talking with several of the other early birds who were out and about in the main hall. He would drive the road to C2c- Brassfield-Mora alone; there was no convoy today from Olsen. He heard a convoy was scheduled to leave C2c to Tikrit and Speicher around noon that day.

He had breakfast with Ryan and Alan; they talked mostly about the civilian contractor evacuation from Basra, which was now to be staged over a three week period. Two weeks, it turned out, was not enough time to get everyone out. There were tremendous logistical problems involving accommodations, and physically moving so many people and materials to the departure points. The military personnel were being airlifted out of the four main US air bases, while the civilians were all going out of Basra.

Murph wandered in after a few minutes and pulled up a bench beside Dakar. He never discussed his orders or what military orders they were given other than in the most general of terms and today was no exception.

Today, he lamented, "Got our assignment location in the US and it means I won't be seeing Mary Lou or the kids anytime soon, but we will beat you home for sure, Dakar. Won't you be lonely on that long trip across the ocean? And, no, Sergeant Simmons can't go with you," he teased. They all laughed at the reference to Dakar's and Simmon's illicit, illegal and nearly public relationship.

"Spoil sport. I put an ad in the Tel Aviv newspaper asking for some company for the trip, but I am not putting much faith in finding a woman to go with me. I'll stop in the Caribbean for a night or two and refuel there, so to speak. Maybe I'll check up on Mick if he made it to Sosua, in the Dominican. Can't be helped, not getting home quickly, but I am going to have a hell of a lot more fun getting there," Dakar shot back.

With that, Murph stood and extended his hand. Dakar got up and took it. They shook, as Murph placed his other hand on Dakar's arm and told him, "Thanks. Have a good life, Dakar."

"That's the plan, Captain," Dakar answered. With that simple goodbye, Murph left the dining hall to direct his soldiers in the business of packing up.

Ryan and Alan had similar wishes of good luck, and Dakar headed out the door on his road trip. He had been at PB Olsen for over a year and a half and his leaving came with a gentle feeling of loss. This had been his home. In Idaho the only thing he owned was an old rundown cabin up in the mountains on ten acres, part of a father's legacy to his only son. Although he loved female company, he could and had lived for many months by himself mostly with little or no contact with anyone for days and was perfectly happy. No—more than happy—at peace with himself and the world.

He reached for the door of the SUV and his mood changed to one of excitement at the new adventure he was starting. The big eight cylinder motor started easily and he crept towards the gate. Simmons was on duty somewhere on the base. They said their goodbyes last night, so he was "good to go." The sentry at the gate waved him through the new gate maze that had been constructed after the attack. Alicia appeared from behind a T-wall carrying a bag, smiling broadly. Dakar rolled down the window and she thrust the bag through the window, and told him, "Bye, baby. Remember me!"

"Of course, always!" he replied, grinning. He swung right onto the road and to the bridge over the Tigris. Opening the bag, he smiled. There was a pair of her panties inside—the sexy ones he liked so much. There would be no forgetting Alicia. Soon, he was through the first IA checkpoint leading out of Samarra and then onto Highway #1, headed to C2c- Brassfield-Mora. The drive was uneventful and took only twenty minutes including going through another IA checkpoint four miles down the road.

Brassfield-Mora was an Iraqi grain storage facility that was due to be returned to the Iraqis soon. Iraq was the bread basket of the Arab world with large irrigated fields of grain everywhere, bordering the Tigris River. When you flew over the fields in a chopper, they looked like circular green oases in a sea of beige. Vegetables were grown under tents of plastic throughout the area. The Tigris River brought life to Iraq.

Ugandans guarded Forward Operating Base- C2c- Brassfield-Mora, employees of a military contractor like him. The Ugandans were good soldiers and he always felt safe while they were on the job. Professional in their attitude and attentive to their duty, they made a fraction of the money he did every month. It was good by Ugandan standards, but their work was different in nature to his. He wove through the entrance maze, and headed towards the far end of the convoy assembly area and refueling point. He parked and walked towards the TOC a few yards away.

Into the TOC Dakar went and asked to speak to the duty sergeant. He explained where he was headed and showed him the letter. The sergeant asked him to wait a minute so that he could check on the convoy for him. He returned five minutes later and let Dakar know the convoy had been delayed after being hit by IEDs coming into Baghdad, and may or may not arrive tomorrow.

"Sir, let me call the FOB Sheriff and get you a bunk for the night," the sergeant said. The sheriff was the unofficial title for the guy who got things done on the base. The sheriff took him over a short distance to the VIP CHUs, containerized housing units. It was nice, with TV, Internet hook-up, clean sheets and a private bathroom. The letter from Lieutenant General Imhoff was paying off. A guy could get used to treatment like this. He thanked him and asked if there was room service, too.

The sheriff laughed, smirked and said, "No, sir, but I understand you had room service at Olsen. The food's not half bad. Not as good as Olsen. Still the guys try." Dakar blushed, laughed and wondered if everyone knew about him and Simmons.

This Forward Operating Base was much bigger than Patrol Base Olsen; it had a larger army-run, DFAC-dining facility, a laundry where subcontract workers did your wash, a big gym and a chapel. He had a few hours to kill, so he wandered the base and checked out what was happening at C2c. Dakar stopped to talk to a few soldiers and noticed a couple of civilian electricians working on reconnecting one of the many generators on the base.

It was his trade, too, and he walked over and commented on their work. "You better make sure the phase rotation is right when you hook up the new one. We wouldn't want things to start running backwards on this base!"

The shorter of the two was pulling hard on a wrench to make sure the connections were tight and almost dropped the wrench he was laughing so hard. The other bigger but younger man was smoking a cigarette. He shot back, "Why change now? Things are already fucked up here and have been since I got here. Maybe we should change the rotation and get things working right." Larry went on to explain they had to change the generator because they didn't have a fan belt to replace on the old generator. A typical story for Iraq: a shortage of simple basic parts due to an impossible, unworkable bureaucratic maze. Truth was if it weren't for the guys on the ground making do with what they had, nothing would get done.

They laughed again at the absurdity and the kernel of truth to the quip, and swapped stories for a few minutes. Jeff hailed from the sunshine state and loved anything with a motor and NASCAR. Larry was an IBEW member like himself, a brother from Maryland. Dakar had kept his union membership and paid his dues every year, even though he had not worked in the trade for six years. The union had been good to him, and he would have a job to return to when he got home and the situation calmed down a bit. They were headed home next week and this base, like all the others, was frantic with soldiers packing up to go. All the other non military stuff was to be abandoned—tools, generators and portable buildings. Only the military equipment was going home with the soldiers.

Another man drove by in a Gator ATV. He was insanely adorned with an aviators' type, fleece lined cap with the flaps up. He stopped, introduced himself as Gary and they talked for a few minutes. He was obviously from the south somewhere. "You all here tonight?" he asked.

"Yes, I will be enjoying the fabulous hospitality of C2c for the evening," Dakar answered.

"Hey man, come git something to eat tonight with us about 7:30. We're having steak, chicken and taters, with some fresh corn bread, grits and succotash?" Gary asked him.

"That sounds great. Thanks for the invite," Dakar agreed. After Gary left, Jeff explained how Gary always made everyone feel welcome at C2c and his barbecues were legendary. Within the hour the generator was back up and running.

Dakar headed for the gym for a mid-day workout. The heat of the day had become intense and as he walked, a small dust devil

131

headed his way. It reminded him of the Tasmanian Devil, from a Bugs Bunny cartoon, the way it twisted and turned. There was no way of avoiding the mini tornado and it blew over him filling his nostrils, hair and clothes with dust before it wound its way through a group of soldiers, trying to cover up the gear they were packing into a container.

The evening was fabulous. The military and civilian contractors all mixed freely and easily at the barbecue. The food was outstanding. He passed on darts, euchre and dominoes, and by 22:00 he wandered back to his CHU, to the strains of "My Girl" coming from the stereo. It was the song he associated with Jenn, and a smile came to his face when he thought of her head on his shoulder, dancing with him on the dock, one perfect summer evening, as the song drifted in on the wind from somewhere far away.

He would sleep in tomorrow, but it was beyond his capabilities to stay in bed much past 05:30. True to his prediction, at 05:00 his eyes snapped open. It was off to the gym for him, then a shower and breakfast. He headed to the TOC to get an update on the convoy situation. On the way he ran into the sheriff, who asked, "Any problems? Everything OK, sir?"

"No problems, Sergeant. Thanks, I had a great time," Dakar said sincerely. Dakar liked the sheriff and this outfit a lot. The soldiers were all professional in their attitude and duties, yet maintained a semblance of civility, common sense and camaraderie in the otherwise insane situation they were thrust into. He witnessed numerous cases of the military working with civilian contractors or vice-versa, both concerned only with helping the other get the job done.

At the TOC, Dakar was informed the convoy was not coming today. It was held up in Baghdad. He let the duty sergeant know he was going to go it alone to Speicher. He had not planned on a solo drive to COB Speicher, in Tikrit, but that was what was going to happen in about two minutes. He threw his bag in the back of the SUV, jumped in the driver's seat and out the front gate, making a right-hand turn onto Highway #1 again and pushed the big beast up to sixty miles an hour. He should be in Speicher in a few hours at most. He wasn't looking forward to his stay there. The base was fraught with the inefficiencies of size, and too many officers and contractor bosses with too much time on their hands.

The road was in good shape: four lanes and traffic was light by US standards—a mixture of cars and transport trucks. He should be able to hit Speicher in time for lunch. He heard the DFAC was contractor run and the food pretty good, a small consolation in that sea of officiousness. The worst thing about Speicher was that the contractor system didn't work well. He wondered sometimes how anything got done there. It was through good will and taking personal responsibility. The workers bent the rules when needed, to the point they were unrecognizable, to ensure the power was on, the plumbing worked, the air conditioners functioned and the hundreds of other things it took to make a military base function.

Dakar had traveled twenty miles. He slowed slightly for a curve a hundred yards ahead and banked the SUV hard into the turn. From behind him came a terrific whump and roar. A split second later, the Tahoe was hit by the shock wave that sent it spinning around and around on the highway. Dakar struggled with the wheel to straighten the vehicle, but the best he could hope for at this point was the truck wouldn't come up short against some obstruction and start rolling. The extra weight of the vehicle armor gave some added stability to the big four wheel drive and it spun twice before finally stopping in the middle of the highway. The SUV was covered in dirt and debris from the explosion.

He quickly assessed what had happened and then heard the sound of small arms fire hitting the side of the SUV. This was no time to shoot it out with the guys firing at him. Straightening the wheel, he punched it and the big diesel picked up speed. He could see at least four muzzle flashes two hundred yards from his right behind a small ditch or depression, as he beat a hasty retreat down the highway. The SUV seemed OK. It was designed to weather small arms fire and provide a modicum of protection from heavier weapons. It was still handling and running fine as his speed hit eighty.

CHAPTER 16

No Choices

T he knock on the apartment door came as a surprise to
Rosie. No one ever knocked on their door, especially in this
apartment block. Perhaps it was Teddy horsing around. It
was already after six and he wasn't home yet. Although, it was
Teddy's turn to cook tonight Rosie had started a basic supper of rice,
beans and a small piece of pork they had purchased yesterday at the
store.

She peered through the peep hole at a woman who was obviously
Colonel Bitch and opened the door. The colonel smiled broadly and
asked, "Hi, you must be Rosie. Can I come in and talk to you for a
minute?" Rosie could smell alcohol on her breath.

Rosie stood aside and let her in. The colonel went straight for the
armchair saying, "Take a seat, Rosie. I've come to talk about Teddy."

Rosie started trembling, when she plunked herself down on the
couch, across from the colonel and asked, "Where is Teddy?"

"Rosie, these are extraordinary times, and all of us need to pull together for the sake of the country and our own best interests. I asked Teddy not to talk to his friend about deserting his job and he agreed not to. You were aware of this condition, too. I also told him that any further contact with his friend and talk about leaving would result in his incarceration in a federal detention center. When he made that call to his friend yesterday, he broke that agreement and he is now in custody," she continued.

Rosie buried her head in her hands and shook her head slightly from side to side, as if the entire scene were unreal, a figment of her imagination, but she knew that wasn't true.

"We have the basis of his new thesis figured out and can continue without him," the colonel stated. "He could be released tomorrow, if I so choose…but I must have some assurances that he will not pull any stunts like he did yesterday. Can you persuade me that that will happen? Can you make sure he stays put and does his job? It is vital to our nation's future he do so. Can you do that, Rosie?" She finished in her best conciliatory tone.

Rosie's heart soared at the prospect of freeing Teddy. There was only one answer Rosie knew and that was "Yes."

"That's great, Rosie, I have only one other thing you have to do for me before he will be released. It is not negotiable and I expect you to do it well, Rosie." The colonel walked to the couch and sat down beside Rosie, put her arm around her, drew Rosie's face to hers, and kissed her full and deep on the lips. Rosie recoiled slightly at the unwanted affections of the colonel, but knowing full well the consequences of not cooperating with the ugly bitch she gave in and let her lead her into the bedroom.

"Yes, you pretty, pretty thing," the colonel moaned, as she removed Rosie's clothes, and peeled off her bra and underwear. She kissed Rosie again, and thrust her tongue into her mouth, took her very small firm breast into her mouth and sucked the nipple hard, biting it before moving on to the other. Her hand was busy exploring Rosie's pussy while she sucked hungrily on her breasts.

She pushed open Rosie's legs, looking at her shaved pussy, and buried her head between Rosie's legs, licking her and penetrating her with her tongue. Then drove one, then two fingers into her, searching for her G-spot to massage. Rosie froze at the unwanted penetration of her body. The Bitch said "loosen up, relax and enjoy yourself."

Rosie let her body go limp and her mind concentrate only on Teddy and getting him home safely. The colonel's roughness hurt her physically, hurt her inside. The Bitch would not stop licking her, pinching her breast and driving her fingers into her harder and faster.

Rosie wanted it to end. She moved her hips rhythmically and moaned as best she could for a few minutes. The colonel continued until Rosie faked an orgasm. The Bitch undressed, making sure her firearm was placed well out of reach. She put Rosie's face to her sagging breasts to suckle and then after a few minutes pushed Rosie's head between her legs. Rosie hesitated slightly and the colonel commanded, "You are not done yet, dear." Her pussy smelled of stale urine, but Rosie started in on what turned out to be a half-hour session of licking the colonel to orgasm. The colonel had Rosie once more, this time also putting one of her fingers in Rosie's ass, before dressing and telling Rosie when she left, "You were wonderful, sweetheart. You kept your part of the bargain. Teddy will be released in the morning, dear. Make sure he behaves."

Rosie closed the door behind her and headed for the shower to get the smell, taste and feel of the colonel off her body. She wept throughout the night, unable to sleep she was so sick with worry for Teddy.

Teddy spent the night not sleeping also, worried about the soldiers perhaps coming for him tomorrow, how Rosie was doing and how to get out of the place. In the morning, they were taken in groups of fifty to a kitchen, given a spoon, some oatmeal in a small bowl and a cup of lukewarm black coffee. The sound of the rain beating on the tin roof of the warehouse made the whole facility very noisy.

Jim told him the food was meager at first and still not great. When the inmates complained, the soldiers beat a few of them with the butts of their rifles, in front of the group, so everyone got the message about the complaint process. The food quantity and quality improved after a few of the inmates got ill and collapsed from lack of nourishment. It was apparently OK to murder them, but not to starve them to death.

Just before 8:00 AM two soldiers came for him. Teddy vowed he would take someone with him if he were to be slaughtered like an animal. To his surprise, they cut the bonds from his legs and told him he was being released. Jim looked at him, as he got up to leave and silently mouthed the words, "Help us." Teddy was led out of the warehouse to the central processing desks and told to sit.

"You are being released today. You are forbidden to speak of the location of this facility, the nature of your incarceration, or what you saw or heard here, with anyone. Failure to abide by these conditions will result in federal charges of treason and a violation of federal secrecy laws. You will be tried by a military tribunal. Possible penalties include death, under authority granted us in this state of national emergency. Sign here..." was all the corporal said, pushing the paper across the desk for him to sign.

Teddy could not scribble his signature on the paper quickly enough. He was handed an envelope containing his personal belongings including his wallet and cell phone. Piled once again in the back of the all black SUV, by men in suits, he was driven out the gate into the rainy sullen world of Washington and he hoped home.

Instead of home, they headed back to his new office, dropping him at the curb with a curt, "The colonel is waiting for you" serving as a goodbye. Colonel Bitch was waiting for him in his office when he entered, and the team was busy at their computers. Rachel was nowhere to be seen. He entered his office, willing himself to be calm. "There will come a time" crossed his mind.

"Teddy, welcome back. How was your stay at Hotel Fed? Not to your liking, I hope," was how The Bitch started. "Time for you to get back to work, Teddy. I'm sure you are suitably impressed as to how seriously we value your work here. You will not come home next time, Teddy, and I will be banging your girlfriend for months before she realizes you aren't coming back. Very nice piece of ass you have. Rosie does swing both ways now. I am expecting some impressive results quickly, Teddy." The whole time she gave her little speech her hand cradled her 45 loosely by her side. The Bitch left the office and facility.

Teddy's faced reddened with anger, his frame shook with rage. The oath changed from a beating to killing The Bitch without mercy. He would play along giving her what she wanted until the opportunity came to literally strangle her with his bare hands. What a pleasurable thought that was for him. People thought of Teddy as strong because of his height and weight, but few people could fathom the terrible strength Teddy had in his body when angry. It would take many men to subdue him physically and they would be doing a whole lot of hurting in the process. He called Rosie at home to ask her how she was, and to let her know that he was out and OK. Rosie let him know she loved him, was all right and that she would see him tonight when he got home.

He sat in his office for two hours, alternating between crying and rage, before venturing out to join his team which was now minus Rachel, "the rat." There was a new face and she introduced herself as Dr. Robin Chambers, the psychologist he had requested. She had an impressive list of credentials, including some research work into mass psychology in relation to politics. President Haines had used her in his successful run for the presidency. She was forty-something and completely average and non-descript in all ways, except for her mind, he discovered.

Meg, the other actuary on the team, looked at Teddy, smiled and said, "Welcome back. How was your stay at the crowbar hotel?" She meant it as a joke. Teddy knew it wasn't.

"You have no idea and don't want to know," he replied, his eyes glancing away when he weakly smiled back.

Robin, the new member, piped up changing the subject, "Your work is fascinating, Teddy. I reviewed some of your older reports to the president, and how you came to your conclusions and your methodology. Solid work. Well done, Teddy! I hope we can adapt it our needs."

"Me, too. I'd just begun to flesh out a plan when we were so rudely interrupted," Teddy said, as the others laughed at how he was able to make light of his predicament. Teddy would trust no one in this office anymore, and put up a good looking front to one and all on his team. For sure, one or more of them would be reporting any suspicions they might have to the colonel.

"Let's start by discussing the basic premise, whether it is achievable, how it can be done and any ideas you've come up with in the past day or so," Teddy said as he threw the project into motion.

The rest of the day was spent doing just that, hashing over the process from mathematical, actuarial and now psychological points of view. It really helped that Robin wasn't one of those touchy feely, "How does that make you feel?" psychologists and appreciated the mathematical nature of their work. A consensus was reached that two areas of the equation had to have fixed minimum values. The first being the minimum psychological component that was needed as a median (average was not a good word) to generate strong confidence in people's lives. They were no longer dealing strictly with economics. They had no control over the second part like stable government, ongoing violence, etc. Even if they discovered a magic formula, it would have to be predicated on those other conditions being stable and of an acceptable level. So they agreed to separate the equation into two parts: one economic and the other, the status quo.

Robin and Teddy would work on measuring methods, and the psychological part of the economics and status quo equations, while the other three members, Meg and the two mathematicians Helen and Glenn, would concentrate on the economic factors available or needed to meet the number Robin and Teddy would come up with for the first part. Helen and Glenn were brilliant in their fields, but none of them had any background in economics. They decided that further help was needed and as much as he hated to he phoned The Bitch to ask for an economist to help with economic modeling. Bernice was delighted to hear from Teddy. It meant he was being a good boy and working. She assured him someone would show up tomorrow.

Teddy went home early, anxious to see Rosie. The physical separation of a single night was bad enough, but knowing what The Bitch might have done to her made him even more apprehensive. He opened the door and Rosie rushed into his arms sobbing. Teddy picked her right off the ground kissing and hugging her. They could no longer share their feelings and thoughts openly in the apartment anymore, so they took a little stroll around the block. Teddy was angry and so worried about Rosie he was having trouble speaking rationally and coherently.

It was the first time he felt he could let his guard down. She told him exactly what the colonel had done to her, and Teddy told her how afraid he was in the detention center that he would be killed and not see Rosie again.

Teddy broke down into tears during the walk and Rosie spent a good half an hour calming Teddy down, cradling his head against her body as he sobbed with the release of the tension he was feeling. They were together. There would be no more mistakes regarding contacting Dakar and that was all that mattered right now. Such was the balance in their relationship, both able at times to be the strong one when needed. A team in every sense of the word. Rosie rationalized it was only her body The Bitch had used.

CHAPTER 17

Speicher

Dakar slowed the Tahoe to a stately fifty MPH a few miles from the scene of the bombing. There was no sense risking stopping and assessing the damage to the SUV until he got to Speicher. The rest of the drive didn't have the excitement of the first twenty minutes, which was fine by him.

Security for the perimeter at Speicher was supplied by an outside contractor, but he was stopped at the gate by a US sentry. The main gate to Speicher was guarded by US troops. He was asked for his CAC card (government military ID) and the first thing he did was let the guard know about the IED attack he had survived. The guard radioed the TOC, and he was directed to go there first and file a report.

After his visit to the TOC, he headed to a common living area that contained the quarters for other ASI personnel living on base. Speicher was a large base of many square miles, with a runway large enough to accommodate jets. He parked the Tahoe at his temporary quarters and inspected the SUV for damage. There were four bullet holes through the side of the SUV. None had penetrated the armor and there was no other visible damage. He was thorough in his inspection, including looking under the vehicle and in the engine compartment for anything that might be amiss.

He bunked in with Tony, a Brit waiting for the call that would get him in a convoy to Basra and then home. Things were still hopelessly backlogged in Basra. Planes sat empty on the runway waiting for passengers or cargo. Personnel and material movement to Basra was held up by insurgent activity near Baghdad. Troops were clearing and patrolling the affected stretches of highway. Tony was told he would be moving in a few days. There was absolutely no reason for Tony to believe any of that bullshit, and he became increasingly frustrated and angry at the delay. Dakar visited the gym in the morning and had a quick breakfast at the DFAC before going back to his quarters.

Dakar's decision to drive looked like the best choice for him. He knew the airlift would be a cluster fuck. He asked Tony to join him for lunch, but Tony's mind was elsewhere and he declined, citing the need to be there in case the call came through. Dakar drove to the DFAC for lunch. It was sweet: his choice of four or five entrées, a couple of different types of soup, tables full of desserts and best of all, really fresh fruit. They had fruit at Olsen, but it often arrived a few days past its prime. He supposed it was because of the extra convoy time, or that Speicher got first choice and took the good stuff.

Lunch was quick. He was always a fast eater. Jenn complained that Dakar gobbled his food up like some street urchin who was not sure when he would eat again. He went to refuel for the trip across the desert. It was another long drive to the fuel point and not like the

144

informal affair of getting your own in Olsen. There was a queue of vehicles waiting their turn and when he got to the front of the line the Indian subcontract worker politely informed him he could not get fuel without a sticker. Oh well, he should have known this would happen. He was in Speicher, where things moved with paralyzing inefficiency. He doubted this group would be on the way back to the States as ordered anytime soon. Dakar wandered back to the TOC where he hoped to get additional intel on the Provincial Road across the desert and permission to fuel up.

The duty sergeant at first told him he was in the wrong place and needed to go to the administration building, on the other side of the base. Dakar asked to see the duty officer, and Sarge went back into the TOC and emerged later with a rather irritated looking captain.

The captain's manner was brusque, when he asked, "Can I help you, sir?" Dakar let him know who he was and what he needed. At the mention of his name, the captain became even colder and remarked, "Aren't you the guy who spilled his guts on CNN? I can't help you. Go to the admin building like the sergeant told you to. We have procedures. You don't get to play the hero card here."

Dakar guessed the process was starting to look like a full day or multi-day mission, and decided to use his letter from Lieutenant General Imhoff. He produced the document for the captain.

The captain scanned the document and said, "Please wait here a moment, sir." He walked briskly to the TOC and entered. When he returned he was accompanied by a full bird colonel whose attitude contrasted sharply with that of the captain's.

The colonel walked straight up to him, shook his hand and said, "The sergeant will accompany you to the fuel point and also provide you with any other assistance you might need. I am sorry for this delay, sir."

"Thanks, Colonel. I didn't really want to use the authorization, but I needed the fuel. I'd also be grateful for any intel you might have on the Provincial Road just north of here from Highway #1 west to Highway #12, the highway from there to the Jordanian border and the border crossing itself," Dakar stated.

"Certainly, sir, when you return from fueling up, I will have that information for you," the colonel answered.

Dakar and Sarge left and on the drive over, Dakar joked with the Sarge that "It helps to know a general in Iraq."

When Dakar told him which general, Sarge whistled softly and said, "That one more so than others." When they returned, the colonel came out directly with maps in his hand.

He was to the point. "Sir, the road to the border is still open. There are delays at the border crossing point with waits of up to twenty-four hours now. The Provincial Road you asked about is another matter; its status has been downgraded from risky to dangerous, not recommended for travel. There are reports of Iraqi travelers being robbed at gunpoint by regular IA soldiers or men dressed as regular Iraqi Army troops. There was even an unsubstantiated report of a missing vehicle containing three people yesterday on that road. The roads in and out of Baghdad are still not totally cleared or safe for travel. Military convoys are not permitted to travel. I've circled on this map where the trouble spots might be on the Provincial Road you asked about."

"Thanks for your help, Colonel. This is great. I will give it a try in the morning," Dakar said.

"No problem. Liked your interview, Dakar," the colonel commented, as he left for the TOC. Apparently, there had been a mixed bag of reactions to his interview with Adrienne Assad. Now it was overshadowed by worry about the domestic situation in the US.

Dakar's stay here would be as he planned, an overnight, before striking out across the desert. For now he would go back, talk to Tony and make a few calls. Perhaps an afternoon nap was in order. Napping was vastly underrated, in his estimation.

Back at the hooch, Tony was gone for lunch, tired of waiting for the call that did not come. Dakar called Simon on the sat phone to check on his progress.

"Hey Simon, how is it going with you? I am in Tikrit." Simon would not know the name of the military base in Tikrit. "Tomorrow I hit the road for Amman. I should be in Tel Aviv in a few days at the most," Dakar said.

"Very well, my friend. I have your gold and the cash in US dollars and Euros," Simon replied. "A Canadian man and woman who are experienced sailors are interested in sailing with you. I will meet them this afternoon at the marina. It is not a young woman, as you asked, but perhaps it is good enough?"

"Yeah, that's fine, Simon. Three people are better than two. I have another favor to ask of you. I have a friend in the States who has some problems with the government and might need to contact me. Trouble is, he's not supposed to be talking to me. He is my closest friend. Would you be my contact person with him? I don't know how to arrange to have him contact you instead of me," Dakar asked. Simon had been true to his word on everything he had asked of him up to this point, and his stomach told him he was a man to be trusted.

"Of course, Dakar. I have a private cell phone number for just such business. Even the Mossad would have trouble tracing it. You need only give him this number or I have a friend in Washington who could help in this matter," Simon offered.

GLENN R. SUGGITT

"That's the problem, getting him the number. I'll take your number and think about it. Perhaps I will use your contact. You have been good to me, my friend. Thank you," Dakar replied.

"You pay me well and in these times your money is good for me. The business is not good now, Dakar. I will see you in a few days," Simon stated as he hung up the phone.

Dakar napped for about half an hour and then played a few games of crib with Tony, while they waited for the DFAC to open for supper. Tony was still upset at the delay and wondered whether Dakar was wise to go it alone through the desert. In the end Tony wasn't willing to take the risk, and he said, "Too many variables for my liking and things are heating up here again."

Dakar went to the main dining facility for supper and ended up sitting beside an Iraqi man. He chatted with the former Iraqi army officer in Saddam Hussein's army who had fled Iraq after the Iran-Iraq war, when Iraq was a friend of the US. A Kurd ethnically, the man was part of the government in exile that was formed after the first Gulf War, Dak suspected. He spoke excellent English, and was obviously a cultured and educated man, his speech refined. A chill went up Dakar's spine as the man spoke and he thought him a cold blooded killer, the stuff mass murderers were made of. No reason for this feeling really: just the man's eyes and quiet manner.

Dakar mulled over Simon's offer over supper and dessert, and back at the hooch he called him. "Simon, how exactly would you work this phone business with my friend? It could be bad for him if he is found out."

"Simply, my friend. I will have my contact in Washington give him a cell phone discreetly with my number only in the memory. He will tell your friend who I am, and instruct him to keep the phone just for outgoing calls, and not on his person or in his home or workplace. Anything else may raise suspicions. It is simple and even if they trace the call to me, who am I, but the owner of a boat repair shop?" Simon said.

Dakar liked the idea and said, "That sounds good. Not much risk to him. Go ahead and I'll pay you when I get to Tel Aviv. Explain where I am to Teddy. Keep him updated. Thanks again, Simon." Dakar told Simon where his friend lived and worked. He described Teddy as tall muscular man with red curly hair and freckles. He stressed again the need for secrecy.

Dakar took the time to rethink his plan, to cross the barren desert north of Lake Tharthan, a deep manmade lake used as a reservoir. The road was paved all the way and the maps showed a rail line and canal running parallel to it for most of the way. It was an eighty mile run from Highway #1 to Highway #12. No military convoys used the road at all. It probably would not attract a lot of insurgent attention. He also thought the IA soldiers would think twice about robbing or hassling an armed US man. A small bribe or the letters that Tariq gave him would probably get him through any checkpoints that were troublesome. It was as good a plan as any, probably safer; no one would be expecting gringo traffic on that road and by the time they knew he was there, he would be long gone.

Dakar was in the sack at 21:00, his eyes closed to thoughts of Jenn and the first night they made love, unable to get enough of each other, drifting in and out of sleep, awakening throughout the night to more lovemaking because of the incredible closeness they felt. It had been impossible to fall asleep when they were falling in love.

Dakar filled up on a great breakfast at the DFAC before driving to the main gate and Highway #1 north. The roads were empty at this time in the morning, and he was past Tikrit going north in no time and checked his map for geographical landmarks that would identify his turnoff a short way down the road. He didn't think it would be hard to find the turnoff. It had to be the only paved road on his left, just before the village of Laqlaq, and then the eighty miles across the open desert.

CHAPTER 18

Work, Work, Work

Teddy had to admit that developing a new formula to fix the economy in the United States was fascinating and engaging work. He was optimistic they would find something or at least prove that it could not be done. The scope of the work had evolved into a complex formula. They were no longer predicting what was going to happen economically based on existing conditions. The group was going to suggest changes to the US economy, and by extension the world's economies. It was becoming a blueprint. He heard President Haines had become interested in his work.

Robin Chambers, the psychologist, was a surprise in her language and work. She was objective in nature, never subjective, and gave Teddy a new perspective on his previous theory. The addition of the economist, Marguerite Coutts, took the whole project up another level. Marguerite was an attractive and amazing woman, and her global insights were startling in their accuracy. Both were brilliant in the extreme.

Teddy was not in their league intellectually, but had assumed the role of leader with reluctance and grace. His presence and counsel were a steadying influence on the team. He directed and focused their energies where needed. Teddy was a natural leader. He was genuine in his praise when they did well, and he never patronized, never demanded, or was sullen or limited in his discussions with other team members. They came to Teddy willingly, for direction and help.

He got to know a bit about everyone on the team. Teddy shared with them his life

with Rosie, and his dreams and aspirations. He was careful never to let his remarks wander to the colonel, Dakar, or to make any negative comments about the government.

Robin was happily married with three children. She had tenure at Georgetown

University, a lovely large home in the suburbs and had been living the American dream.

Marguerite had a long term relationship with her partner, Gwen, and lived in a luxurious apartment in New York. She often traveled because of her job as a senior economic analyst with the Federal Reserve. The violence in New York had subsided to manageable levels, but it was still worrisome for Marguerite. She called Gwen a few times a day to make sure she was safe.

Helen lived an alternative lifestyle: young, Goth, and into some really weird stuff. Her lifestyle choice had undergone some radical changes in the last few weeks. Teddy didn't judge her, and thought to himself, "It's not like I don't also live outside the box. So, what the hell?"

Glenn, the other mathematician, was in a world unto himself. He was single, brilliant and a loner in every sense of the word. Teddy didn't really know much about him other than the fact that he was really good at crunching numbers.

Meg, who had replaced Rachel, was very young and flighty. She loved the outdoors and had a boyfriend who was a doctor. She hoped to get a ring for Christmas. All in all, it was a nice group of people and under different circumstances he would trust them, but he couldn't—his life depended upon it.

They were making real progress. The Bitch was ecstatic and sickeningly profuse in her praise. She had pizzas sent to the office one day, but Teddy would not eat the pizza. It stuck in his craw to take anything from her. He kept imagining her face as his hands tightened around her neck and he slowly squeezed the life out of her. That gave him some comfort.

On his walk home the next day from the drop-off point to the apartment, he was approached on a corner three blocks from his home by an older man walking in the same direction. The man wore a fedora, and walked with confidence and grace along the sidewalk. He pulled his collar up against the cold, damp, November wind.

As he strode abreast of Teddy he spoke. "Hello, I bring greetings from your friend Dakar. Keep on walking, Teddy," he ordered. "It's OK to talk, but we should appear casual, just in case."

Teddy did not know what to think. It could be a setup by The Bitch. It was not beneath her to do that.

The old man continued, "My friend Simon in Tel Aviv, who repaired your friend's Decker, asked me to give you a cell phone. It has his telephone number in it. It's very important you listen to what I have to tell you, Teddy. Call only him on the phone with your messages for Dakar. Do not keep the phone with you at your home or business—place it somewhere they will not find it. Your surveillance is only electronic now. They lifted the team following

153

you and Rosie. Still, be careful. Good day." When the two of them rounded a corner he slipped the phone into Teddy's pocket and walked briskly away.

It seemed very unlikely The Bitch knew of Dakar's sailboat, and there was no reason she should try and trap him with the work going so well. Teddy would try the cell phone when he got a private moment. He glanced in his jacket pocket to make sure it was off.

Rosie was home. He could still not believe how his heart felt every time he saw her. God, she was spectacular and had the looks of a model. He particularly liked the way she brushed the hair off her face so that it stayed behind her ear. Rosie would catch him sometimes as he marveled at her beauty and she would blush.

They left on their evening walk, holding hands. They talked in a subdued manner about the new treasure they had and where to hide it. The first area he would start looking for a hiding spot was the underground garage where the Honda was parked. He would not look in the car, but perhaps there was another nook or cranny he could find somewhere. Rosie was excited since they were back in business. There was risk, but it was low, she thought. Besides, who would think a phone number in Tel Aviv would be tied to Dakar?

The violence in most of the US had subsided. The use of lethal force by the National Guard and The Patriot Force had accomplished that. There were soldiers and the newly formed "Patriot Force" everywhere in the cities. Now the authorities were turning their attention to armed groups holed up in enclaves and "communities" in rural America. Using the pretense of the National Emergency and armed insurrection, they were brutal in their attacks on the enclaves. The residents were given one opportunity to surrender or face annihilation. Sometimes with gunships, sometimes artillery, they reduced the enclaves to rubble. Then hundreds of infantry assaulted the positions. It was over in hours for most of them. The smart ones gave up quickly, the less enthusiastic members were then allowed to go free, and the fanatics were sent to detention centers. One group in the community called Jefferson's Ideal held out for three days in their mountain fortress in Tennessee. Twenty-seven out of forty-five of them had been killed when it was finally over. The tunnels they had carved out of the mountain, now sealed shut, served as their tombs.

Many outspoken radicals in the US had been rounded up and imprisoned without criminal charge or reason. Few managed to escape into hiding. Some were arrested as threats to national security while others were incarcerated using existing mental health laws as "a danger to themselves or others." By using these laws, it cut the official number of detainees at federal detention centers by thirty percent. The opposition was effectively silenced in the aftermath of the attacks. Their arrests and detentions were hardly noticed by the American people. There were some senators and congressmen and women who spoke out against the continued imposition of martial law, and the wholesale arrests. Their forum was limited to friends and family. Certainly no national media was allowed to carry too critical a view of the current situation. The language had to be constructed and delivered in the broadest of terms.

One instance that stuck in Teddy's mind was Senator Jane Collins from North Dakota who used these words, "It is the hope of all Americans that peace and order will be restored to our communities, so that we can return to the freedoms guaranteed us by the Constitution, which we so deeply cherish and need." He supposed the senator only got it on air because she was a Republican from the west and was touting the peace and order angle.

Teddy was haunted by the last words he heard Jim mouth, "Help us." The only way he could think of helping was contacting someone in a position of power and then letting them know what was going on. However, websites were now being censored nationally and certain of his online news sources had dried up. Too overt a censorship was bound to raise the ire of the American public so most of it was done in a micro manner, only allowing some criticism of the government or president. Criticism saying, "The president had exercised too much restraint and not gone far enough in cleaning house," was especially welcomed.

The world scene was a mixed bag of weirdness and contradictions economically, including the prevalence of violence and government reactions. The Chinese workers who had benefited from the economic miracle in China were now demonstrating in front of their closed factories, the promise of a better life snatched from their grasp. In typical Communist Chinese fashion, the military and police put down the demonstrations with brutality in almost the same manner as the United States. Leaders were rounded up and sent to jail. Ethnic troubles in Nepal and Western China were starting to raise their ugly head again.

Much of Africa ploughed along as it had for decades, the major difference being the rich no longer had the income they were accustomed to, and were destined to join the middle and lower classes shortly.

Europe was mostly calm, but frozen economically. Businesses opened because they always had. The trains ran for the same reason. It was business, for the sake of doing business, and absolutely nothing was usual about it. Teddy couldn't remember exactly how many, but six or more European nations were now dictatorships. It was none of the biggies, just former countries from behind the Iron

Curtain and some in the Balkans. Poland of all places had a military dictatorship now and Russia may as well have had one, too. Everyone was being very careful with their nuclear weapons and acting extremely responsible.

He hadn't heard what was happening in the rest of Asia. Latin America was as unstable as it had ever been, except for some major unrest in Mexico. One huge benefit of the chaos was that the drug trade was taking a real beating. When there is no money, there are no drugs. It was a direct cause and effect relationship. America had millions of strung out addicts looking for drugs or help from an already overburdened healthcare system. The world had entered a twilight zone between reality and the past, with no clear path or direction imagined.

The underground parking garage in their building did have a good hiding place for the phone. The charger he bought could be plugged into the Honda to recharge the battery when necessary. The plastic pipe he hid the phone in had a cap that could be removed easily and there was no reason for anyone to look in there. The underground parking garage had no cell phone signal, so Teddy was forced to use a small alcove at the rear of the building that was mostly protected from view to make his first call to Simon in Tel Aviv.

"Hello, my new friend Teddy. I am Simon, a friend of Dakar's. So you trust me, know that your friend has left Tikrit, and is headed for Amman and Tel Aviv," Simon said after answering on the third ring.

"Thank you, Simon. I will use this phone sparingly. Things have gone badly for me here," said Teddy, as he went on to explain about his detention, The Bitch and the real threat to his life.

"I understand. I will tell Dakar what happened to you when he phones me or gets to Tel Aviv in a few days. Teddy, please be very careful and safe. It will be many weeks before Dakar comes to America. Trust no one, be silent. Please, my friend," Simon said, as the call ended abruptly.

CHAPTER 19

A Sunday Afternoon Drive

Dakar sped along Highway #1 at fifty for a half an hour, until a small town came into view when he rounded a curve in the road. Sure enough a paved road appeared just before the entrance to Laqlaq. It helped that he had used Google Earth and the satellite view to see the exact location of the road. As he made the left-hand turn, he thought that it was a perfect day for a drive in the desert. The road was good so far, paved with a few patches here and there, and he had not gone three miles when an IA checkpoint appeared.

Dakar slowed for the guard at the forlorn location. He rolled down the window and spoke to him in Arabic saying, "*Sallam Alykom* (Peace on you)." He had picked up a lot more Arabic in the last year, but it was only basic. He got the gist of the conversation by picking up on keywords someone was saying. The guard asked for his papers and he produced the travel authorizations, his military ID and the letters from Tariq and the president of Iraq. The guard nodded and looked long at the papers. He then said it was going to be hot today. He did not have much money, and had a large family and sick father to care for. Dak produced a US twenty dollar bill to aid in his plight and the man smiled broadly and handed him back his papers, saying "*Shukran jaziilan ma`a, as-salaamah*" (Thank you very much, goodbye) and waved him through. *That worked well,* Dakar thought to himself.

Dakar reduced his speed to forty; the road was getting progressively worse the farther he went. The evidence suggested road maintenance was not as frequent outside of town. Ten minutes later, there was a large whump when his right front wheel hit the "mother of all potholes" that sprung up out of nowhere. The steering and wheels seemed OK, but Dakar pulled over to take a look. The rim was bent slightly, but the tire looked intact and on he went, only to feel the vehicle starting to pull to the right about ten miles down the road. He got out to change the flat tire; there were a good spare and jack—everything he needed. Dakar had made sure of that before he left Olsen.

It was past 08:00 and the sun had already started to heat the place up. The wind was very strong and the sweat evaporated from his body before it made his shirt wet. He often took off his shirt at night and found salt stains on it. That was why it was so important to drink lots of water; he had already started on his second bottle of the day from the cooler. He changed the tire rapidly and was back on the road, now slowed to thirty miles an hour. He figured at that speed he should be able to avoid the bigger potholes, which were looking like they should be measured in yards instead of feet.

Within five miles he came upon another IA checkpoint. Part of the Iraqi government strategy to decrease the level of violence and keep the roads safe was to put lots of checkpoints on all the highways. US military convoys did not have to stop, but he did. He did not like the look of the guard and his partner at this checkpoint, and the bribe he had to pay increased to one hundred US dollars. At this rate he would be out a thousand by the time he made it to Highway #12. He vowed to take a tougher negotiating stance at the next checkpoint. It took time, too, to check his papers and make small talk at each of the checkpoints. The eighty mile desert cake walk was looking like an all-day affair.

He neared a wadi and bridge that crossed a seasonal river which fed into the northern part of the lake. Dakar noticed another checkpoint in the middle of the bridge. This time the guards waved him out of the Tahoe and were intent on searching it. He let them know that was not possible. He had produced the letters again and they had little effect on the four guards who were asking for one hundred dollars each. The one guard also said they would be searching his vehicle regardless of what he said, if he wanted to pass their checkpoint. No one was pointing their guns at him, but they were all too nervous for his liking. His rifle was slung loosely over his shoulder, muzzle down as he gripped the stock near the safety, which was on for the time being. There was no telling how much of his shit would go missing if he let them search his truck and the situation looked as if it could turn violent at any moment. Trusting his instincts he made a snap decision. He thanked them in Arabic, hopped in the SUV, turned it around and headed back down the highway towards Laqlaq. The guards appeared surprised at his choice.

When he was out of sight over the next hill, he pulled out the maps that the colonel had given him in Tikrit. He would try and skirt the checkpoint by driving cross country to the irrigation canal that ran parallel to the road about four miles away. It had a dirt track running beside it, and then he could cut across country back to the road four or five miles southwest. The desert was crisscrossed with tracks everywhere and he kept his eyes peeled for one that would suit his needs. He didn't have to wait long. Within two miles he spotted a fairly well-used dirt road on his right. The road was a lot better than the ones he traveled in the mountains in Idaho, and the big SUV would have little trouble with it. Within five miles it ended at the dirt track that followed the now dry irrigation canal and he turned right onto it. His speed was reduced to a crawl and it was beginning to get very windy.

As he crested the hill where the wadi should be, he noticed a building and structure. There was movement in the front of the building. He backed up the SUV out of sight and crawled to the top of the hill with his binoculars. It was about eighty yards across the wadi. The road ran on top of an earthen dam and a control structure for regulating the water graced the middle part of the dam. The building was on the other side of the wadi. It was small: no more than twenty by thirty feet. The movement came from an Iraqi soldier who sat facing away from him and doing nothing in particular. Two vehicles were parked to one side of the building, one a small black pickup truck, the other a small blue car.

So much for his idea of trying to skirt the roadblock. Perhaps the guard here would be cheaper and not as much trouble as the four on the main road. He continued to look through the binoculars intently, as the guard smoked a cigarette. From inside the building another IA soldier appeared leading a blindfolded Arab man whose hands were bound behind his back. He heard the guard shouting at the man, apparently asking him questions. All he could hear clearly was the word dinars, the Iraqi currency. The man was now kneeling and answering the guards increasing hysterical questions in desperate language. Suddenly the guard raised his AK-47 and shot the man in the back of the head without warning, apparently tired of not getting the right answers.

Damn, Dakar thought, *another jackpot. How the fuck was it, he was involved again in more of this shit?* He could shoot the men from here with his regular rifle, but there was a chance he would miss one or both at this range. He returned to the truck for the sniper rifle and set it up using the bipod on the front of the barrel. By this time the guard had brought out another prisoner, a woman by the looks of her chador, and had her kneeling on the ground. Dakar hurried to get the rifle ready to shoot, the clip in and the scope properly focused for the range, which was about a hundred and fifty yards. An easy shot with this rifle; he was too late. A shot rang out. The guard had killed the woman before he was ready. Both of them stood smoking and looking at the bodies of the two people they had just shot. When Dakar pulled the trigger on the first one, he dropped like a rag doll. The other turned to see where the shot came from instead of dropping to the ground and Dakar hit him in the body. Dakar waited for two hours to see if other soldiers would exit the building. When he was confident the coast was clear he walked across the dam and control structure, his rifle at the ready. First, he inspected the two soldiers. The first had died instantly from the head shot; the second must have been alive for a few minutes. He could see where his boots had scraped the earth as he lay thrashing his legs. The man and woman were both dead, of course, from head shots.

Dakar then turned his attention to the building. The door was closed. He approached from the side, opened the door and yelled in Arabic, "Come out or I will shoot you." There was a faint muffled cry in response. Dakar kicked the door wide open and entered, carefully checking the corners and all his vulnerable spots. The front part of the building contained a cot and a small kitchen area. The muffled cries were coming from the room in the back and he entered that room the same way he did the first.

In the corner on a soiled mattress lay a girl, one hand tied to a metal pipe behind her, the other handcuffed to the pipe. Her face was bruised and beaten, her mouth gagged with a cloth rag. She was clad the same as the woman, in a black chador that hung loosely from her body. There was a small room in the corner, which he took to be the latrine, and when he got closer the smell told him he was right—a hole in the floor serving as the toilet. It was clear in that room. The girl was trembling with fear and when he looked at her eyes they pleaded for mercy. He put up one finger in the air, and then to his mouth to tell her to wait and to be quiet. Dakar went outside to find the key to the shackle she wore. Most likely in the pocket of one of the dead guards, was his idea.

He returned to release the girl and un-gag her, and was met by a barrage of questions and comments from the girl, in between her sobs. He could not understand what she was saying and kept her at arm's length, indicating with his hands to take it easy and slow down. Using sign language she showed him she was thirsty. He held up one finger again to indicate time and went over again to shackle her to the pipe while he went for the SUV. She recoiled at the prospect, but he was firm with his voice and grabbed her wrist and shackled one wrist to the pipe. He was back quickly with the SUV and a large bottle of water from the cooler for the girl. He un-cuffed her and she gulped the water hungrily from the bottle.

In his limited Arabic he managed over the next little while to understand a little bit of what she said. Her name was Hajirah. She was a nineteen year old Sunni girl from oil rich Kirkuk and was being taken to a village one hundred miles from here to marry an old man her parents had given her to. Hajirah was small, almost childlike in stature, and couldn't have weighed more than eighty or ninety pounds at most. She was being forced to do this because she refused to dress in a modest manner, left the house frequently to be with her friends, spent much of her time on the Internet and, horrors of horrors, had a boyfriend. The dead man and woman outside were her aunt and uncle who had been tasked with the job of delivering her to the waiting groom. The handcuffs did not belong to the guards, but were used by the aunt and uncle to keep her under control. The chador was not her idea either, but an attempt to persuade her new groom she was an obedient, pious woman. The IA guards had stopped them on the highway and two had brought the group here.

Dakar could not take her along and told her he was leaving her there. She had the car and could drive. He was sure the four dead people outside would have some money. She could go home or do whatever she wanted to do. It was not his problem. Hajirah got up and went to the other room to use the toilet, such as it was. There was no door on the toilet, and Dakar sat cross-legged on the floor facing away from the entrance out of respect for her privacy.

He heard her walking back to him, and then the shuffle of her feet as she started to run the last ten feet to him. He was barely able to deflect the small knife from his back and it sliced into his shoulder. He turned and reached with his other hand and arm to throw her to the ground in front of him. His shoulder hurt like hell and she still grasped the knife in her hand. His blood stained the blade. Dakar drew his 45 and she whimpered when she tossed the knife away.

He cocked the hammer on the 45 and she cowered, covering her face with her hands. Then she reached down and pulled up her chador to reveal herself, spread her legs open invitingly and thrust her hips upward. Hajirah's eyes begged for her life and she was offering all she had to give at the moment in exchange for it. He liked her delicate, slim frame, small ass and her pussy did look promising. Dakar cuffed her once again to the water pipe. She fucked him like her life depended upon it. One thing was for sure—she wasn't a virgin, which was a mortal sin for many Muslim women. It didn't take him long to fill her up with his cum and when he pulled out of her, his sperm ran out of her hole onto the filthy mattress.

When he was done with her, the pain returned to his shoulder and he went out to the SUV for the first aid kit. Hajirah cried out in Arabic, "Don't leave me."

"Fuck you," he said and Hajirah understood exactly what that meant. When he got outside, the wind had become ferocious in its intensity and to the southeast he could see a solid wall of dust headed their way.

CHAPTER 20

Two to Tango

Dakar set about securing the door as best he could against the approaching dust storm. The windows were already boarded up and there was little light to be seen infiltrating the structure anywhere. It didn't matter. A dust storm as severe as the one that was approaching would drive dust into the building from the tiniest opening or make its own openings. He brought with him the first aid kit, some water, and MREs and made his way into the back room. Hajirah was sobbing and saying over and over, "Don't leave me!!"

Finally Dakar told her in Arabic to "Shut up." He broke open the first aid kit and realized reaching the spot on the back of his shoulder was not going to be easy. He un-cuffed Hajirah. She stopped crying, and set about cleaning and bandaging the deep wound she had inflicted on him. He scowled at her every time it hurt. The wound had stopped bleeding and she did a passable job patching him up. He cuffed her to the pipe again and she nodded she understood when he told her about the dust storm approaching, using the little Arabic he had and sign language.

Dakar broke open a couple of the MREs, heated them using the heating packs supplied and gave one to her, along with another bottle of water. Again she started with "Don't leave me" and he glared at her once again to shut her up. She wisely stopped that tact, and started in on her life again and how she would rather die than marry the old man. Not his problem, he thought, when the storm started to howl and rage outside with a terrible whistling sound and dust infiltrated the building. It got darker as the storm obliterated the sun. He lit a candle he found in the other room as the twilight of the storm was replaced by the darkness of night. He dragged the cot in from the other room and prepared to catch some sleep. He couldn't travel in the storm and wouldn't travel at night. The dust storm might last four or five hours at most. By morning it would be gone.

She lay manacled to the pipe looking at him intently, as he got ready for sleep. Once again she lifted her chador and opened her legs. This time she spread herself open with her free hand and begged him to come to her. Sweet Jesus, she was hot and although the first time had been quick—a revenge fuck for him—he couldn't resist, if it was being offered. He left his weapons by the cot and went to her. This time was passion-filled and gentler, and Hajirah caressed him and held him close to her with her free hand.

In the morning Hajirah's petite, perfect little body beckoned him again and they ate another meal as the sun rose and filled the building with light from the now open door. In the light he could see dust everywhere on his body, gear, weapons, etc. She was covered in it, too. He went outside, and policed the area where the bodies were, for weapons and money. He locked the guns in the old truck and dragged the four bodies out of sight around the side of the building.

He released Hajirah, giving her two bottles of water to clean herself up. He did the same. There was lots of water, and he cleaned his weapons and shook the dust from his clothes.

Dakar would have to leave soon. There were no radios anywhere to be seen, on the guards, in the building or in the truck, but the two guards might have buddies who would come to check on them or relieve them. Hajirah would have to strike out on her own with the car. She peered out of the building at him and he waved her out, throwing the keys to the car to her. She went to the car, unlocking the trunk and dragged a bag out with her belongings half hanging in and half out of the bag. From the glove box she retrieved her passport. Hajirah had not a thought for her murdered aunt and uncle. She said they treated her badly. She also said through sign language that she could not drive, which made sense; few women of her age were allowed to drive and didn't have the opportunity even if they could.

Dakar did not know whether to buy that story or not, and he went to the car, put the keys in the ignition and tried to start it. It turned over well enough, but that is all it did for about a minute before the battery gave out. Chances were the air filter or carb was plugged with dust and dirt from the storm. He glared at her once again, knowing full well she would ask him again to take her along.

He could leave her here, but he was starting to have some guilt about their first sexual encounter, and whether it was consensual or not, a cocked 45 was a great incentive to a woman. He also reasoned that Plan A, which was this road, was not working out so well. There had to be another three or four checkpoints along it before he reached Highway 12, and so far each one had become progressively more hostile and dangerous. At least he knew he could go back the way he had come and have a fair chance of bribing the guards again. He could dump the girl in Laqlaq and work on some sort of Plan B.

With that thought, he went to the passenger side of the SUV and opened the door. Hajirah could not get to the SUV fast enough saying, "Thank you" every second word. He went to get in the driver's side as she peeled the chador off. Her naked body showed scars and bruises on her back and arms. Some were nasty looking. She was into a pair of jeans and a trendy but discrete blouse, in a moment. She tied a scarf over her head to further enhance her stylish, yet pious, Muslim image.

As Dakar drove, he planned his story for the two checkpoints they must pass before getting back to Laqlaq and Highway #1. Girlfriend would not cut it in this Muslim country; therefore, she was his wife who he had picked up in Ramadi where she was visiting her sister. They were now returning to Mosul and her parent's home. Because he had legitimate travel documents and she was his wife, she did not require travel documents. Only the head of the household did. Hajirah did have a passport, which helped a lot. He took the passport from her and stuffed it into his shirt pocket. Muslim women did not carry their own documents. Besides the guards would not focus on the story so much, as the bribe he would give them and the fact he was American and armed.

Hajirah chattered incessantly and did not stop until her told her to "Shut the fuck up." Being subtle with her was not succeeding. She was excellent at the first checkpoint, never uttering a word, looking away from the guards and refusing to make eye contact with them like any respectable Muslim wife. The guards, likewise, observed protocol and avoided looking at her too closely. He managed to bargain the bribe down to fifty dollars and at the last checkpoint before the highway he shoved twenty out the window and the guard waved him through.

During the drive Dakar decided he might try the route north to Turkey, driving through Syria was out of the question. The highway, he heard, was very safe north of Mosul and he could then make his way to Tel Aviv by sea perhaps by chartering a boat for the journey. Hajirah had also managed to persuade him that he could not abandon her in Laqlaq, that he owed it to her to get her closer to home which was Kirkuk. She seemed to have him figured out, as she caressed his dick through his pants while asking him to take her with him. No doubt about it—women were his great weakness, especially ones like Hajirah.

Just before the turnoff back onto Highway #1, Dakar stopped and called Simon. "Hello, Simon, how are you?" he asked.

"Fine, my friend," Simon replied. I have contacted my coworker in Washington, and he gave your friend a cell phone with my private number and instructions to use it to call me only. There will be no direct tie to you."

"Great, that sounds like it will work fine. Unfortunately I've run into a snag with Plan A. I can't make it to Amman by the road I've chosen or by any road, for that matter, and I'm going to drive north to Turkey and the coast. Then I'll try to make my way by sea to Tel Aviv," Dakar said. He thought the word "coworker" was a strange word for Simon to use.

"I met with the Canadian couple at the marina yesterday and they are good sailors, Dakar, and wish to go with you to America. George and Sheryl are nearly sixty years, but very healthy and anxious to leave," Simon continued.

"I trust your judgment, Simon, if you think they're OK. I'll call you tonight when I get to Mosul," Dakar said.

"Perhaps they could sail to Turkey and meet you. I think they can be trusted. Do you wish me to ask?"

"Yeah, that sounds great, Simon. I'll let you know tonight for sure and tell you where I'll be," Dakar said as terminated the call and put the sat phone back on charge.

There were three more checkpoints on the main highway before he reached Mosul, none of which required a toll; in fact, he was waved through all of them. On the way she had unzipped him and given him a blowjob while he was driving. She was certainly a grateful girl. He would drop Hajirah at the edge of Mosul before continuing to the military base.

Hajirah abruptly looked at him an hour into the journey, just after the BJ, and asked him in broken English, "You go Turkey?"

"You speak English?" he asked.

"Yes, I work American base Mosul for massage, but no work there now. Me, Turcoman, no Sunni. My name Jennet. My family is Turkey. You take me Turkey, I suck and fuck you good, baby," the new Jennet blurted out.

"What are you—a hooker?" *Damn,* he thought, *that makes sense.* She was much too good sexually to be a misguided Sunni girl. "No, I'm not taking you to Turkey." He pulled her passport out of his shirt pocket and sure enough she was a Jennet.

"Please, baby, I have passport and help with border. I know many truck driver for the convoy. They can smuggle for you and I treat you good, baby. I speak Turkey and Arabic very good," she said as she smiled coyly and arched her hips off the seats suggestively.

Dakar changed the subject and asked her what she was doing in the middle of the desert with the couple and handcuffed in the back of the car. Jennet told him the couple was her aunt and uncle, and taking her to Amman where they could make money pimping her out to rich Arabs. She was banned from working on US bases. She again asked him to take her with him.

"I told you NO, baby," he said, noting to himself he had called her baby and continued, "Why do I need to smuggle across the border?"

She explained in her limited English that the border guards were very corrupt because of the huge volume of materials coming out of Turkey for the US military. The convoys rolled through unchecked both ways because they paid large bribes every month on both sides of the border. There was smuggling, but mostly booze and other small items going into Iraq; rarely was anything ever smuggled out of Iraq. She said Dakar's SUV would be torn apart at the border unless he paid a large bribe and even then they would steal whatever they could while searching it. He could never get his weapons across. Paying a truck driver to take her, his guns and his most valuable things would save him money and a hassle.

Jennet could travel with the truck driver concealed behind the seat because she was so tiny, and she could watch his things and meet with him on the other side of the border. He could then pay a small bribe to the guards, who would not find much of value in his vehicle.

It all sounded good, but Jennet was, he thought, a consummate liar and manipulator. On the other hand, she wanted to get to Turkey and would probably stay with him because it was in her best interest to do so. Sweetening the pot might help a little bit, so he made her an offer she couldn't resist. "I take you to Turkey, to the coast, and give you two hundred American if you are good. Do you understand?"

She looked at him long and hard, especially his eyes and said, "Sure, baby, I be good. We go Turkey no problem. You pay me now?"

"No chance of that, baby," Dakar laughed.

Jennet smiled in return and laughed slightly. *No harm in a girl trying*, she thought. Then amazingly she was quiet as her mind worked over the details of what she would need to do. Reaching Mosul he dropped her off where she wanted, on the outskirts of the city. They agreed she would meet him at the same spot at 7:00 AM the next morning and continue their adventure. He kept her passport as insurance.

Dakar continued to the military base in Mosul, where getting stuff done was a hell of a lot easier than Speicher. He refueled and had something to eat. At the TOC he asked about the highway to Turkey and what Turkey was like. He was told that it was absolutely no problem. The border was close. Once he crossed, the roads were great, some of them four lanes, and Turkey was very stable compared to the US and parts of Europe. He stopped by the medics who looked at his wound, bandaged it, gave him some antibiotics and told him whoever had patched him up had done a good job. Then he went to the MWR and got on the Internet, checking where a port might be on the Mediterranean coast and the route he would have to use to get there. Iskenderun looked like the port that was closest to Israel. There was also an e-mail from Mick, telling Dakar he had made it to the Dominican Republic to a place called Sosua. Dakar was to call Mick on his cell phone if he wanted to stop in for a visit on the trip home. Dakar made a note of the number. It was after 20:00 when he made it back to his temporary sleeping quarters and called Simon.

"Simon, what's happenin', bro?" Dakar said, as Simon answered on the first ring.

"Always the joker, my friend. There is good news and there is bad news. George and Sheryl will sail to meet you in Turkey at Iskenderun in three days, maybe four." He continued, "Your friend

Teddy says hello. Things are not so good for him." Simon went on to explain that Teddy had been imprisoned and to describe what was happening at the detention centers. How he was out now, but needed to keep a low profile and not to make contact unless absolutely necessary for the next little while.

"Jesus, Simon, make sure he keeps out of trouble till I get there. I told him last time he called to keep his nose clean," Dakar replied.

At 07:00, Jennet was waiting for him and they headed north on Highway #2 out of Mosul for the border.

CHAPTER 21

Breakthrough

O ver the course of a week, The Bitch dropped in more frequently than ever, always pressing for something she could take back to the White House. Teddy could barely hide his disgust and revulsion when he looked at her. She kept her distance and was mindful of how big he was. Her gun was always at the ready, if Teddy should snap. The Bitch thought to herself, *Maybe I shouldn't have done his girlfriend. That man looks like he could do some serious damage to me.*

After three days of working the numbers, very heated discussions and a lot of trial and error, they came up with part of the equation that set out the minimum psychological state and a number needed to generate confidence in the economy. It was only one part of the plan and a useless thing unless a way could be figured out to make that happen. Teddy joked with the other members of the team that he and Robin had done their part; why hadn't the other group done theirs? Marguerite had assumed the role of leader in the other group. Meg and Glenn were too academic to be interested in who was in charge, and Helen was preoccupied with something in her personal life. She did her work well enough, but that was all she wanted to do. She had no enthusiasm.

Marguerite went to his office one Wednesday, closed the door and went straight to the point. "Teddy, we can present this formula to the powers that be, but it'll be without value unless we provide a blueprint on how to achieve the numbers we want. I have a theory, or plan if you like, that I've been working on for some years now. I haven't shared it with anyone else yet."

She laid it out in plain language. "I have an economic model I think we can adapt to the present situation. I'd been skeptical of it ever being of use before. It involves radical change in the way the stock market, banking institutions and other financial sectors operate. Plus, changes to the capitalist system have never been high on the agenda of the wealthy, especially if it limits their ability to make money. I am sure the administration's plans to fix things don't involve any real changes because of this."

"Okay, lay it on me, Marguerite. What are you proposing?" Teddy asked.

"I was reluctant to show it to anyone because of my job at the Federal Reserve, but if this country is going to get back on track, we're going to require big changes to the way the economic system operates. I'm willing to present the idea now because we can include it as part of our overall package, rather than my idea alone. Besides, if we don't act soon there will be no economy to fix, which seems ludicrous, given that we have all the labor and materials we need to have economic stability in this country. Instead of being based on greed and manipulation, I am proposing a system that regulates the manner and scope of financial dealing. There is plenty of room for entrepreneurship in my model, just no room for useless speculation based upon hype and lies. It'll need to be adapted to our current situation and phased in slowly. I'm sure it will work. The fact the government can have a workable plan is bound to generate some of those precious confidence numbers we seek."

"It's outside our scope of work, Marguerite, but I agree without some sort of economic plan, what value will the prediction part be to anyone?" Teddy answered.

"Which brings me to another point. I know some of your story, Teddy, and I know you are being careful, but be especially discrete around Meg and Helen. Neither of them seems to me to be exactly as they appear. I think you, Robin and Glenn should work with me on this, if you decide to include it in the overall report."

"Thanks for the heads-up, Marguerite. I'll keep it in mind," said Teddy. It was his way of letting her know he would keep his own counsel.

Marguerite passed Teddy a memory stick and said, "I trust and value your opinion. I know economic planning may not be your area of expertise, but you are involved in economics per se. Let me know what you think."

"I'll do that, Marguerite. I take it this isn't light reading and I'll get to it right away," Teddy promised.

Teddy spent the best part of the rest of the day reading the overview which, thank God, was written in layman's terms, before starting on the meat or theory part. It was a massive document over three hundred pages long. He could not fathom some of it, and ended up skimming those pages that made no sense to him or were too detailed. The entire next day he sat in front of his computer finishing the job. He was exhausted mentally from the process.

The plan was broad and comprehensive. It called for a new watchdog agency to oversee all financial institutions and corporations in the US, and stiff fines and substantial jail terms for corporate executives exceeding set personal remuneration levels. It made corporate executives criminally responsible for the actions of their companies—no bailouts for large businesses and banks, and breaking up monopolies. Certain patents, inventions and innovations were to be made public domain; the practice of suppressing new ideas would end if they were deemed in the public interest, such as new battery or energy saving technologies. The most controversial part dabbled in the political arena and called for the separation of politics and the corporate world by eliminating corporate donations to political parties, limiting the maximum amount any one individual could give to a political party and federal legislation to ensure everyone's vote was counted fairly by banning the use of voting machines.

Every day as he walked home, his thoughts were of Rosie. They used to get together with friends for dinner once in a while. Now it was always dinner at home when they entertained. "Entertained" was not an accurate term, either. They ate and played cards or games, and talked about almost everything except what was not allowed.

The one thing that really bothered Teddy about Rosie was the fact that she was never ready to go anywhere on time, it took her forever to get ready. She seemed unable to leave for any appointment at the specified hour. Her supervisor had already spoken to her about her tardiness at work.

Rosie and Teddy agreed to wait a week before calling Simon for an update. The phone remained safely in the hiding place.

The next day, he decided he would get in touch with his uncle, the congressman, instead of the good congressman from North Dakota, and tell him about what was going on in the detention centers. One day he slipped out for lunch to meet Uncle Billy at the Lincoln Memorial, which was not far from his office. It was cold and an early light snow fell as he walked briskly. He thought to himself, *Isn't this where all conspirators meet in the movies?*

Uncle Billy was old, seventy-two to be exact. His face looked like the furrows on a newly ploughed field, they were so deep.The dark brown in his face refused to fade even after many years in Washington. A full head of Braxton hair carpeted his head, now as gray as the sky. He spent summers on his ranch in Western Idaho. His tall frame was lean and tough. He had the strength of a Braxton, a man who spent his whole life working with his hands. Filling Uncle Billy in didn't take long. He simply nodded his head when Teddy related the story of his incarceration, what he had seen, and the extra judicial killings that were taking place.

He paused after Teddy finished, raised his voice and said, "We know, Teddy. Many of us are working to get marital law lifted at least in some states. There is no reason for it to continue, but until it is lifted, the president has extraordinary powers using executive privilege—almost that of a dictator. Don't forget Lincoln used the very same power to start the Civil War. The president can ignore court orders, or even the directions of the Senate and Congress. There are no clear lines of authority. Martial law will end when the American people are aware of what is occurring at these detention centers, in the streets of the nation, and what has happened to their rights. Many of us are working towards that end. Even though there is censorship, we speak out on a personal level where ever people will gather and listen. Several congressmen and at least one senator have gone missing from our ranks. There is a growing body of us: Democrats and a few Republicans, who are standing up to the reactionary elements perpetrating these crimes. We will prevail and much more quickly than you think. Have hope, Teddy. Please be very careful. I can't help you with the Homeland Security Gestapo. They are the ones responsible for most of the killings." Uncle Billy finished his speech, as always, with a nod and left.

Teddy walked back to the office, thinking to himself that the normally gentle, reflective Uncle Billy was pissed and hoped he would also be careful. Teddy didn't want Uncle Billy to become another of the missing congressmen by doing something stupid.

After lunch he gestured to Marguerite to join him in his office. She came in a few minutes later. Teddy took a deep breath and said, "Damned if I know whether it will work, Marguerite, but it might and it's brilliant. I still can't understand all of it in detail, but your overview was very good. The four of us can work on it together. Meg and Helen can finish up the mathematical part and a bit of actuarial work to finish the Predictive Formula. Nothing is to be secret from them; it will only raise suspicions. Because the Economic Plan is really not integral to the Predictive Formula, it can be detached from our work. Hopefully the colonel will not be concerned about it. One more thing, for obvious reasons you are in charge of this part of the project. You ready to start?" Teddy knew The Bitch was happy with their work. She knew they were very close to finishing, so it was also unlikely she would know they were working on something outside the scope of the project.

Marguerite was stoic in her acceptance of what was to be. Teddy called in the rest of the team to inform them of the broader extent of their new assignments. Tomorrow was the day they would start on their new job.

It is an axiom of troubled times that the production of the nation increases dramatically because of need and is spurred on by a desire to be patriotic: to do one's part and more. The team worked hard on their new assignments. Meg and Helen called on Teddy constantly for guidance and help with their work while Marguerite directed the rest of them in the task of changing her theory to suit the times. They had worked three days on the new project when The Bitch showed up at the office.

"Hey, Teddy, how are you?" she drooled sarcastically. "Got a minute?" She nodded her head in the direction of the office. She closed the door and in her best sugary voice said, "I understand you and other members of the team have become diverted by some work outside your assigned project, Teddy. Get the work done you were assigned to do. You can do whatever you want on your own time, after you finish the job. You will be returning to your old position." She did not want to sit on him too hard especially when he was so close to finishing the job. She made herself heard, she was sure.

Teddy responded, "Our work will be completed in five days. If you leave us alone, I can guarantee you we will be finished. The other thing is an economic theory that we think the president will like."

The Bitch thought for a few moments. "OK, you have a deal. Five days, but you better be finished, Teddy." Teddy would have strangled her right there if she had threatened Rosie again. Sensing this, the colonel wisely avoided any confrontation.

Well, we definitely have another rat or two in the office, Teddy thought. He wondered if they were being paid extra to be a rat. Hell, maybe The Bitch was paying all of them.

That night Teddy had turned the TV on so they could watch a rerun of *Jeopardy*. It was pointless. Rosie and he already knew the answers to the questions Alex spouted. The president was having a news conference and the network cut away to the White House. Teddy had grown sick of listening to the president's platitudes and clichés, which said nothing of real substance to the nation or gave anyone any hope. He debated about changing the channel to watch a rerun of some other program. Everything was a rerun now. But he left it on for background noise as he worked a Sudoku puzzle. It was Rosie's turn to cook tonight. Tuna casserole was on the menu.

The president came on and started, "I have some hopeful news for the American people tonight. We have established relative calm and order in our cities and nation as a whole. It is time now to start the process of returning our great nation to normal and the lifting of martial law..." He went on to explain that he had appointed a joint committee made up of members of Congress and the Senate to meet to determine when to lift marital law. They were to report back to him within sixty days with their recommendation.

CHAPTER 22

Driving Ms. Jennet

From the look of the map, it was about seventy or eighty miles to the Turkish border and Jennet heard that the drivers, their rigs mostly empty, often stopped at a small café a few miles from the border for strong coffee before continuing on to Turkey. With the pullout of the troops, some truckers got work transporting non-strategic supplies out of the military bases in the north of Iraq to the US base in Incirlik, Turkey.

Mosul was Iraq's second largest city and getting busier by the month. Dakar had little trouble finding the highway north or traversing the city streets. There were two more IA checkpoints on the highway and he was stopped at both. Jennet did a masterful job of playing the dutiful wife again and a twenty at each was enough to get him through. About thirty miles from the border, the truck stop appeared. It wasn't much—a small shack with a single window, and a few plastic tables and chairs under a tarp completed the café. They pulled in and knocked on the window of a truck where two drivers were sleeping. Neither driver was the least bit worried about being searched at the border, and agreed to five hundred to hide Jennet and a duffle bag containing Dak's sidearm and other weapons behind the fold-up seat in the truck. They asked for the money up front. Jennet said "No!" at the same time Dakar did.

They agreed to meet Dakar just before Silopi, the first Turkish town over the border. Dakar had a little over three thousand cash on him, which was more than enough to get him to Iskenderun.

This left him defenseless, other than his boot knife; the gold he brought with him was sewn into his flak jacket. Even if they searched the SUV, there were only a few items the border guards might be interested in and he could afford to lose them. The highway north of Mosul was lightly traveled. He drove ahead of the truck.

Within forty-five minutes he was at the border crossing and there were no line-ups. One truck was just pulling away in his direction while another rolled away from the crossing into Turkey. Iraqi Customs and Immigration stopped him, and he slipped twenty into his passport. The twenty dollar bills were coming in handy. Onward he rolled to Turkish Customs and Immigration. The border guard spoke some limited English. He tried the twenty dollars in the passport.

The guard said, "This is Turkey. It costs me much more to keep my family," as he handed the passport back unstamped. He upped the ante to one hundred and handed it back. The guard said, "I will have to search your car." Dakar handed him the twenty dollars he had just retrieved. The guard smiled and said, "Enjoy our beautiful country, sir" while he handed him back his stamped passport.

He drove until he spotted a small turnout on the same side of the road and there he waited. Forty minutes later the truck rounded the bend and pulled into the turnoff. Several trucks rolled by and the two drivers got out of the cab; one held Jennet firmly by the arm. The other produced Dakar's 45 and with Jennet translating from Turkish, told him the price had just changed for his bag of goodies and they were keeping the girl. The other driver had a pistol tucked in his waistband, but appeared a reluctant participant, doubting the wisdom of holding up an American soldier for money. They wanted five thousand. Dakar doubted he would get anything for his five thousand, certainly not his weapons.

Dakar laughed at the driver with his gun. The driver scowled and told him, "I will shoot you and take your money. Maybe you not laugh then."

Dakar figured he would go for the guy with the pistol in his waistband. The 45 would not fire since he had disabled the gun. It was only six short feet to the other driver and he could handle that easily enough. He stepped forward to rush the second man, when from nowhere Jennet produced a small knife and stabbed the man in the leg. He was doubled over when the first man pulled the trigger on the non-functioning gun. Surprised, he pulled the trigger again. Jennet already had the pistol out of the waistband of the second driver and was about to shoot the first when Dakar yelled, "No!" He took the 45 from the first driver, smashing him hard in the head a few times. The driver slumped to the ground and whimpered, holding his hands up to protect himself. He pleaded with Dakar in Turkish, in a universal plea: "Please do not shoot me." Jennet held the gun on the driver with the leg wound and spat on him. Her hand was steady and the look in her face deadly. Dakar again told her "NO!!" and he took the gun from her.

He ordered the two drivers to sit on the opposite side of the truck away from the road, not to attract attention should someone drive by. Jennet stowed the duffle bag in the Tahoe. She returned and translated, as Dakar told them, "I should kill you both, and I will kill you if I see you again or we have any trouble in Turkey." Dakar had them produce their passports and driver's licenses. Jennet wrote down their names and addresses. With that he gave them a hundred, and he and Jennet drove off in the SUV.

As they sped away down the highway Jennet asked, "Why you no kill those bastards and then you give one hundred? You crazy?"

"Baby, baby, baby, much trouble with bodies and give money, then no problem," Dakar said.

Jennet fell silent for a moment, her brow creased in thought. She smiled and nodded that she understood.

"You do very good. More money for you, baby," Dakar replied.

"You give me five hundred? I am very good with knife," Jennet asked.

"No, one hundred," Dakar answered and continued. "I go to Iskenderun and sail then to America."

Jennet said she was from a small fishing village just south of Iskenderun and had often helped her father with his fishing boat that had a sail. She continued, "Me good sail."

More Jennet bullshit he was sure, and to catch her in the lie, he questioned her about her sailing experience. Although she didn't know the sailing terms, it was obvious she knew how to sail. The road got better as the miles passed. Noon approached and they stopped in Cizre, first at a money-changers where Jennet negotiated with the man to get the best exchange rate from American dollars to Turkish liras. Dakar then fueled up the big SUV with diesel and bought a road map. A little farther down the road, they had a typical Turkish meal of manti, a delicious dumpling filled with meat, pilaf rice and a couple of Efes Pilsen beers at a roadside stop and poured over the map, planning their route to the sea.

Dakar calculated they could make it to Kiziltepe easily or even Sanilurfa by nightfall. The Tahoe's windows were all tinted and it was almost impossible to see in any of them except for the front windshield and only then if you were very close. The SUV was licensed in Turkey. The Turkish plates and the appearance of the vehicle lent it a mysterious appearance, a "don't fuck with me aura," which might keep the cops from bothering them and petty thieves at bay. He took the opportunity to change out of his combat clothing into something a bit more touristy: long pants and a short sleeve shirt. He kept the now functional 45 tucked within easy reach. Once again Jennet unzipped him and gave him a terrific blowjob while he drove. Dakar was sure this was the way all travel should be. They made it easily to Sanilurfa with no problems a little after 18:00. The big armored SUV consumed copious amounts of fuel and they filled up first thing, for the next day's travel. Jennet asked about hotels and they checked into the Akgol Renaissance Hotel. Even though the hotel parking lot was gated and guarded twenty-four hours a day, they left nothing of any value in the SUV. The room he rented for eighty dollars was spectacular with a Jacuzzi and large king size bed.

They would not leave the hotel. The first thing he did was order room service, a bottle of champagne first and a dinner of chicken and beef kabobs with vegetables to be brought up in a hour. He and Jennet soaked in the tub drinking champagne and fooling around before toweling each other dry and making love. It was surprising to him that the sex kitten could be so gentle and tender. There were a lot of things he didn't know about the girl. Jennet was smart, no doubt about that, and had acted swiftly and decisively when their lives were in danger. Her survival instinct was off the scale. Perhaps it had to be for a single woman working as a hooker in a Muslim country like Iraq, especially given her petite size. She could not have been over four feet, tem inches tall and weighed next to nothing. She was exceptionally pretty, with fine facial features and long black hair.

They lay on the bed. She curled up in the crook of his arm with her head resting on his shoulder. Supper arrived and they ate the delicious kabobs. A more precise description was Dakar gobbled, as he always did, while Jennet nibbled away. The TV had several English language stations and one had a movie on with Turkish subtitles that Jennet settled in to watch. Dakar took the opportunity to use his cell phone to call Simon and get an update on when his sailboat that he had renamed Jenn would arrive.

Simon answered in Hebrew, and then realizing it was Dakar, switched back to English. "Hello, my friend. How are you and where are you?"

"I'm great. Just got out of the tub with Jennet, drank some champagne and had a great supper of kebabs. We are in Sanilurfa and should make it to Iskenderun by tomorrow night. What news have you got for me?"

"Another woman, Dakar. Do you pick them from the tree?" Simon said teasing him and continued, "I have very good news, Dakar. George and Sheryl went early this morning for Iskenderun and the winds are very good for the next few days. They will arrive in three days at the most, I think."

"They will be good sailors if they make it in three days. I have my weapons with me, and I have to find some way to get them past Turkish customs and onto my boat before I sail for America. The world has become a dangerous place," Dakar said.

"Yes Dakar, very dangerous especially in America and now I hear that private boats are being robbed near the Tunisian coast and people murdered. You must also stop in Tel Aviv. I did not want to put your gold and money on the sailboat going to Turkey. You can get more water, fuel and food if you stop. I have a friend in the customs department. He can look away for a small fee when you arrive."

"I already owe you much, Simon. Thank you! Maybe you will want my boat in payment when I come," Dakar joked.

"No, it is a small thing and will not cost much, Dakar. George and Sheryl have a phone on the boat. Call me when you arrive in Iskenderun," Simon said, as he gave Dakar the number.

Whenever he slept or had sex with a woman he almost always thought of Jenn at some point. That night for the first time, he slept without a thought or dream of Jenn. They awoke to lazy morning sex. They were out the door and on the road at 06:00, picking up some food at a local stop. Traffic was light until they got near the coast and the speed limit was sixty-five on the bigger highways. Dakar kept it within the posted limit and noted that Jennet had dressed once again very discretely and appropriately. Jennet was so beautiful; he imagined in a little black dress she would be something else. Maybe he would buy one for her in Iskenderun before he left. A few hours later she had her head in his lap once again, swallowing everything he had to offer and sating him quite quickly.

There was one more stop for fuel and lunch. Jennet had quit babbling on incessantly, sensing how much Dakar hated the constant chatter and they talked about her life in the small fishing village as a girl. She was an orphan now. Jennet had not started her new profession until after she started working on the US base. One day a man had offered her five hundred for a blowjob when she was giving him a massage. It was more money than she made in a month. Word spread quickly and soon she had amassed a string of clients and over seven thousand dollars. Word spread so fast that within six weeks she was found out and escorted off the base. Her aunt and uncle in

Mosul had stolen her money and taken her prisoner. It was only a week later when she met Dakar.

The trip passed uneventfully. They pulled into Iskenderun in the late afternoon. Dakar paid for a nice room with an ocean view and settled in for the evening. The hotel was very upscale and had a lockable storage closet where he stashed the bag of weapons, safe enough for the time being. Dakar took Jennet's hand and they walked on the seashore to the point, enjoying the sunset and ocean breeze. The rock work was hundreds of years old. It lent an air of antiquity to the port. The walkway was filled with other couples doing the same as they were. They kissed briefly and discreetly at the point, and dined at the superb Oceanside restaurant in the hotel. Tomorrow he and Jennet would go to the docks to bribe a fisherman or charter boat to bring his bag of goodies to him when he was far offshore and away from Iskenderun.

It was almost 9:00 PM when he remembered to call Simon. He had become enthralled with Jennet. When she laughed it came from deep inside her, lighting up her face. He remembered after they had made love, she whispered his name over and over again when he was inside her. Her orgasms turned him on intensely and there seemed to be no end to her gentle sighs of pleasure.

"Simon, we are in Iskenderun, and I will be ready to go when George and Sheryl get here," Dakar said.

"I help you with your problem to get your things on the boat; it's very risky if you don't know anyone. I have a friend in the Turkish customs. I will make sure he only inspects your boat before you go. You do nothing. Just give him one hundred dollars when he comes. I have a special surprise for you in Tel Aviv. You will like, Dakar, and it is a good price."

"Why doesn't that surprise me, Simon? And, of course, the man owes you a favor and there is only a small fee." Dakar laughed at his patter. He wondered about the other types of businesses Simon might have. Smuggling, gunrunning. Who knew? Maybe a little of everything. He disconnected and turned his attention to the lovely Jennet, naked in his bed.

Jennet peered into his eyes and then tears started to run down her cheeks as she said, "Dakar, I no family, no mother, no father. My brothers know what I do and will kill me if they see me. Please take me to America."

Dakar knew this was the truth; his intuition told him so. He should have known that question was coming sooner or later, and his automatic response was "NO!" He continued, "It's too dangerous and what can I do with you when we get to America? It is not safe there either."

Jennet said nothing, but the sadness in her eyes told it all when she said to him, "OK, Dakar," and she drew him down to the bed and her waiting arms.

CHAPTER 23

Sailing

D akar awoke late the next morning. He was never late waking up. Jennet was propped up on one elbow wide awake and smiling at him. He ordered breakfast from room service. There was little for them to do until George and Sheryl arrived. He was excited at the prospect of finally starting his journey home. The idea of leaving Jennet behind was not sitting well with him and he knew why. He had feelings for her. He questioned the sanity of his feelings, to fall for a woman with a name almost the same as Jenn's. He could plainly see Jennet loved him, that the bullshit had stopped long ago and Dakar knew Jennet wouldn't leave him like Jenn had. Clinically it was wrong in so many ways, but Dakar always followed his heart and the feeling was loud and clear. True to form, in speaking to the point, he turned to her and said, "I am falling in love with you and I can't leave you behind. You come with me to America, please?" Tears formed in his eyes.

"Yes, I come, Dakar," was all she said, when she kissed him. In an uncharacteristic display of emotion, he sobbed out loud and buried his head into her chest. Dakar was in love again, something he hadn't felt in six years.

Breakfast arrived. Afterwards they went shopping for some sailing gear for Jennet. It was still mid-morning when they back to the hotel room and his cell phone rang.

"Hi, Dakar, it's George. We are here and just sailing into the harbor now. Sheryl and I are looking forward to meeting you. Look for us at the marina on the west side of the harbor, in about an hour."

"Wow, George you made good time. Great sailing. See you in an hour," Dakar answered. Dakar could not stay another night. He was anxious to get started. He decided to load up the Tahoe and head to the marina. They would take George and Sheryl out for a seaside luncheon and this afternoon set sail for Israel. Jennet could not stop smiling and laughing. The two of them joked all the way down to the marina about everything and anything that came to mind.

It wasn't hard to spot "Jenn" at the marina; the pictures did not do the boat justice. She was in superb condition and looked better with every step Dakar took down the wharf. George and Sheryl were climbing out onto the wharf. A Turkish customs officer stepped off the boat after them.

Introductions were short and sweet. George and Sheryl were glad to be there, and grateful for the lunch invitation. George was completely bald, fit, tanned, lean, about five foot nine, slightly forgetful and laughed a lot. Sheryl was blond headed and thin, just as fit and healthy at five foot and quieter in nature. She was one of those women whose being exuded sexuality at any age. Simon had been accurate in everything he said about them. Sailing the distance they did in a little over two days was excellent. Dakar took an instant liking to the pair; both were comfortable with each other and very easygoing.

George and Sheryl were retired school teachers, who were visiting Israel when the worldwide troubles started. Air travel was supposed to resume shortly, but they did not want to risk staying put. Hoping their chances would be better making their own destiny, the pair decided to throw their lot in with Dakar. Sailing had always been their first love and crossing the Atlantic was another adventure to them. Both were creatures like him, enjoying life to the fullest.

The first thing he did was take a tour of his new boat. Everything was ship-shape on board and stowed properly. The boat was moored to the dock correctly, the sails properly furled and tied. The galley and head were clean. Jennet talked and chatted very comfortably with both of them, in her broken English.

Over lunch, at the same waterfront restaurant they dined at the night before, they went about the business of updating each other. Sheryl said Simon had called them and let them know about the customs guy and they had given him a hundred dollars already, although there was nothing on board that would attract his attention. The Turkish customs officer had given George a phone number to call when they were ready to go. Dakar let them know Jennet was coming along and there should be no problem with the Turkish customs guy for another hundred. He would figure out some way to get her ashore when they got to the US. He assumed Simon would take care of the Tel Aviv end. He had no clear plan of where in the US he would end up. A lot would depend on Teddy. Teddy, he explained, was his friend and needed some help in Washington.

George and Sheryl told him they had no clear idea either of what they would do once they were on the other side. Just getting there was the first priority. A few friends who were scattered along the eastern seaboard would help them make their way back to Canada. Over lunch, his intuition said good folks—no problems here. It was likely the crossing would be safe, fun and relatively stress free.

Back to the Jenn they went. He parked the Tahoe in the marina parking lot, leaving the keys in the marina office after telling the owner they were sailing to Greece for a few weeks and would return. The formalities with customs took five minutes and they were out of the harbor tacking eastwardly towards Israel by 15:00. He got a firsthand look at how George and Sheryl handled his boat, and realized they were better sailors than he was. He was still the master and captain, but knew he would defer to their superior knowledge and skills if any tight sailing situation arose.

They sailed night and day, constantly tacking into the wind. Jennet knew the wind and was an eager learner when it came to the work of sailing. Dakar only had to show her any particular task once and it was always done correctly thereafter. He often left her at the helm. She looked almost dwarf-like against the huge wheel at the stern of the boat and was thrilled to be piloting the vessel. The interior of the Decker was magnificent—polished mahogany graced the walls, the fittings were brass and the master cabin was spacious. Food preparation was a shared responsibility, with all eager to help with whatever or whenever they could.

Dakar and Jennet slept and made love many times in their twelve hours off. Jennet asked him the first night, as they lay in bed, "You have other girl, Jenn?," her eyes clearly conveying her concern about the name of his sailboat.

"Yes, but many years ago. She is gone now many years," was all he could say. He seldom shared his thoughts and emotions with anyone, but with Jennet he did. He was amazed he had fallen in love with her so rapidly and easily. Teddy would have been surprised, too.

George and Sheryl enjoyed the voyage as much as Dakar did, and sometimes he heard them making love below. He showed George how to use both of the rifles he had with him and the 45. Sheryl refused to touch the guns. Jennet could barely pick up the rifle, yet she fired alongside George when they test fired both rifles. Jennet would not hesitate to use a gun. Dakar wasn't sure about George. Perhaps he would if they were being shot at.

They took four days to sail to Tel Aviv. The weather was fine. It was only the wind that slowed their progress. Even a quartering wind would have helped. In the late afternoon they sailed into Simon's boat repair wharf and tied up near the end of the pier. Simon's "friend" in the Israeli Customs and Immigration office did not search the boat. She was friendly and stamped all their passports without comment, including Jennet's.

A balding, slightly overweight, fiftyish man smoking a huge cigar walked intently down the wharf towards them. It could only be Simon. "Ah, my friend, Dakar, it is good to meet you and Jennet. You have done well on the trip. Come, we will have some cold drinks and food at my home," he said. He greeted George and Sheryl with "Shalom," and they returned down the wharf to the office, and discussed the uneventful trip from Iskenderun.

The four of them followed Simon to the end of the pier, where a shotgun wielding security guard stood and piled into his old Toyota Camry waiting near the office. Simon's home was a modest one bedroom condo on the tenth floor of a building a few streets away from the ocean. It had a spectacular view of Tel Aviv and out to sea. His wife, Rachel, had started the preparation of lunch, and they relaxed with some cold beer and a nice red wine. Lunch was a very simple affair: a great Greek salad and some hot panini . Rachel was a pleasant woman with a matter of fact manner and ample hips. She was regaling George, Sheryl and Jennet with stories from the sixties and seventies when both she and Simon were young, foolish and idealistic and Israel was at war with their neighbors. Both had served with the IDF (Israeli Defense Force) and were glad for the relative peace and stability they were enjoying in the last ten years.

Simon wandered out to the balcony where Dakar was enjoying the view and sunshine.

"My friend, I have your gold and cash for you." He took out a very small amount of gold and an envelope containing the US dollars and Euros Dakar had asked for and continued. "It will be dangerous on the sea for you. There are more reports of killings and robbery off Tunisia. The pirates use high speed boats, attacking with two or three. They leave no one alive and burn them after."

Dakar interrupted, "My small arms will not give us much protection against multiple attackers…"

Simon piped in, "Yes, I know and my surprise for you is a 50 cal. machine gun that I can supply for a very reasonable price. I can also install a mount for the gun on the rear deck. I have it made and ready to go. My men can install it this afternoon, while we resupply and refuel your craft, if you wish."

Simon had too many friends and connections for Dakar's liking and he said to Simon, "You sure as fuck aren't a simple boat repair shop owner. What the fuck do you do for a real living? I'm sure the price will be very reasonable, but what the fuck is going on?" Dakar demanded.

"My friend, you do not want to know and it is better you do not. My business is my business. Take the gun and use it to keep safe," Simon answered.

"No, I am not feeling very safe with you anymore. I think you should keep the gun, and George and Sheryl will not come with us to America. They cannot be who they seem to be."

Simon paused for a moment, weighing his options and took a puff on his cigar. It had been fortunate that Dakar had called him to look at the Decker, but further lying to Dakar was not going to work. Dakar was intelligent—that was for sure—but his intuition was phenomenal, almost psychic. Simon had not lied to Dakar, until a few minutes ago. He just hadn't told him everything. Now that he had met the man, he would have to trust Dakar. He had been given complete discretion in this matter by his superiors.

Simon chuckled, as he puffed on his cigar and said, "Okay, my friend, like you say, here is what is happenin'." Laying out the covert activities of his government in the United States that led up to today took Simon a few minutes. Someone with information on US foreign policy and direction in the Middle East had contacted Israel. Israel was not interested in military secrets, firstly because the US shared most of their new weapons technology with Israel already and was a staunch ally, and secondly the US would be furious if they attempted to do so. They were aware of Israeli espionage activity in the US, regarding foreign policy initiatives and direction. While the US didn't like it and did what they could to stop the spying, it didn't piss them off enough to cut aid to Israel.

The person who contacted Israel had an outline of all proposed US foreign policy direction and initiatives in the Middle East. There was also sensitive information about the governments of many of Israel's Arab neighbors. The spy had agreed to supply information to them for the next three years for the all-inclusive price of five hundred pounds of gold, worth over nine million dollars at the time they negotiated the deal. The original information that was supplied was a taste, they said, of what was to come. It was priceless information to Israel. Now with the world in turmoil because of the bombings that gold was worth a lot more: perhaps eight or more times that amount. What was odd was the request for a specific weight in gold rather than a dollar amount.

Dealing with an American who wanted money was no problem, but striking a deal with one who may have been responsible for the trouble the world had descended into was out of the question. The United States could not even suspect Israel had any part in the bombings. Their ally had been attacked and Israel needed to know who was responsible. It seemed insane that the person would do such a thing simply for money.

Mossad had intended to buy the gold through intermediaries, but this was now impossible and they needed to get the gold to America from Israel. A Mossad agent would identify the person when he delivered the gold. Dakar was the only answer they could think of to get the gold to America. Simon and his superiors knew, it also put distance between Israel and the gold if he should be caught. Simon stopped talking for the moment to let what he said sink in.

Jennet could see the look on Dakar's face had changed and stuck her head out the balcony door to ask if everything was all right. Dakar smiled and said, "Yes, it is Jenn," and instantly regretted his slip as Jennet blanched and returned to Rachel's story. He asked Simon some pointed questions about why they couldn't use another method to get the gold there, like a plane or yacht. Simon filled him in on their reasoning, and also let him know that although George and Sheryl knew there was going to be Israeli gold on board, they did not know why or where it was to be delivered. That information was to come later. The mount for the 50 cal. was a large diameter pipe filled with the gold. It would look like a mooring point for towing a small boat. It was well constructed and powder coated, painted gray, with a single hole in the top serving as the point to affix the gun to. It looked as if it belonged on the deck.

Dakar looked directly at Simon and asked, "So you want me to commit treason, by working with the intelligence service of a foreign government?"

CHAPTER 24

When All Is Said and Done

Teddy informed Marguerite about the new deadline to finish the project he had agreed to with The Bitch. Marguerite had grown to dislike The Bitch, completely independently of the feelings Teddy had for her. Marguerite had four days to finish the changes that would be required on her Economic Renewal Plan. She worked steadily for twelve and fourteen hours a day. For the most part, Teddy and the rest of the team could only do the grunt work of providing the mathematical proofs for various segments of the plan, after she feverishly finished with each part of the financial sector. Teddy had taken to fetching coffee and food for Marguerite as she worked, and moved her into his office to minimize distractions. Marguerite finished on the afternoon of the third day, and fell sound asleep at the desk for three hours before Teddy woke her up and sent her home to sleep.

The next day, Teddy assembled all the components of The Plan and at noon, Marguerite drifted in. They polished the presentation and as a group reviewed both parts of their project, Marguerite's Economic Renewal Plan and Teddy's Economic Predictive Formula. One could be separated from the other, so that any Economic Plan could be plugged in.

Later in the afternoon, they toasted their success with some Dr. Pepper Helen had found in the back of the refrigerator. Teddy was effusive in his praise to all of them and delivered his own impromptu speech telling them, "The Plan and Formula are ground-breaking in their brilliance and scope. If implemented, I believe our work will have a tremendously positive impact in our country and the world as a whole, and I am proud of each and every one of you. Tomorrow we will turn our work over to the Administration."

Making a backup copy of the work on a smuggled memory stick, Teddy stuck his prize in his pants' pocket. It was strictly verboten for him to do that and he risked everything. Marguerite and he spent a few minutes at the end of the day in his office and she asked him point-blank if he had a copy of their work. He told her he did not and would not make a copy; it was illegal for him to do so. Marguerite told him she had made one and hidden it where it would not be found. All that remained to be done was to phone The Bitch and let her know they would be finished first thing in the morning.

All of them were ready to call it a day and go home, when The Bitch and her entourage of men in suits walked in.

"Hi, everyone, I understand you are finished and right on schedule. I've come to congratulate you on behalf of the president and the nation. Tonight we will review our work and let you know in the morning what further action, if any, is required. Teddy, let's go into the office and have a look at what you have." The colonel gestured towards his office and in they went. The other members of the team were leaving and being thoroughly searched by the goons she had brought with her.

The Bitch was direct. "Let's see it, Teddy."

Teddy reached into his pocket and handed her the memory stick saying, "I have your copy ready for you." Then he got up to leave.

"That was thoughtful of you, Teddy," she said facetiously. "See you tomorrow." Teddy exited the office and was subjected to a body search before he left. There were still rats in the office.

Rosie was always glad to see her man and today was no exception. For them the mundane was also the sublime: the day-to-day tasks of living a shared experience of mind and body. A promise of all that was good in life waiting for them in the future. Teddy and Rosie were living the meaning of life, reveling in their companionship, and the love of friends and family.

Social networking sites such as Facebook and Twitter were filled with stories of what was happening at the detention centers, and pleas from the relatives and friends of those who were taken and missing. Teddy logged into his e-mail account that night and noticed a friend request from Jennifer Flood and recognized the picture as that of Dak's Jenn, her last name changed from Olmstead. He logged onto Facebook and confirmed her request. He had not heard from her in many years. He liked Jenn and although Dakar was hurt badly from their split, it wasn't her fault—just part and parcel of life. He returned to answering his e-mails, always careful to watch what he wrote in response to his friends, and comments about the president and the government.

He was barely ten minutes into his routine when he received notification of a message on Facebook from Jenn. The message confirmed his friend request and asked him for his e-mail address, which he sent. He spent a minute looking at her profile on Facebook and pictures. Jenn was single now and the mother of a beautiful boy with blond hair and a mischievous grin. Teddy always imagined Jenn would be a good mom. Her pictures showed that time had made her even more beautiful, if that were possible. Her blond hair was shorter now and in her pictures she often wore it in a ponytail or with a ball cap. She still enjoyed hiking and sailing, he noted, and there were pictures of her, her mom, dad, brother and two sisters. Some recently over Thanksgiving: all together and enjoying themselves.

He didn't have to wait long for an e-mail from Jenn. It popped up in his inbox ten minutes later and read:

Dear Teddy,

Hope everything is going well for you!! What have you been doing with your life? I am well and a mom of a six year old boy who brightens my life every day. I've been divorced for five years, and lately I've been thinking of Dakar and hoping he's all right. A few years ago I heard he was in the army, and knowing him I couldn't help thinking that he went to Iraq or Afghanistan or some other silly violent spot. I don't want to intrude upon his life, but I would like to know if he is safe and healthy. The troubles here recently make me worry for his safety.

All the best,
Jenn

Teddy typed out a quick, matter of fact, but not too detailed reply.

Hi Jenn:

Dakar is great and on his way back to the States, as we speak. You know him. He had his share of excitement in Iraq and now is trying to live some of his adventure dreams. Everything is great with me. I have a good job in Washington and I'm in love with a woman named Rosie. We have plans for a big house with lots of bedrooms and to fill them up with children. This summer, we're planning a trip home to do some hiking and spend some time up at Dak's cabin.

Motherhood has treated you well and I always knew you would be good at it. Your boy is beautiful.

Teddy

Teddy finished up his e-mails and went to the kitchen for a kiss and to harass Rosie as she prepared supper. He got the kiss while groping her at the stove and then was promptly driven away by the threat of a gooey spoon. She called to him in the living room, "Set the table, honey. Supper will be ready in a few minutes."

It had been many weeks since marital law had been declared and the only thing that appeared to be stabilizing in the States was the level of violence. The financial system was still paralyzed. The markets were all closed and banking restrictions were in effect for all except the very wealthy who had multiple domestic and foreign bank accounts. Airlines were mostly grounded, interstate trucking and the railways operated because they were ordered to, but you needed a permit to travel. A few radio and TV stations were attempting to circumvent the censorship laws by exposing what was happening at the detention centers. The people that did were hauled away to those same places to join the thousands already in the concentration camps.

Teddy heard nothing from Uncle Billy. In many colleges across the United States students were starting to protest. Not wanting to deal with the children of the elite in the same brutal manner as those in the poor, urban areas the government opted for tear gas, rubber bullets and truncheons. Things were not going well for the riot police on many campuses as groups of ten thousand or more students were now protesting. In law and order Texas and in the name of Jesus, the Presidential Patriotic Force had been called in, opted for violence and killed eight student protesters on the campus of the University of Houston. The original protest demonstration had only consisted of five hundred students. The killings enraged the student population and now organizers were preparing a massive protest the next day. The crowd was expected to reach twenty thousand.

That night after supper Teddy and Rosie went out for their walk and discussed what they should do next. Both agreed they would sit tight, but call Simon to get an update on where and what Dakar was doing and to let him know their situation. Teddy would be back at his old job in a day or two—for now, he was relatively safe from The Bitch because he was being a good boy and keeping a low profile.

They got back to the apartment and Teddy went to the parking garage, retrieved the phone from its hiding place and went to his secret spot at the rear of the building to make the call.

Simon answered on the second ring. "Hello, Teddy! What's new?"

Teddy updated Simon on his situation and that he was safe for the time being. He respected Jenn's wishes and did not pass along her inquiry about Dakar to Simon.

Simon answered, "Dakar left two days ago for America with a Canadian couple and a woman, for company. I think your friend is falling in love. With good sailing in a few months he will be home. Can you last that long?"

Teddy was glad he didn't let Simon know about the e-mail from Jenn, especially if Dakar was in love. Love was a word he hadn't associated with Dakar since Jenn.

"Yeah, we're fine, Simon, and will keep ourselves safe for the next few months." Teddy finished off and hung up the phone. The battery was a little low and he put it on charge in the CRV under a folded blanket in the rear of the vehicle, plugged into the power outlet located in the back. After supper he went back downstairs and stashed the phone and its charger back in the hiding place.

Teddy reported for work the next morning at 9:00 AM as usual. This time he was surprised to find everyone standing around in the office that had been stripped of all the computers and office equipment. There was not a scrap of paper anywhere and The Bitch sauntered in the door at 9:15.

She was as always, brief and to the point. "You are all done here. The Economic Predictive Formula shows great promise. The extra work you did on the Economic Renewal Plan has been rejected outright as too socialist in nature, almost communist in its attempt to fetter the Free Enterprise System, which is at the heart of our great democracy. It was also outside the scope of your work. It will be destroyed and all of you are forbidden to discuss or disclose to anyone or have in your possession any information about either of the projects. Any attempt to do so will be viewed a violation of the Official Secrets Act and treason against our country. You are all to return to your previous assignments." Looking straight at Teddy, she continued, "You got that, Teddy?"

Teddy, reacting coolly and calmly, said, "Yes." Noticing that Marguerite wasn't there, he asked her, "Where is Marguerite?"

The Bitch glared at him and said, "She had an opportunity to return early this morning to New York and took it. Sorry, but you won't get a chance to say goodbye to her. You all have thirty minutes to clear your stuff out. Report to work tomorrow at your regular time. Everyone has the rest of the day off." She turned and left.

Teddy was glad to see the end of her and wanted to look at her only one more time, to see the shock and surprise in her eyes when she died by his hand. That day would happen sometime in the future; for now it was all about making sure Rosie was safe. Teddy would have liked a copy of their work. Maybe Uncle Billy would be interested in it. Marguerite might have a copy but how could he get it? Teddy still wasn't sure whether Marguerite might be working with The Bitch. He thought not, given the way she felt about her Economic Renewal Plan. It had really been Marguerite's baby. The rest of them had only been helping her in a support role.

CHAPTER 25

Almost Nothing but Clear Skies

Simon banked on his confession, and the aid he had given Dakar so far, swaying Dakar. Simon returned all the money he took from Dakar in commissions and handed him an additional eighteen one-ounce silver pieces to cover his expenses and trouble. Simon told Dakar, "The letters in Hebrew are numbers and number eighteen means life. To wish you a safe trip."

Dakar spent a wonderful evening at one of the many hotels that lined the Tel Aviv shore. He and the crew sailed from Tel Aviv the next day headed for America. It would be hard enough sailing across the ocean. The threat of a pirate attack seemed bizarre in the 21st century and this was not the coast of Somalia, but the civilized Mediterranean. They rotated shifts with at least one person on deck at all times. The winds shifted and were now from the northwest. The auto pilot worked well and a comfortable operating routine evolved. George suggested they use a couple of bungee cords on the helm instead of the autopilot to save battery power and it worked! They sailed well and would have been faster with a following wind, but they made good progress.

Dakar insisted they drill every day in the procedures they would use if attacked at sea. In addition to more firing of the rifles, he assigned everyone a job. Sheryl steadfastly refused to use a gun and her assignment was the helm. He instructed her to stay low behind the protection of the hull. Jennet's task was to lug a box of 50 cal. ammunition up to the deck mounting point and hand Dakar the end of the ammunition belt. Dakar was to get the 50 cal. out, mount the big gun and use it. The big advantage of that gun was its range; the shells would carry a great distance with accuracy, tremendous velocity and energy. George would retrieve both the rifles. The sniper rifle was his to use, Jennet the other. Both were instructed to use the ammunition sparingly, George to shoot only when he had a good shot and Jennet in short bursts.

The first few days they practiced the drill three or four times a day until Dakar was sure they knew instinctively what to do. Dakar also discussed the strategy they would use in battle; the closest boat would be engaged first, then the next and so on. The 50 would do almost all the work. There was a good chance the pirates would break off the attack when they heard and felt the 50 tearing into their craft. Dakar knew he would. George and Jennet were to stay low behind the protection of the hull, firing only when ordered to do so.

They had little choice of route. They could not skirt the area where the pirates were operating, by going north around the island of Sicily. To do so would mean traversing Italian waters and an inevitable search by the Italian authorities. Their best hope lay in staying north of the Tunisian coast closer to the Sicilian coast, and to keep up the pace. Once they got a few hundred miles west of Tunisia the boat would be out of danger. There were many miles to travel to Tunisia and days before they got there.

Every day they drilled with the weapons until Dakar was confident in their abilities. There was a greater chance they would be able to perform correctly if they acted in a rote manner. Combat and coming under fire did strange things to people. Some froze, others ran away and still others acted erratically. It was impossible to tell how a particular individual would react. Jennet had already faced a gun and would probably be fine. Both George and Sheryl admitted they were apprehensive about the whole idea, but both acted proficiently during the drills.

The days and nights Jennet and he spent together were heavenly. She was strikingly beautiful; her long black hair, smooth facial features and olive complexion were bewitching. He could not get enough of her or she of him. The sex was fantastic, and bliss was when she lay curled up in his arms, her head on his chest sleeping. He often made her giggle when he kissed every square inch of her face, and then worked his way down her body to her breasts and beyond, at which point the giggles turned to sighs and moans of delight.

Jennet was also amazingly intelligent and kept abreast of world news and events. She and Dakar shared similar opinions on the US invasion of Iraq, and her insights into the benefits of membership in the EU for Turkey were insightful. She felt the move helped Turkey develop its industrial potential, but hurt its agricultural sector. She loved playing cards and they would sit for hours playing a card game her father had taught her. She was tough to beat.

An uneventful week of clear skies and clear sailing passed. They passed the time in conversation or playing card games for money. Dakar owed Jennet almost one million dollars as they neared the danger zone. Dakar instituted a rotating watch on the radar set, although small craft might not show up clearly if the seas were rough. It was worth having some sort of warning. An attack would probably come in the daytime, but not necessarily so. They passed a few ships within sight on their trip, mostly freighters or the occasional tanker bound for some European destination. A few ships appeared on the radar, too big and too far off to be a threat to them. One medium sized vessel showed itself. It was probably a large, motorized yacht. It moved very quickly on a course parallel and a bit south of their own.

On the morning of the ninth day, George came on deck gesturing for Dakar to come below with him. As Dakar descended the stairs, George said, "I have three small craft heading rapidly in our direction coming from the southwest."

Looking at the track of the boats on the screen, Dakar agreed. "This doesn't look good, George. Too fast and they are headed right for us. Let's get our little surprise party ready." George went up the stairs to tell Sheryl, who was already at the helm. Dakar went to wake the napping Jennet and fetch the 50 cal. from the forward storage compartment. All the sails were furled and they traveled under power now. The three boats were still a few miles away and everything was ready. George continued looking at the radar and yelled up from below. "Two have slowed greatly and are moving apart. The other is running parallel to us."

Dakar knew this was it—one coming at them from the starboard, the other the port and the third guy their vulnerable stern area. They would start their attack when the boat speeding south made its turn to attack from the stern.

"Come on up, George, or you'll miss the show!' Dakar ordered. When George came on deck, he continued, "Yo, ho, ho. Prepare to repel boarders, ye scurvy rats!" He looked towards Sheryl who was obviously nervous but stoic at the helm. George was also apprehensive, but took up his firing position alongside Jennet. Jennet was peering over the edge at the approaching boat on the starboard side. Dakar yelled at her. "Get your fucking head down!" Dakar would engage whichever boat was closest and start firing first. Their attackers were obviously good at their job. It was going to be a coordinated attack. In all probability they would face ten or twelve weapons, for sure.

The boat speeding along parallel to them had just passed their stern and would soon be turning to attack. They would be abreast of the other two boats in a few minutes. Dakar ordered Sheryl to bring her about. It would change the attack angle the pirates had planned, leaving one boat attacking from off the bow, the other two at an angle from the stern and port side. It should enable him to engage both of them without having to change course, and by changing the angle the boat was to the waves he would have a more stable platform to fire from.

The change in direction precipitated a change of tactics from the three boats. The third boat that planned on a stern attack was now parallel with them on the port side. It turned for a direct attack coming at them from slightly off the bow. It would be the first to close the gap, at eight hundred yards. The first boat turned slightly, to allow the four men on board to start firing. It was obvious they had a light machine gun as he saw the tracers spurt out of the muzzle and fall very short of their target. The muzzle flashes from the other weapons showed all were now firing. He again ordered Jennet and George to stay down. Sheryl was already crouched low in the stern. She was very vulnerable in the stern, but there was nothing that could be done about that at the moment. Some bullets began whistling harmlessly overhead, and a couple struck the hull. At this range there would be little energy left in them.

Using his best Scarface impression, Dakar said out loud, "Come an' say hello to my littl' frien'." He cocked the big gun, and sent a burst of five or six shells in their direction to gauge the range. The noise was deafening and frightened Sheryl more than the incoming. His next burst of ten or twelve rounds tore into the hull of the small craft. He could see where it was penetrating the hull. Two seconds later he fired three long sustained bursts of ten rounds each. The machine gunner was hit and out of action. Another man was missing his arm and shoulder. The M2HB was a devastating weapon when used on humans. It had an impact force five times greater than an ordinary shell, and an effective range of one and a half miles. Many men receiving even simple wounds died from shock because the force of the impact was so great. At eight hundred yards even from the rolling deck of the sailboat he was able to make short work of the first boat which was now stopped in the water. The two other riflemen were still firing, and he fired another burst in their direction and then the firing ceased.

"Yeehaaa! Next!" Dakar yelled.

Sheryl looked at him as if he were insane. He swung the big gun over sixty degrees to meet the second boat. The deck was littered with hot shell casings and it was about to get messier. The second boat was coming in mostly bow first, but at enough of an angle that the four men could start firing at them. The range to this target was six hundred yards, and with no further fanfare he opened up on the gunmen. He took the head clean off one man and he swore another single round took two of them out. He never stopped firing, pouring forty rounds or more into the boat and started a fire in the process before it too was dead in the water.

The third boat was dead astern and within three hundred yards when it turned slightly to let the men fire into the vulnerable stern on the sailboat. Everyone in the sailboat was exposed to fire from the third craft. His ammo was getting low and he yelled to Jennet, "More ammo, Jennet." She bent over the next box of ammo opening the cover and stood with the belt when Dakar was ready for it.

He ordered the boat brought about twenty degrees to the port side to offer more protection for them by using the broadside of the hull as a shield. As Sheryl swung the boat, he could see the telltale bursts from another light machine gun on the third boat. He picked it as his first target shooting a long burst in its direction, but failing to silence the withering fire as the pitching sea made his firing platform less stable. He could see where his shells were hitting the hull. The direct fire from the third boat was becoming more accurate as the distance decreased between them. He fired the last of his rounds in their direction before pausing to put the next belt into the gun. Before he did, he ordered George and Jennet to open fire. Perhaps they would keep their heads down a bit while he reloaded. He could hear the two of them firing, George with one shot and Jennet with short bursts.

George's second shot elicited a, "Yeah, got one." from him.

Dakar yelled back an, "Atta boy."

He pulled the bolt back on the gun and swung the muzzle over to start firing again. The 50 barked long and hard. He could plainly see his shells tearing into the hull, but again failed to silence the machine gun. Its shells were hitting their boat frequently. Sheryl cried out and crumpled to deck. Dakar yelled, "George, help Sheryl. Jennet, take the helm." He kept up the bursts and another gunman was blown apart by a round. George had dragged Sheryl in behind the shelter of the hull and Jennet was at the helm, but standing up instead of crouching to lessen her profile. Dakar yelled at her again, "Get down." His last burst tore the machine gun on the speed boat from its mount and there was no more incoming direct fire coming from any of the boats.

A man stood up in the boat and he killed him, and continued firing into the boat until it was torn to pieces and sinking, he hoped. As he swung the 50 to finish off the other two, Sheryl yelled, "That's enough, Dakar!!" He stopped firing.

Sheryl held a bandage to the wound she received in her thigh. The bullet had passed through, but her face reflected the pain she was feeling. Jennet turned on the autopilot and went to help George take care of Sheryl. The boats were no longer a threat and rapidly receding in their wake.

CHAPTER 26

The Plot Thickens

Teddy left for the comfort of his home and to await the return of his beautiful fiancée. He often looked at the engagement ring Rosie wore as a symbol of how much she loved him. She wore it with pride and on more than one occasion, he caught her looking at it and smiling, which made his heart soar.

Teddy returned to work the next day, feeling like a fish out of water and unsure of what he should be doing. He opted to look busy and attempt to use his old formulas to produce some meaningless reports. How could he predict anything using as a basis an economy that wasn't functioning? At lunchtime he decided to retreat to the indoor fountain, in the lobby of the building, to eat his bagged lunch. The sound of running water always soothed him. He drifted downstairs, sat on one of the benches near the fountain and opened his lunch bag to see what surprise he had packed today. *Oh goody,* he thought, *tuna sandwiches and an apple.* He thought of Rosie seated at the nursing station digging into the lunch he had packed for her.

A woman with closely cropped hair, and a lot of hardware decorating her face and ears, including a very stylish nose ring sat beside him. Smiling at him she said, "Teddy, my name is Sigrid. Marguerite sends her greetings. She wishes she had a chance to say goodbye to you and asked me to give you this little gift." She palmed a small thumb drive and dropped it into his lunch bag when she reached inside and took out one of his sandwiches and started to eat it.

"Thanks, I hope she's all right. I was worried about her," Teddy said. He talked with her in such a manner that it appeared they were old friends or a couple meeting for lunch.

"Marguerite is OK and back in New York. She was unsure of what to do with the information she had and left it with me, with instructions to get it to you where you worked. I hoped you would come out at noon for lunch today. She called me later to say it was a good thing she did. They searched her and all her stuff before she left for New York and threatened her," Sigrid said.

They spent a pleasant fifteen minutes talking. Then Sigrid got up, hugged him, kissed him on the cheek and said, "Stay safe and good luck, Teddy." She left as quickly as she had appeared. Teddy closed his bag up a few minutes later and went upstairs. He could not keep the thumb drive at work or at home. He would get it to Uncle Billy and, for the time being, it would be stored with the cell phone. A fast check upstairs on his computer confirmed it was the Economic Renewal Plan and the Economic Predictive Formula.

Teddy and Rosie went for their walk after supper, and Teddy told her about the thumb drive and his plan to give it to Uncle Billy. Rosie thought an invitation to dinner tomorrow night might be a good way to get him the thumb drive and they settled on that idea. Rosie called Uncle Billy later telling him they had managed to score some meat at the supermarket and asked if he would be interested in a roast beef dinner tomorrow night.

Uncle Billy laughed. "Would I? Of course I would, my dear girl. What time do you want me there?"

President Haines was starting to get a lot of pressure from prominent members of his own party and there was talk of impeachment, if marital law wasn't lifted soon. Haines had a problem, though. The lifting of martial law would mean exposure of the atrocities and summary executions by the media on a nationwide basis, and he was unaware of the magnitude of the abuses. Most of the deaths had been explained as rioters or looters killed in the process, some as suicides by the thousands of people detained under the mental health laws as a danger to themselves or others. For some there were no records they had ever been detained and they were listed as missing. Still some hundreds of deaths appeared very suspicious. Cracks had also appeared in his support; some members of the Christian Right did not share the same views as their brethren who had so willingly joined the Presidential Patriotic Force. They thought Christ's message was not about killing their fellow Americans, and that the Constitution was to protect the rights and lives of its citizens, not to imprison and murder them. A few had gone so far as to stand up in church, and criticize the words and behavior of their pastors and fellow parishioners. Still others had left their congregations to join ones that stood against the totalitarian regime that had developed in the name of law and order.

The real threat, however, came from the traditional sources of opposition to tyranny; trade unionists began to demonstrate and picket federal government offices and suffered dearly for their defiance. The police brutally broke up the picket lines. Unfortunately for the police, these were not students they were dealing with and often they paid a dear price for their violence. Union members were not willingly beaten. Work stoppages and strikes were still dealt with using the military and mass arrests.

Uncle Billy showed up at 6:30 for his roast beef dinner, kissed Rosie on the cheek and said, "Teddy, you don't deserve such a beauty. She needs an older, wiser man."

Teddy said, "She's taken, you old goat" and shook his hand heartily. Dinner was filled with laughter, stories of home, Uncle Billy's bullshit and, for Uncle Billy, a second helping of the roast beef.

"Damn, Teddy, I surely do appreciate this dinner. That filly of yours can sure cook!" Billy chirped.

"Hey, I cooked supper tonight, Uncle Billy. Give credit where credit is due!" Teddy answered.

"Point taken. Thanks for the great feed. How about joining me for a smoke outside?" Uncle Billy asked, as Rosie was busy clearing the dishes from the table. Teddy noticed Uncle Billy wasn't all that old, after he caught him stealing a look at Rosie's ass when she took a load of dishes to the kitchen.

"Come on, let's go. You'll just get into trouble if you stay here," Teddy said. They bundled up against the cold temperature and headed for the front of the building.

Billy rolled a cigarette the way he always did, with one hand expertly folding the papers back into the pouch of tobacco and slipping the pouch into the inside pocket of his jacket.

"What the fuck is going on, Teddy?" Billy asked.

Teddy explained the projects he had been working on with Marguerite and the results. He also related the restrictions that had been placed on discussing or disseminating the Economic Plan and Predictive Formula.

"I have a copy for you." And he palmed the thumb drive, slipping it to Uncle Billy when he shook his hand. "If this is made public or you're caught with it, I could be in a world of trouble. The Bitch suspects me already and I believe I will be executed if caught."

Uncle Billy warned him, "Teddy, don't take any more chances. I will make sure that if I do distribute it, it will appear as if someone else was responsible. Just so you know, we are getting closer to having the numbers necessary to impeach the president in the Congress and Senate. We really don't know what to charge him with. The powers of executive privilege are so great, he can argue he had the authority and duty to commit these crimes. Our hope is he will resign if faced with impeachment. We know Vice President Emily Johnson is a good woman. I will meet with her to gauge her reaction to possible impeachment. So much rests with the support of the American people for our actions."

Billy continued, "Thanks again for supper. Say goodbye to that lovely girl of yours. I'm headed home for some light reading. Take care of Rosie and yourself, and be safe, Teddy. We will put the run on the bastard in the end. I am confident of that."

Uncle Billy was an intelligent man, but the technical parts of The Plan and Predictor were beyond him. The overviews were brilliantly written and they made sense. It might be a powerful tool if used correctly, creating hope for the country and adding momentum and support for their cause. Widespread distribution would require planning to keep suspicion away from Teddy. Billy knew an aide in the White House and he would use his contact to send four copies to certain senators and congressmen on memory sticks from the White House. Those select four could then make multiple copies and distribute it widely on the Internet. The documents would have to be digitally washed and changed slightly from what Teddy had given him. It should be enough to protect Teddy from reprisals. A day or two at most would see it done. Tomorrow he would meet with Vice President Johnson. Billy had no fear of Homeland Security or the disappearance of some of his colleagues.

The extreme right still dominated the television and news reports, spewing shrill reactionary rhetoric advocating more violence against the enemies of America and greater restrictions to freedoms to keep the country safe. Right-wing radio talk show hosts reveled in what they saw as a cleansing of undesirables from the America mosaic, a start in the cathartic process ending in a return to American core values. They railed against the false accusations being made against President Haines. Military units returning from Iraq and Afghanistan began arriving in the United States, but many did not go back to their home bases and were reassigned to sensitive areas.

Captain Michael Murphy, Murph, and his company were assigned along with the rest of the 25th Infantry Division, 3rd Brigade, 2nd Battalion 35th Infantry Reg. to Malmstrom Air Force base near Great Falls, Montana. When they arrived a tent city had been established near the closed runway to house them, along with portable generators and a temporary dining facility. Malmstrom was home to forty-two hundred people and the 341st Missile Wing and 819th RED HORSE Squadron responsible for part of America's Minuteman nuclear deterrent. Murph was told their mission was to safeguard the nukes from all enemies, foreign and domestic.

The locals filled Murph in on the tension that had developed between President Haines and the people of Montana, including the shootout at the state capitol in Helena. The Montana State militia now stood at eighty thousand volunteers and it was doubtful the National Guard would obey any orders from Washington that involved suppression or violence against its citizens. The Western

Coalition had gone from four states to eight with at least six other states leaning that way. Arizona had joined the Coalition, in spite of some rioting in Phoenix. Murph was shocked at how far things had deteriorated in the country. He doubted his company was being used for protection of the nukes. Ample security measures were already in place and being supplied by forces on the base already. Murph was genuinely afraid he would be ordered to fire upon his own countrymen. Helena, the state capital, was less than two hours away.

CHAPTER 27

A Change of Circumstance

J ennet took over the job of bandaging Sheryl's wound. It wasn't
serious and the bleeding stopped. Because of Sheryl's slight build
and weight, however, her overall physical condition was poor.
The shock of the wound affected her badly. George picked her up
and carried her below to their berth. He came back on deck and
looked very serious and worried.

"Dakar, we have to get Sheryl to the hospital," he said.

"I know, George, we are sailing northwest to Sicily to Marzara del
Vallo. They should have a hospital or she can be taken to Salerno.
Let me call Simon and ask if he can help us," Dakar replied. He went
below to get the sat phone. The disabled, sinking or burning pirate
boats were now far behind them.

Dakar had Simon on the line in a few minutes. "Simon, we had
our visit from the pirates and Sheryl was injured in the attack. Her
wound is not life threatening. She needs to get to the hospital. We are
headed to Marzara del Vallo. Our position is about fifty miles off the

coast." Dakar went on to describe the attack by the three boats and the outcome.

"This is not good. Sheryl needs a doctor. Let me make some calls. Keep out of the Italy waters and I will send a boat for her. It will be faster if we take her to Marzara and then to hospital. I will call back in less than one hour," Simon said.

"George is going with Sheryl. I am willing to carry on with Jennet if you wish. What do you want to do? Let me know when you call back," Dakar replied.

"OK, thank you, Dakar. Soon I will call you," Simon said, as he hung up.

Dakar went over to check on Jennet and gave her a hug and a kiss, telling her "You did great, baby!!" She looked back at him with love in her eyes, grateful they were all alive. Dakar and George went below to check on Sheryl. Sheryl looked a little better, not so pale and weak looking. Dakar let them both know that Simon was to call back shortly. Dakar went back up to clean the 50 and the other weapons and stow them below.

He had just finished cleaning the weapons when George called up from below, "Dakar, the radar. There is a ship coming our way very fast." Dakar raced below to check out the contact. There was indeed a vessel headed their way from the Sicilian coast and very rapidly, eight miles away, and closing fast: almost twice the size of the speed boats and coming from the wrong direction to be a pirate ship. If it were an Italian patrol boat, he was breaking no law and outside their territorial waters. The Jenn was flying an American flag. The Italians had no jurisdiction over the weapons they carried on board, but an armed pleasure boat in waters with known pirate activity might not bode well for them with the Italian Navy. Many small patrol vessels were armed with a small cannon and he wanted no conflict with the authorities. Dakar's options were to stow the weapons below and take his chances with them understanding, or to chuck them overboard. He had to make the decision quickly. Maybe it was the boat that Simon had said he would send, he mused. They would know in short order. In less than half an hour the ship would be alongside.

The sat phone rang and Dakar answered without giving Simon a chance to speak. Dakar asked him, "Have you sent a boat for us? We have a boat approaching fast from the Sicilian coast."

Simon was brief. "It cannot be the boat I sent. I just finished talking to the captain, of a small boat, who will meet you."

"Ok, thanks, Simon. I have to deal with this approaching boat. It is probably an Italian Patrol boat. I'll call you back when I am finished with them." Dakar terminated the call chuckling to himself. Knowing Simon, he would be shitting bricks worrying about a situation he had absolutely no control over.

Dakar could not bear to part with his weapons. For the past eight years he had never been without a weapon close at hand in a tight situation. He risked everything if they decided to take him into port. At the very least they would be detained for days, maybe weeks, or even charged with some sort of crime. They should not need the weapons for any other part of their voyage; the rest of the crossing would be as safe as could be reasonably expected.

Dakar decided to keep all the weapons on deck and on the starboard side of the boat, away from the approaching vessel, and deep six the lot if it was a patrol boat. The task at hand was to get all the weapons and ammunition on deck, and loosely tie them to the rails with some cord and then release them to a watery grave if it was a patrol boat. He had to keep his 45 for his own sanity. It was safely concealed behind some paneling below. The stanchion that served as a mount for the 50 cal. was solidly anchored to the deck and the gold it contained was inside the steel pipe, safe from prying eyes. The 45 and gold were calculated risks he was willing to take.

Jennet helped him get rid of the shell casings overboard and clean up Sheryl's blood. George finished tying the last of three slip knots securing the weapons and ammunition to the railing on the starboard side. The vessel appeared vaguely on the horizon, headed straight for them off their port side. Using his high-powered binoculars he could not make out what kind of ship it was. They were as ready as they could be, even with a story about Sheryl's wound should they be boarded. In the event it wasn't a patrol boat, they could prepare for another potential encounter with bad guys. The guns were close at hand.

Three minutes passed and the view he got through the binoculars could not clearly distinguish what type of vessel it was. Dakar thought it might be a warship. Another minute confirmed it was a patrol boat. That along with the horn that was blaring was all the proof he needed as it bore down upon them. He could see two men looking at them with binoculars from the deck of the patrol boat, watching them intently and what they were doing. He ordered George to back up to the railing and discretely release the weapons and ammo. Jennet cut off the engine. Being compliant would help them, although the obvious damage from the bullets to the hull would be hard to explain away.

Within minutes the patrol boat was alongside with a sailor manning a 50 cal. aimed at them and a half dozen sailors on deck with automatic weapons pointed in their direction. They were hailed in English, and ordered to halt and prepare to be boarded. Dakar had the three of them stand facing the boat with their hands on their heads. The men with guns never wavered in their aim or attention to their every move. Within a few minutes, an inflatable with four men on board sped to the Jenn, which lay motionless in the water. They came on board off the stern and the officer in charge introduced himself as Lieutenant Armando Fellini, had them lower their hands and stand in the stern of the boat. His eyes relayed a friendly air and an underlying intelligence. His actions spoke volumes to his competence. The patrol boat had approached, ready for any eventuality. Dakar would have done exactly the same thing. Two men went below and discovered Sheryl in bed, her leg covered under the blanket. They conducted a brief and thorough search below deck, and one emerged with an all clear report for the officer. The other remained below to watch Sheryl.

The officer politely asked in excellent English, "Signore, we have come to investigate reports that three boats have trouble ten miles to the southeast of here. There have been many problems from pirates in the last few weeks and we offer help to small vessels and to search for weapons on pirate boats. You are not pirates. We know this much. Where do you go, Signore?"

"I am sailing to America on my new sailboat that I bought in Tel Aviv, with my friends from Canada and my girlfriend," Dakar answered. Telling the truth in all things, except the basic lie was important. It was too easy to get tripped up if you manufactured too many lies. He also kept the information he gave to a minimum, stated verifiable facts where possible, and never offered opinions or comments if he could help it.

"I see, Signore. You have your passports?" he asked.

"Yes, they are below in the cabin. George will get them," Dakar said. George went below to fetch the passports with a sailor following.

"You have damage to your boat from guns, Signore?" the officer stated in the form of a question.

"Yes, we had some men fire at us from their boats, but we managed to get away," Dakar said.

George returned with the passports and the officer examined them, checking the exit stamps. He spent some time on Dakar's, taking interest in the many entrance and exit stamps to Iraq. Glancing to the stern, he said, "Ah, what is this, Signore—blood?", as he spotted a smear of red on the wheel of the helm that they had missed in the cleanup. "And this," he said, as he stooped to pick up an empty 50 cal. shell casing that was semi-obscured in a coil of rope lying on the deck, a casualty of the hasty cleanup.

Dakar knew the man had pieced together the story or at least had a good theory as to what happened. He decided to throw caution to the wind and give the officer a basic truthful overview of what transpired.

"We had a brief encounter with some armed men who did not get what they wanted before we escaped, and Sheryl has been injured. We are going to Sicily to get some help for her. She needs a doctor," Dakar said.

"Ahh, I see and the shell casing is a trophy from Iraq perhaps," he said and then stopped for a moment to think, as he stared at Dakar. For almost a minute he said nothing. Then he said, "You have no guns on board or drugs, and I have no authority or reason to hold you, but I can offer to take the injured woman and her husband on board and to port immediately. We have an excellent medic and the woman's wound must take priority over the disabled boats. Perhaps we investigate them tomorrow."

"George, what do you think?" Dakar asked.

"I'll get Sheryl and our stuff. Thank you, sir, for your kind offer. I am worried about her," George answered and went below to gather their belonging and bring Sheryl upstairs. The officer ordered the sailors to stand down, and help George with Sheryl and their bags. The four had brief goodbyes and in a few minutes George and Sheryl were on board the small boat ready to leave.

As the officer turned to leave, he looked at Dakar and said, "I'm amazed, Signore. The men in those boats were very dangerous. They have chosen the wrong boat and man to attack, and now maybe we have fewer problems with pirates. Good luck in your trip." They were gone. George and Sheryl waved as they headed to the patrol boat, and Dakar hoped some prompt medical attention for Sheryl and a safe journey home.

Dakar called Simon to let him know Sheryl and George had gone with the patrol boat, and were headed to port and a hospital. The gold was safe. He also let him know they were defenseless now, having ditched the weapons.

Simon was thankful that Sheryl and George were safe, and the gold not found. He went on: "If you take the gold to America, I thank you. I will give you delivery instructions when you get to America. It is best you know little. Please call me often." Simon hung up thinking, *What a man. We should have so many soldiers like Dakar. He must have some Jewish blood in him.*

Dakar and Jennet raised the sail, and they snapped taut with the following wind and set course for the gates of Gibraltar and the Atlantic.

CHAPTER 28

Secrets Exposed

T eddy spent the next week doing next to nothing at work and keeping abreast of the news as best he could on the Internet, which was now severely restricted in content. Few anti-government sites could be accessed and the only way people were getting information was through personal e-mails. Stories of disappearances were rampant and almost everyone knew someone who had disappeared or had friends that knew of someone. The atmosphere of distrust and paranoia made many people afraid to be specific in e-mails or negative in any way about the government's behavior.

President Haines spent a lot of time praising the sacrifices Americans were making and the great job its security forces were doing keeping Americans safe from terrorism. One story caught his attention on the regular TV news. It was the discovery, in the upper peninsula of Wisconsin, of four bodies believed to be the three men and one woman suspected of exploding the container bombs that triggered the global meltdown. Phillip, Diane, David and Wayne Scranton were three brothers and a sister well known for their anti-government sentiments and a long history of criminal activity. The FBI was investigating the circumstances, the story said.

President Haines's political problems with the Congress and Senate presented bigger difficulties for him. His attempt to stonewall the lifting of martial law by appointing a committee to recommend when that should happen was being fought at every turn by all the Democrats in the House and Senate. In addition a portion of his Republican compatriots, especially those from the Western Coalition States and some northeastern states, were joining the Democrats. Thirty-three states had experienced little if any problems with riots, looting or violence and were demanding marital law be lifted in their states. The house had formed its own committee to recommend when to lift marital law and how it was to be done. The findings of the committee were to be presented to Congress in two days.

The Patriotic Community and other sundry paramilitary groups that had not been decimated were between a rock and a hard place, hunted and reviled by most Americans. The perpetrators of the bombings had all been members of the Patriotic Community. Much to their chagrin, the Patriotic Community had been betrayed by those who they thought were their traditional allies: the Christian Right and right-wing Republicans, who they imagined would rise up against the hated government. The only ones who appeared to be standing up for freedom and the Constitution were those damn socialist-commie-liberals, union members, academics, misguided college students and a smattering of old-fashioned Republicans.

Some of the paramilitary groups had managed to orchestrate a series of what they called counter-attacks on federal government buildings in the last few days, in retaliation for the destruction of their armed enclaves around the country. Three small groups of armed men and women burst into federal buildings killing everyone they could, armed or not. Federal buildings were now well guarded and the firefights that occurred were bloody messes. Teddy noted, as was usually the case, the Patriotic Community did exactly the wrong thing at the right time, violence being their only response to the present injustices. President Haines was now able to say that the threat from terrorists was not over and martial law was needed, in the short term, to keep Americans safe.

Uncle Billy thought the Economic Renewal Plan might be the answer or a good start on the road to recovery. The Economic Predictive Formula could be an important tool in monitoring the progress they were making and to adjust, where necessary, the dramatic action the government would need to implement to revive a devastated US economy. First Billy would get the information to greater minds than his for their evaluation.

Billy's meeting with Vice President Johnson was bizarre; she was not very forthcoming, answering vaguely. He asked her directly, "If the president steps down or is removed from office through impeachment, will you lift martial law?"

Johnson answered, "I see no signs that the president will step down or be impeached, and there are no impeachment resolutions in either the Senate or House."

Billy pressed her for a more definite answer, "Emily, I am going to ask you again: If the president steps down or is removed from office through impeachment, will you lift martial law?"

"I will perform my duties according to the Constitution, if that should happen." Johnson said, "I know the nation and world face grave problems, and martial law has caused serious rifts in the country."

Billy left the meeting wondering if she had the strength and character to be president. The coming months and years would require a leader of vision, courage, honor and integrity.

Teddy had made one call to Simon in the past two weeks. Simon told him Dakar was well on his way, was making great time through the Mediterranean and was headed towards Gibraltar and the Canary Islands. Simon also said that Dakar and his new girlfriend were alone now. George and Sheryl had been taken off the sailboat near Sicily.

Teddy and Rosie were enjoying the almost stress-free time, cuddled up on the couch watching movies, the diminutive Rosie lost in the great arms of Teddy. In the recently cold, clear days, walking was still an enjoyable part of their routine. The restrictions on travel and tightness of money had brought about an unexpected benefit — more people on the streets, doing exactly what Teddy and Rosie were doing: walking. They made friends with several young couples and sometimes went to the local Starbucks for a latte together. An older couple in their building had befriended them and they got together several evenings a week for cards.

Teddy continued to send and receive e-mails from Jenn. She had been divorced for some years, and laid off from her job as an alcohol and drug counselor in Spokane. Financial pressures had forced Jenn and her son to move into her parent's home in Coeur d'Alene. She now worked part-time as a receptionist in a doctor's office. In one e-mail she wrote; "Dakar changed so much after the death of his father. He was irritable, withdrawn and sullen at times and not the man I had fallen in love with. I had other pressures and the stress became unbearable. I became very unhappy living with him. I had to leave even though I knew he still loved me."

Teddy did not tell Jenn about the depression Dakar was suffering as a result of the death of his father or how much worse it had become after she left. He would never betray his friend's confidence and it would have been unfair to Jenn to burden her with the thought that she may have been responsible for Dakar's depression. Dakar was responsible for himself. Instead he wrote, "I understand, Jenn. The death of his father was a big blow to him. He is a much different man now and still my best friend, but radically different in his outlook on life." That was as far as he was willing to go in discussing his friend. Jenn would have to contact Dakar if she wanted more information. He did say that Dakar was incommunicado because he was sailing across the Atlantic.

Jenn e-mailed back, "Well, some things haven't changed about him. Sailing across the Atlantic is something the old Dakar would do."

Billy began to get feedback from the Senators and members of Congress he sent the Plan and Formula to. Several had been in contact with noted economists for their opinion on the legitimacy and likelihood of success the Plan offered. Marguerite had been summoned by a certain senator from New York and asked for her opinion on her own Plan. Rather than give away the fact that she had authored the Plan, she gave a glowing review on how great it was. A Nobel Prize winner in economics also gave a thumbs-up to the idea. He recognized right away that it was probably Marguerite's work, but said nothing to the congresswoman who asked his opinion.

Billy presented the Plan and Formula to all the committee members the next week for their consideration. His group already had the support of forty percent of the members of Congress including most of the influential ones. The Republican allies he knew were also brought on board and the word was out that the Plan was workable.

The administration was not happy about the leak of the Economic Renewal Plan and behind the scenes had launched an investigation into where the information had come from. The president was said to be furious that the leak had apparently come from inside the White House.

The president no longer trusted the FBI and Homeland Security had been given the job of finding out where the leak was. Colonel Bernice Guay had her own idea about where the information might have come from. She started her investigation by having Marguerite Coutts pulled in for questioning. The men that came for her late that night knocked on her door and identified themselves as being from Homeland Security. They handcuffed and arrested her in front of her partner, Gwen, and dragged her into a waiting SUV. Gwen was aware of the whole story and without a moment of hesitation picked up the phone and called Teddy at his apartment in Washington the minute they left.

Rosie answered the phone, in a sleepy daze. It was midnight, and both she and Teddy had been sound asleep. "Hello?" she asked.

"Hi Rosie, I am a friend of Teddy's. Can you put him on the phone, please? It's urgent," Gwen said.

Teddy took the phone from Rosie, thinking to himself, *Who the hell is calling me at midnight?* He was wide awake in a few seconds and answered, "Yeah."

"Teddy, this is Gwen, Marguerite's partner. They just came and took her, Teddy!! Homeland Security took her, Teddy!!" she said sobbing into the phone. "You have to go, Teddy. Leave. They will come for you next!"

"Took Marguerite! Did they say anything, Gwen? Do you know anything else?" Teddy asked.

Gwen had stopped sobbing, but was obviously upset. "They didn't say anything, Teddy. They handcuffed her and told her she was under arrest and left. I don't know where they were taking her. They left a few minutes ago. Leave, Teddy. Go now before they come for you. Please, go! Marguerite really liked you, Teddy. Get out now, please. Don't let them take you!" she pleaded again.

"Thank you for the warning, Gwen," Teddy said as he hung up the phone.

Teddy turned to Rosie, who had heard Gwen's words and said, "Get dressed. We're leaving now. Take one small bag. We have to be out of here in five minutes."

He was dressed in twenty seconds, grabbed two bags and then screamed at Rosie, "Get fucking going!!!" This was nothing like Rosie's Teddy. Rosie did exactly as she was told, dressing and having her stuff together a full ten seconds before Teddy was ready to go. They were down in the garage in five minutes, retrieving the cell phone and charger before driving out onto the street with nowhere to go. Teddy turned right and headed for parts unknown. It was impossible for them to take to the highways. Travel was restricted and the police had roadblocks on the main highways stopping all small private vehicles to check for travel authorizations. As he drove down the street he turned to Rosie and said, "I'm sorry I screamed at you, sweetheart, but our lives are in a lot of danger." Tears were in his eyes for having spoken so harshly to her.

Rosie answered, "It's okay, Teddy. It's okay!" She caressed his neck and head as he drove.

"I hope Uncle Billy has some suggestions for us about what to do. We're on the run now," Teddy commented. He turned on the cell phone to call Uncle Billy at home. There was no answer and Teddy panicked for a moment before deciding they would find a place to park the CRV and wait till morning to call Uncle Billy at the office. Teddy picked a parking garage at a shopping center to spend the night. They spent a fretful but quiet night in the parking garage, and got a coffee and breakfast at a small restaurant that was open early the next morning. Teddy tried Uncle Billy's home number and there was still no answer. They would have to wait till 9 or 10 o'clock when he should be in his office.

CHAPTER 29

We Sail the Ocean Blue

Dakar and Jennet had nothing but blue skies and a following wind that propelled them to Gibraltar in less than a week. At Gibraltar, they needed to make their turn south towards the Canary Islands to catch the easterly trade winds. Life on board was idyllic and they often used the autopilot at night to sail, making sure their course was well away from land. There was still little in the way of shipping. Every few days they would take in the sail and swim off the stern of the boat, and Dakar would use the barbecue to make steak or chicken for them. More often than not they had simple basic meals of oatmeal or pancakes in the morning, and a larger meal later in the day. Lunch was often nonexistent, or snacks of peanut butter and crackers, or a can of sardines. The lovers had nothing to do but enjoy each other and talk.

The test of a relationship can often be by enforced times together and if the past week was any indication they would do just fine. Jennet's English was improving as the days passed, and the sex was getting better and better for Dakar. He guessed it was because he loved Jennet so much and it was plain to see she loved him, too. He loved the smell of her on his body and would often not wash after their lovemaking, so that he could enjoy the smell of her vaginal juices on his hands or face.

Dakar told her he wanted to return to the mountains of Idaho near Coeur d'Alene someday and live a simple life with her. Jennet was excited about the prospect of living in America and ecstatic she had found Dakar. Mostly, she was grateful he could love her: a whore who had sold her body to men for money. He did things to her sexually that gave her so much pleasure she thought she would pass out from the orgasms and imagined it would be a lovely way to die.

When they sailed through the Alboran Sea to the Strait of Gibraltar, the water color began to change, becoming a mix containing the deep blue of the Mediterranean and the darker blue-black of the Atlantic. Surface currents in the Alboran Sea flowed eastward, bringing water from the Atlantic into the Mediterranean. Deeper subsurface currents flowed westward, carrying the saltier Mediterranean water into the Atlantic. Bottlenose dolphins started to follow the boat or, more correctly, lead as they criss-crossed in front of the boat playing chicken with the bow as it cut through the water. One leapt out of the water to a height of fifteen feet and could tail walk, the majority of its body above the water. They were thrilled to see the dolphin play; sensing it had an audience and hung around for most of the afternoon. The Rock of Gibraltar loomed into view, as the setting sun reflected off its side, giving it a reddish orange tint and great contrast between light and shadow.

Eight miles later they passed Tarifa, Spain, and made their turn south for the Canary Islands. Dakar had decided they would stop in Santa Cruz de Tenerife, to top up their food, fresh fruit and vegetables and fuel. The guns were no longer a problem and the gold would not be found where it was. They had used little fuel, but Dakar liked to keep the tanks full and would store some portable containers of diesel in the aft quarters now that George and Sheryl had gone. He hated being becalmed from no wind, stuck going nowhere fast and would use the engine if need be. Being becalmed was bound to happen on their journey across the Atlantic.

The wind had shifted the previous day to the north and they once again had a following wind. The wind brought with it a small storm, and they spent an uncomfortable day and night riding out the huge waves it produced. The wind was so strong they took in some sail. The gale went as quickly as it had come and they covered the six hundred sea miles to Tenerife in four days with ease. Dakar was a mere thousand miles or so due north of the place he was named after—Dakar, Senegal. It would have been nice to see the place that bore his name. Perhaps they would come back this way someday.

The desalinator was working fine and producing ample fresh water for them. It used power, and the length of their voyage dictated its use. He didn't like to turn it off once it was operating. The membrane tended to clog up and didn't function as well. It was expensive to replace and he left it on. This meant the generator had to run every day to recharge the batteries. The wind generator and solar panels were often not enough to make up for the power they were consuming on board. He called Simon a few times to let him know their position and his planned stop in Tenerife.

Although he used sunscreen frequently and wore his hat, Dakar's face and neck had become red and weather-beaten from the weeks at sea. He took off his shirt for an hour each day, and his chest began to take on the same rosy hue and texture as his face. They sailed into the harbor in Tenerife and through customs on a beautiful sunny day.

Refueling took only a few minutes. The waterfront was deserted from the lack of tourists and they had their pick of seaside restaurants to eat in. Dakar and Jennet were besieged by vendors of all types eager to make a sale. Tourism was dead and would be until some sort of sanity and stability returned to the world. The desperation he saw in the eyes of the merchants and people of Tenerife was frightening, and he began to doubt the wisdom of their layover. It didn't matter all that much. He planned to set sail before nightfall.

For now, there was time for lunch, a visit to the botanical gardens, and then shopping for fresh fruit and vegetables, more meat for the freezer and some assorted snacks and canned goods. There were a few impulse buys that seemed impossible for him to resist: stuffed green olives and taco chips with salsa, to name a few. He regretted taking Jennet into a women's clothing store, but not the few items she bought, including a little black dress that was stunning on her and some very sexy lingerie.

The afternoon wore on and they drifted back to the boat with their small mountain of supplies. After stowing the food in the galley, he took the roll of duct tape he had bought to repair the few small holes he hadn't been able to fix since the pirates had attacked. There was no real damage to the hull other than cosmetics. It was obvious they had been shot at, and the customs and immigration officer had noted the damage, but she said nothing. Jennet and he had patched the main sail so it would hold for the rest of their trip.

There was not much to do, for an hour or so before the customs officer returned, so they had sex, with Jennet lying on her side and him spooning her from behind. He teased her by slowly entering and removing himself from her. Jennet let him know that the pace was unacceptable by pushing back against him and wiggling her ass to take him inside more deeply. She complained loudly, "Dakar, do not tease me. Fuck me, please." He got the message and furiously finished with a loud groan and a large serving of his sperm inside her. Jennet loved the sensation of him coming, and the thought and feel of his cum dripping from her.

By 17:00 they were motoring out of the harbor, sailing north around the top of the island and setting the sails for America. The weather was wonderful and the wind steady at twelve knots from the north, not the expected trade winds they hoped to catch to push them hastily westward.

They sailed day and night, setting the autopilot and sleeping soundly; occasionally Jennet would wake in the night to use the head and wander topside to look at the moon and stars, or check the sails and helm. For four days they sailed with a north wind until the wind changed direction coming from the east north east. They made better progress and more sea miles. Jennet prepared a great fruit salad which they picked at for two days, and they ate the mountain of fresh vegetables and the fruit that wouldn't last. Other fruits and vegetables would keep for a week or more in the refrigerator. They barbecued every manner of meat and enjoyed each other's company. At the start of every day he told her he loved her. One evening she came on deck in the little black dress looking stunning and they danced a slow waltz to the music coming from his iPod in his shirt pocket. Her arms draped around his neck drew him in close, so she could rest her head on his chest as they swayed to and fro across the deck.

On the fifth night, Dakar was rudely awakened when he was thrown violently from the bed to the floor. For a second, through the fog of half sleep, he thought the boat might turn over entirely. It righted itself rocking crazily back and forth until settling down. He picked himself up and called for Jennet who wasn't in bed with him. First loudly and then screaming, he raced from the forward cabin through the living area and onto the deck, where one of Jennet's deck shoes lay up against the hull. Jennet was nowhere to be seen and he bellowed her name hoping she was in the head or the forward cabin, thinking to himself that she must have been on deck when the wave hit.

Dakar ran to the helm and stopped the boat noting the position on the GPS. She must have gone overboard when the wave almost toppled them. He screamed and screamed her name, listening in between for some sort of reply above the noise of the ocean. They could not have traveled far since the wave hit three or four hundred yards at most, he guessed. Dakar took in the sail and started the engine. Running the boat on engine power alone made it easier to conduct his search for Jennet. He returned to the GPS coordinates he noted and started backtracking on a easterly course, all the time calling her name and listening intently for some sort of reply. After five hundred yards he turned west and one hundred yards south and started back towards the GPS coordinates again. For an hour he concentrated on a quarter mile grid size and found no trace of Jennet. He then expanded the grid to a half mile criss-crossing the area, hoping she had a life jacket on, and was unconscious but alive out there somewhere waiting for him to save her. He thought, *She probably hit her head. I have to find her soon. She is hurt. I know it.*

After four hours the grid was two miles square and he was sure he would find her soon. He became frantic in his calls, his voice wavering from the constant effort to make himself heard above the crashing of the waves. After eight hours, he wept for an hour, inconsolably sobbing and calling her name between the sobs. Still he pressed on. For two days, he went back and forth on the grid which had expanded to four miles. He took no breaks, eating whatever he found lying about in the galley and drinking water. After forty-eight hours his mind, body and spirit broke and he collapsed on the deck, exhausted.

He woke four hours later, the boat plowing through the water to God knows where. He turned off the engine, went below and collapsed onto the bed for another two hours before waking up to the realization that she was gone. Jennet had been taken from him, swept overboard by a freakish rogue wave and drowned. He cried for her until he could cry no more. Then he went topside to set the sail and autopilot for home. He felt the familiar stirring of the sadness again, the darkness which would be followed, he knew, by thoughts of dying and the release death offered him. He doubted he could survive another bout of depression.

CHAPTER 30

On the Run

T eddy and Rosie were lucky to be free. The parking garage might have had a security patrol, which would have brought the police. They left the restaurant where they had breakfast, and parked the CRV at a Park and Ride next to a train station and decided to walk around the platform area for an hour until Uncle Billy arrived at his office. Rosie would keep an eye on the Honda that contained their bags with clothes and personal effects, making sure it wasn't spotted by the police.

Marguerite's nightmare began the moment she was hustled into the SUV and a bag placed over her head. She was taken to a federal detention center somewhere in Jersey. She bypassed the normal registration process and went straight to a special area marked Anti-terrorist Unit. The area was not guarded by the military like the rest of the facility and was run by Homeland Security. The two men who interrogated her were blunt in their language. She would tell them whom she had given classified information to, or they would hurt her until she did.

The bound and brave Marguerite was determined not to say a word. Her explanation that she didn't know what they were talking about, and that the work she did was not classified, fell on deaf ears. They did not care, and in the end, did things to her that no woman should have to endure. Both men raped her. What followed was hours of horrific pain and screaming—she was always screaming. The more she screamed and pleaded, the more the men hurt her and enjoyed doing it. For six hours Marguerite hung on; in the end she betrayed everyone and told the men everything. Marguerite told them she had passed a copy of the Plan and Formula to Teddy. Gwen knew and her friend Sigrid had delivered the information to Teddy.

There was no physical record she was ever there, and no military tribunal or trial for Marguerite. She sat moaning and weeping softly in the chair she was bound to, bleeding from every orifice in her broken and twisted body. Her reward was a single bullet to the back of the head. Her body was taken from the room, destroyed in a nearby crematorium and her ashes flushed down a toilet.

By 9:00 AM, Homeland Security had issued a nationwide arrest warrant for Teddy and Rosie. Colonel Bernice Guay was able to report to her boss, Lincoln Lancaster, the head of Homeland Security, that she had found the leak and stopped it and was in the process of rounding up all the conspirators. Lancaster called the president.

President Haines was pleased, very pleased, that once again Lancaster had come through. Lancaster was a key man in the Tea Party, an intellectual lightweight who had kept his nose clean so far. His appointment had helped him gain support from the growing Tea

Party movement. He was a "get'er done" sort of guy. Lincoln Lancaster's appointment as head of Homeland Security had not come without some criticism from his political opponents, who said he was a radical, rough and a political neophyte. President Haines trusted Lancaster; he had been a key player in his election victory. He was rough, but he had delivered the vote and Haines owed him.

Teddy and Rosie called Uncle Billy's office a little after 9:00 AM. He had not arrived yet. His assistant, Linda, knew Teddy and told him he might have spent the night at his girlfriend's apartment. Linda promised to call her and ask if Billy was there. Uncle Billy never carried a cell phone or pager, or any of those other stupid little gadgets. He was computer literate to a point, but only because he had to be to do his job. Linda called Teddy back, and said he had just left his girlfriend's apartment and she expected him at work within the hour. Teddy wondered how many girlfriends the old goat had.

Loitering around the parking lot had become a risky proposition. It was past nine and most of the commuters had already caught the train into the city. There were only a handful of people waiting when the last train arrived at the station. Rosie noticed a police car stopped behind their CRV and they decided to leave. Teddy bought them tickets for the train and they boarded a minute before it pulled out of the station. Now they had lost their transportation and clothes. Both had taken cash out of their accounts and between the two of them they had a little more than six hundred dollars. It was not much, but there was little they could spend it on. On the train they talked about their strategy, and decided before the train reached downtown to get off at some stop and walk a distance away to make the next call to Uncle Billy.

Three stops later, they got off and walked ten blocks to a little diner in an older row of commercial buildings. Seated in a booth

Teddy made another call to Uncle Billy's office. It was past eleven. Linda still had no idea where Billy was. Rosie and he could not risk staying out in the open much longer. Sooner or later they would be caught; perhaps their pictures would be on TV, as wanted terrorists. He was out of options, when he called Simon.

"Simon, Rosie and I are in trouble. Homeland Security and all the police in Washington are looking for us. Can you help?" Teddy pleaded into the phone. Fear was starting to cloud their judgment, and they needed to get somewhere safe quickly.

"Yes, I will help you, Teddy!! Where are you? The older man who gave you phone will come for you within one hour," Simon replied and added, "Stay inside. Less chance the police will see." Simon thought it could spell big trouble if US authorities found out Mossad operatives were harboring known fugitives. He had no choice. He owed Dakar. He marveled at how single-handed he had crossed the Atlantic. Perhaps helping Teddy would be useful in the future.

Mossad would have to let someone in the US administration know the name of the person who had probably masterminded the bombings. The question was, who could be trusted? His superiors would have to make this decision. The person who instigated the bombings was surely in the innermost circle that surrounded the president. Simon wanted the information he was buying, before exposing the traitor. Shame it had to happen that way. Such an information source would have been useful to Israel. How could the informant have been so stupid and not reason out that such acts might cause the problems that beset the world? Yes, better to be rid of such an idiot.

Rosie and Teddy had been sitting in the diner for too long and decided to wander into some of the stores that occupied the row of older buildings on the street. In the second-hand store, Rosie saw some things she thought would be great in their apartment while Teddy imagined the apartment would be torn apart by now. The mobile phone rang and Martin asked where they were. Within half an hour they were safe in Martin's small one bedroom apartment near the river. Martin took their phone from them and destroyed it along with his own phone. A trace of the location, however remote, remained a probability. Bad enough the phone records would show calls to Israel. When they called Uncle Billy, it was out of desperation and they had not thought of the consequences; they should have used Rosie's or Teddy's phone. Martin had gone out to get them something to eat for supper. Teddy and Rosie sat entrenched on the couch wiling away most of the afternoon, watching TV, upset and apprehensive. Teddy had to talk with Uncle Billy.

Martin returned a little after 5:00 PM and made them supper. Teddy told him he wanted to call his Uncle Billy. Martin agreed to take him to a pay phone a few miles away to call after supper. The risk they would be spotted was small. Rosie was to wait in the apartment.

"Billy, it's Teddy!" He stammered into the phone in his desperation.

Uncle Billy answered the phone with the gruff, "Linda told me you called. How are you?"

Teddy described the fix they were in and that they were at a friend's place for the night.

Uncle Billy said, "Tomorrow at 10:00 AM, I want you and Rosie to go to the same place we met for lunch some weeks ago. Friends of mine will find you there and get you to a safe place. You can't call me anymore. The assholes will have taps in place within a few hours, if they haven't already. Take care and stay low, Teddy."

The next morning Martin drove them to the Lincoln Memorial. An elderly couple approached Teddy and Rosie as they sat on a stone bench on the cold winter day. Their breath and words seemed frozen in the vapor they exhaled. Annie and Matt looked like a pleasant couple; they shepherded them to a large commercial van, emblazoned with the name "Fox's Fine Handmade Virginian Pine Furniture, Purkins Corner, Virginia." They told them to hide behind some furniture in the back of the van.

The van started and stopped frequently as it made its way to I-95 and then south for a few hours. Rosie and Teddy had taken a few furniture blankets to wrap themselves up in for the journey. When Teddy suggested it would be a good time for sex, Rosie glared at him and told him, "Now is not the time." Teddy saw nothing wrong with a little tension-reliever on their journey. The speed of the van reduced and there were a lot more turns and finally a short bumpy ride before the van halted.

The back door of the van rolled up and Annie called out to them, "Come on out, folks. You're safe here." Rosie and Teddy scrambled out, shivering, into an overcast midday beset by a heavy snowfall. Matt told them, "We have some hot soup on the stove and Annie made some fresh homemade bread this morning, if you are interested."

A quick glance around showed an old stone farm house, the sides of which were covered in vines. The barn had been converted to a workshop from the look of it, with a sign above the door that echoed the markings on the van. Matt had the hands of a carpenter or furniture maker, rough with the odd healing cut here and there. His missing finger showed he was a careless carpenter. Annie's graying hair was tied back in a bun and she looked every inch a matronly farmer's wife. The whole setting was very private, in a grove of trees that obscured the view of any other dwelling or the main road. Teddy thought to himself, *Now this is more like the type of place I'm comfortable in.* He slipped his arm around Rosie's waist when they ambled into Annie and Matt's home.

A little after 10:00 the next morning Linda got a call from Vice President Johnson's office asking to meet with Billy within the hour. Billy was in the office and promptly agreed, wondering to himself what this was all about. Emily Johnson was in his office by 11:00, beckoning from the doorway to walk with her and talk a bit outside. It was a hell of a day for walking. Wet snow was falling heavily. She motioned for the Secret Service agents to stay back, when she started to speak.

Vice President Johnson was brief. "I am through living in fear, Billy. The president chose me because of my age, gender and lack of presidential aspirations. A safe choice, a woman in the twilight of her political career. I am expected to remain in the background, supportive, yet mute in my criticism of all things. Over the past week, I have received veiled threats from the president and Homeland Security regarding the safety of myself and my family. I will not stand for it; I should have come forward sooner. Fear made me a coward. Not any longer. I will do whatever it takes to stop this madness."

Billy paused for a moment and said, "Fear robs us of courage. My fear is that the future is not clear. My sources in the Pentagon tell me the president has moved large numbers of troops into the Western Coalition States or close to their borders. I think the fool means to use them and that cannot be allowed to happen. Many of the Joint Chiefs are very concerned about what will happen next. In two days, our congressional committee will recommend the immediate lifting of martial law in forty-five states and the other five within the week. It will preempt the committee the president appointed. I expect after we do, all hell will break loose. Be ready, Emily. We may have to move quickly and decisively," Billy answered.

"I am ready, Billy. I'll keep in touch. They have already cut me out of the loop, so I have no real idea of what is going on. There are at least two other members of the cabinet who are leaning our way. Let me feel them out. The head of Homeland Security and the secretary of state are not. Sometimes I wonder if the secretary of state isn't advocating nuking half of the Western States to the president and the Joint Chiefs," Emily said, as she rolled her eyes back in her head and laughed.

The truth was that the president had become isolated from the American people and relied too heavily on his inner circle of friends and advisors. A group that could best be described as reactionary: people who frequently turned to violence as an option to solve problems. Corporate America was afraid and they pushed for a rapid return to the status quo or business as usual. It was the business leaders who were unable to see that America had long since passed the point of a quick fix. Marguerite's Plan would never be accepted by Corporate America and President Haines had assured them it would not see the light of day.

CHAPTER 31

Home

D akar called Simon a few days after Jennet had been lost and related dispassionately the details of her freakish death. There was work to be done on the sailboat, work cleaning and getting rid of Jennet's passport, clothes and personal items. He kept nothing of Jennet's, in a futile attempt to cut himself off emotionally from her memory and the pain of losing her. His goal now was to get to America, help Teddy and Rosie and to fulfill his promise to Simon, to deliver the gold.

At times in Dakar's journey, the sadness seemed to seize him by the throat, choking the breath from him. He had not yet experienced the same sort of constant wish for death he experienced years ago: the thought he wished he could have given into, but lacked the courage to now. Up until he met Jennet, at times he had a slight feeling of loss, for being cheated out of death, that it had been stolen from him. Living in the moment meant living with the emotional pain he was now suffering, not reveling in it, but recognizing it was there. Rationalizing and denial had not helped before. His only relief had come from giving up, literally turning his life over to God. He had no religious beliefs or faith per se: just an abiding knowledge of God's love. Letting God make the decision, he would carry out the death sentence, when he felt it was right in his heart. Up to this point Dakar had lived his life as well as could be expected and he was ready for that moment.

Physical exercise helped keep him focused during the time it took of sailing day and night to cross the Atlantic. Dakar exercised four or five hours a day. He could not watch movies. He had no interest. His days and nights were confused, and his sleep pattern fitful at best. He had to post and keep a schedule to make sure he ate at least one proper meal a day.

The lack of light pollution, the absence of the frequent dust storms that blanketed the upper atmosphere and no moon, had rewarded Dakar with a few amazing nights on the deck of the Jenn, when the skies were crystal clear, and broad swathes of stars and galaxies covered the sky from horizon to horizon. Small storms beset the craft on two occasions; he had ridden them out, in relative comfort below deck.

Dakar toyed with the idea of stopping in the Dominican Republic to see Mick and to take on supplies for the short hop to the US mainland. Feelings of duty and responsibility to Teddy banished the thought and in any event he would have to clear the layover with Simon.

Simon was mulling over his chances of getting Dakar to deliver the money to the informant. The operatives Mossad had in America were not soldiers. They were businessmen and shopkeepers whose training in the espionage trade centered on managing their network of informants or running errands. All of them had little training in the use of firearms and no experience in combat. None had the skills of Dakar and anytime millions of dollars in gold was being exchanged, there was a danger of violence. Simon needed Dakar.

Mossad maintained a modest arsenal of weapons in the US including the ubiquitous UZI. The two goals Mossad had were finding out the identity of the traitor and to get their hands on the information that person was supposed to bring to the exchange. The taste the informant had given them was outstandingly useful intelligence and Israel wanted it badly. It was a simple money for information deal; Israel had to know the identity of the informant to verify the validity of the intelligence given to them. Otherwise it could be false: an elaborate hoax perpetrated by one of their not-so-friendly Arab neighbors.

Theoretically, if the informant was genuine, there should be no reason for the informant to want anything other than the gold. Simon knew violence was messy, uncertain in outcome, invited retaliation and usually never achieved the goals he wanted when dealing with informants. From time to time informants were stupid, watching too many movies and talking themselves into doing irrational things. There was a good chance this person was in that category, if he or she had orchestrated the bombings, solely to manipulate the price of gold. Simon would wait before asking Dakar to help him. The loss of Jennet would be hurting him badly right now.

Dakar called Simon ten days later, laying out his position as two hundred and fifty nautical miles east northeast of the Dominican Republic. He needed instructions on when and where Simon wanted his gold delivered and to get word to Teddy he was almost home. Since talking with Dakar last, Simon had helped Teddy and Rosie escape the clutches of Homeland Security and into the care of Uncle Billy. Simon knew Dakar would be appreciative of his help.

Intimidation or bribery would not work with Dakar. The other thing he counted on was Dakar's wish to expose the traitor. He would use one of Mossad's operatives to handle the physical exchange of the information for the gold. Mossad would keep possession of the information. Dakar would be out of sight and provide security.

Simon picked up his mobile phone with a cheery, "Dakar, my friend, how do you feel now? I have some good news for you." Simon went on to describe Teddy's situation, how he had helped and to pass on to Dakar Teddy's new mobile phone number. Then he popped the million dollar question, "Dakar, can you help expose the traitor, the one who started all the problems? I cannot trust such a person and I cannot go to your government without the name. We need security for the exchange and the agent I send to meet the informant."

Dakar thought, *That fucking Simon knows exactly what buttons to push when it comes to me!* Simon had not lied to him, and had refunded all the money he had charged in commissions for the gold and services he had supplied. Dakar knew Simon was right when it came to the informant; he paused for a moment and said, "OK, asshole, but I can't do that by myself. I need a three man team, minimum, and you will pay extra for this work—fifty thousand per man. My friends Mick and Teddy will be the team. Yes or no, the terms are not negotiable."

"Yes, I agree and from now on, you call me Mr. Asshole. I have weapons, some automatic weapons, few UZIs, grenades if you want, when you get to America." Simon replied, laughing at his humorous Mr. Asshole remark. Whoever the informant was, he was now at a disadvantage. Dakar was playing for his team.

"I am going to Sosua in the Dominican to pick up Mick, if he accepts, and then on to the States. Where do you want me to go?" Dakar asked.

"You clear customs in Florida and then go north to Teddy, and I will arrange the exchange. Dakar, where do you think is the best place?" Simon said.

"I will let you know after I talk to Mick and we get a chance to scout out the area—certainly somewhere that lets me see people coming and gives us a tactical advantage," Dakar said as he ended the conversation. He was already going over in his mind possible scenarios to do with the gold for info exchange. Somehow he didn't think it was going to be easy. The great part of the operation was he had the two men he trusted the most helping him. Mick was solid and fearless. When Teddy and he hunted big game they were like one. Teddy had served in the National Guard for a while also. For a big man, Teddy moved through the bush like a ghost. He always intuitively knew where Teddy was. As a team, the two were unbeatable. His first call was to Teddy. Dakar had not talked to his friend directly for some weeks.

Teddy answered cautiously, "Hello."

Dakar said, "Teddy, did you miss me?"

"Yes, matter of fact, I did and I almost wasn't around to hear your voice again." Teddy told him Rosie and he were living the good life, at their new digs, safe and sound, waiting for Dakar to come and get them, and whisk them away to Idaho. The only glitch he could foresee was being a hunted traitor. He continued, "Dakar, where are you? Come and get us. Rosie and I want to go home," knowing full well he and Rosie couldn't do that while they were being hunted.

"It's good to hear your voice again, Teddy. I'm coming to get you. I will be there in a few weeks at most. Simon told me what happened, but we have some work to do before we can go anywhere, Teddy. After we finish, pack your bathing suit and we'll hang out in the Dominican with Mick until this blows over."

Dakar went on to talk about the pain he was suffering over the loss of Jennet, the woman he loved. He described the fifty thousand they would each receive for a single day's work. "I can't tell you what we will be doing or the reason until I see you in person. Can't say this will be easy either, Teddy. This time the game we hunt will be shooting back if things go sour. Are you in?"

Are you in? What a dumb question to ask him, Teddy thought. Of course he was in. He was always in for one of Dakar's adventures. He would not knowingly have his friend at risk without having his back.

"OK, Dakar, and when does the action start?" agreed Teddy.

Dakar knew he would agree and knew he was putting Teddy's life in danger by asking. Teddy would always protect Dakar if he could, just as he had in high school from the bullies, even sacrificing his life if need be. Dakar felt exactly the same way.

"Gotta see if Mick wants to join us first and there is still a bit of sailing time left, Teddy… couple of weeks, as I said, before I arrive. Don't be a stranger for so long this time," Dakar said, thinking of the time he could see his friend again and get a Teddy hug. Teddy was the only person left in his life that he loved and who loved him.

Dakar's next call to his Scottish buddy was predictable. Mick asked him why he should leave his beautiful, twenty-two year old girlfriend in Sosua, to possibly get his ass shot off in the States. Things were rough in the Dominican with the collapse of the tourist trade, but nowhere near as dangerous as the States right now.

Dakar responded, "How about fifty thousand for a few hours work at most?"

Mick had heard that story before from Dakar. "It will be easy" and "it" never was. On the other hand, Dakar was as lucky as a shit house rat. Mick was coming also. He just had to moan and bitch a bit before accepting.

"I'll be in Puerto Plata in two days. Come meet me, one night in the Dominican Republic and then we're leaving," said Dakar. The one night layover would allow him to get some more fuel, fresh fruit and vegetables, and supplies on board for the next leg of his journey.

Sosua was interesting: a stunning beach, lively night life, hundreds of beautiful women and Mick smack dab in the middle of the lot. Mick had decided not to buy a bar; instead he rented a small home in the El Batey section of Sosua and had moved Mirabela in. Mick had offered to have one of Mirabela's friends come over for company for him. Dakar had turned the offer down.

Mick hadn't stayed long in Scotland when he returned. Somehow Cynthia had gotten wind of his arrival and had taken all of his antique furniture with her when she left. There was nothing for Mick to do, except hire a solicitor and file a complaint with the police. The lawyer would file a civil action against her for the cost of the antiques and the police would file criminal charges for theft. *Stupid bitch*, he thought to himself, *you steal from an ex-SAS*. Maybe she wasn't so stupid. She knew he was not a violent man in his personal life.

Mick and Dakar were on the water the next day, the boat loaded with fresh bananas, pineapples, oranges, melons and whatever else was ripe that they could get their hands on. The hurricane season was over and there was a moderate easterly breeze. It was a short hop to the Florida Keys, and the voyage offered fair winds and good weather. Dakar and Mick had used Google Earth to decide on a few options for the exchange. All were located south of Washington in

Virginia close to where Teddy was. They would investigate the three possibilities when they arrived in the Washington area.

They cleared customs easily in South Florida. Customs had brought the drug dog on board and found nothing. Not many people were smuggling drugs these days. There was little if any market for the stuff. Disposal income was at an all time low.

After clearing customs, Dakar called Simon, telling him they were in the States and making their way up the Florida coast. Dakar told Simon, "I'll need a few days after I arrive to scout out potential exchange locations and decide on one. After I do, you can schedule the exchange."

CHAPTER 32

The Heat Gets Turned Up

Teddy and Rosie were very comfortable in the home of Matt and Annie. They had an airy, bright, east-facing upstairs bedroom, furnished with antiques including a graciously crafted pine chest of drawers. A down duvet and heavy handmade comforter covered the antique bed adorned with a plain wooden head board. It was cool in their room in the morning, and the warmth of the bed kept Teddy and Rosie ensconced under the covers. The stone walls of the farm house held the heat well, and early every morning Matt got up to refuel the wood stove and open the damper to get the fire burning well.

The meals Annie prepared were as delicious as they were amazing in their simplicity. Rosie helped Annie in the kitchen. In addition to the gas stove they had in the kitchen, there was also a wood-fired, cook stove that Annie was showing Rosie how to stoke and cook on. Rosie found it was almost an art form. Rosie dreamed of the day she could cook on the wood stove in the cabin, high in the mountains of Idaho.

Teddy hung out in the workshop trying to ensure Matt didn't lose any more fingers and learning about building Fine Handcrafted Virginian Pine Furniture. Annie and Matt were Quakers who deplored violence and were very politically active in days gone by, in the peace movement. They still dabbled in causes they were passionate about. Rosie and Teddy were safe for the time being.

Uncle Billy was safe also, even though Homeland Security was aware he had been in contact with Teddy and Rosie. The president was not aware of the role Homeland Security had in the disappearance of several members of Congress and a sitting senator, although secretly Haines was pleased several of his most virulent critics were silenced. Officially, they were missing, and presumed kidnapped or murdered by terrorist elements. The president was so engrossed in the domestic situation he failed to see the incongruity of the explanation. President Haines always had a strong sense of right and wrong and loyalty to his friends. Above all, in the current malaise, he imagined he had a manifest destiny, to save the nation.

The Secretary of Homeland Security, Lincoln Lancaster, noted the domestic situation was calming down and further disappearances of any federal politicians would spur that pesky Jew Boy at the FBI to step up his campaign against him. Right now he had the ear of the president and had been able to argue successfully that desperate times required strong action. The head of the FBI was no longer welcome in the White House. The FBI director, Allan Hoffman, had spoken out against the imposition of martial law on a nationwide basis, and was now aghast at the mounting evidence of extra-judicial executions and incarcerations. He had reluctantly handed over the FBI's domestic watch list to Homeland Security, after a verbal clash with the president had resulted in him being ordered to surrender the list or be removed. Thousands of those on the list were now missing. Some were dead and others incarcerated in the camps.

The attempt to arrest Governor Maier had not been the director's idea either. The president had ordered him to do it. Lancaster had argued Hoffman did not "execute the warrant properly, unnecessarily exposed his agents to harm and failed because Hoffman had not wanted to succeed."

Lancaster was right about Hoffman not wanting to succeed. Arresting the Governor of Montana was a stupid idea that could have plunged the country into a civil war. Sending FBI agents to the State Capitol building in Helena had been his plan. He suspected they would fail. Hoffman was genuinely sorry about the unforeseen death of the state trooper killed in the resulting brouhaha, but it was a small price to pay for avoiding a civil war.

The threat of dismissal had not mattered much to him either; he had been appointed to the job by the previous administration. Allan expected he would be turfed well before the troubles started in favor of someone "more in tune with the ideas of the present administration." For the time being he could do more good from within than outside the Bureau, so he stayed.

Of interest to him were the deaths of the four home-grown terrorist suspects found murdered in the Upper Peninsula of Michigan that the Bureau was investigating. The area their bodies had been discovered in was remote and there was little physical evidence. The locals reported four strangers in town driving a black SUV, a week after the bombings, and none of them was female. It was hard for him to imagine that anyone other than crazies would do anything as stupid as setting off those bombs. Now, it was beginning to look as if someone else had orchestrated the whole thing. The suspects didn't have the money or wherewithal to have designed and constructed the large container bombs. He wanted to get to the bottom of that mystery. Perhaps solving the crime would increase his influence at the White House. Hoffman desperately needed allies and there were none to be found in the White House.

The House committee that Billy Braxton chaired came out with its report to Congress and the recommendation that martial law be lifted immediately in forty-five states, and in all states in two weeks. The timing could not have been worse. The attacks on the federal government buildings by the Patriotic Community had just taken place, and the proposal was lost in a storm of criticism from the right wing and the office of the president. The mainstream media carried all proceeding of the House of Representatives and the Senate. Censorship was loosened slightly to allow an illusion of free speech. The right-wing talk show hosts had a field day with the report, branding it an example of how out of touch liberal Democrats had become with the actual situation in the country.

Peaceful demonstrations and protest marches were now allowed. The presence of the police and members of the Presidential Patriot Force was a constant reminder to those involved of the willingness of the government to use force at the slightest provocation. Colleges across the nation had become hotbeds of unrest and President Haines ordered them all closed for two months "to allow the country to stabilize."

One protest in Chicago turned into a national fiasco when a contingent of the Patriotic Force opened fire on union members peacefully protesting martial law, who were taunting them with cries of, "Go home, Nazis" and "Freedom Now." Twenty-two protesters were killed and two members of the Patriotic Force were found beaten to death later by vengeful union members who took exception to their brothers and sisters being killed. The major TV networks carried the story and footage of the incident. The statement from Homeland Security was that the police and Patriotic Force had only returned fire when they were fired upon.

The news footage of the incident clearly showed otherwise and the Chicago Police quickly issued a news release saying they had nothing to do with the killings. Privately the Chicago cops were angry at their new allies in the fight on terror. During the melee, several cops had to be restrained from attacking members of the Presidential Patriotic Force. Some cops went so far as to tell their superior officers they felt like firing on the Patriotic Force during the slaughter and would not work with them again.

At least one person wanted to meet the authors of the Renewal Plan and Predictive Formula. With Marguerite missing, Teddy was the only one left to meet Vice President Emily Johnson. Teddy was transported to Washington in the back of the furniture van again and deposited in a small office building somewhere in Washington he did not recognize. As instructed, the vice president ordered the Secret Service agents assigned to her to wait outside the door. Then she entered to question the man responsible for such a masterful piece of work.

"Teddy, it is a pleasure to meet the man responsible, or at least partly so, for this Plan to put our country back to work," she began.

Teddy answered, "The Renewal Plan is solely the work of Marguerite Coutts. At best I made some not so great coffee for her. My contribution had mostly to do with the Predictive Formula."

"I have two questions for you, Teddy. First, do you believe the Plan will work and secondly, why?" Emily asked.

"My answer is fairly short, Madame Vice President. I think it will work because it is brilliant in its scope and audacity. Yet it does not alter the fundamental nature of the free enterprise system, but rather changes it to make it fair for everyone including the American people. No longer will corporate power be able to dictate to Americans how they live their lives. Corporations and their officers will be legally limited and responsible for their actions including the suppression of and withholding innovations or discoveries deemed in the national interest . The slow return Marguerite envisioned to normalcy and the changes we will have to make will generate the numbers we need to reestablish confidence in the economy. My area of expertise is the process, and according to my Predictive Formula it should and will be successful. Not perfectly perhaps, but well enough to get us going again. Sorry, that was not short at all. I'm starting to sound like my Uncle Billy!" Teddy answered jokingly.

The interview ended with the vice president thanking him for risking his safety and leaving out the front door. Teddy was hustled out the back door to the waiting van for another couple of cold hours in the back. Rosie ran to him when he stumbled out of the van cold and stiff, wrapping her arms around his waist and hugging him desperately. Her clothes were covered in flour from the baking she and Annie were doing, and Teddy now showed a trace of white up and down his body where Rosie enveloped him. The sweet smell of burning pine permeated the clear, still, winter sky as they walked arms around each other's waist back to the house, chattering to each other like a couple of Virginian squirrels.

The number of congressman and senators who stood in opposition to the president had grown substantially and more had joined on the rumor the vice president was with them. Someone had suggested a name for their movement and Freedom America was born. Fully half of the Congress were members and another thirty reluctant Republicans were solidly leaning their way or committed, but unwilling to say publicly. The Senate was more evenly divided. Billy suspected up to an additional ten senators would support their cause when the time came. Freedom America had the numbers; they only needed the right time and circumstances to act.

CHAPTER 33

Reunion

Dakar and Mick sailed steadily northward up the intracostal waterway towards Virginia. Dakar used the engine frequently when there was little or no wind. There was lots of fuel on board and he was anxious to see Teddy. Because they had cleared customs and the Jenn flew a US flag, they sailed without being stopped again by the coast guard. Travel restrictions had never been applied to marine traffic. Restrictions had been limited to vehicles on the highways and had been lifted in many states several days before because of complaints from people unable to visit family or conduct personal business. That did it, along with the mountain of complaints the president was receiving from Corporate America including the airlines, bus companies and vertically integrated companies invested in the travel industry.

The lifting of travel restrictions had given President Haines some badly needed good PR and he was able to say that the country was moving towards the complete restoration of normal life in America.

Polls the government commissioned indicated the number one issue people were concerned about was "a return to normal life." All his media releases now used the phrase as often as possible.

Moving north meant cooler weather. *To hell with the word cooler*, thought Dakar. It was cold, especially after his time in Iraq. He'd purchased a cheap, light jacket in the Dominican and layered up, but the wind cut through the thin material and chilled his slight frame to the bone, if he was outside for more than a few minutes.

Mick was not much of a sailor; he did what he was asked to do, but had no interest in sailing. Dakar had to be on deck often, even when the auto-pilot was engaged. The Jenn held up well to the voyage and he was happy with his new purchase. The attack by the pirates had damaged the hull, but he thought it added some character to the boat. The cabin was toasty warm with the heat cranked way up and Dakar retreated to below deck whenever he got the chance. Mick made a large pot of soup and one day a beef stew, and they sopped the gravy up with their last loaf of bread. Dakar loved stew when the weather turned nippy.

Dakar was becoming more subdued throughout the trip. Mick understood the loss of Jennet was still hurting Dakar, and was there to listen and support his friend. Dakar wore his quietness as a veil, masking the pain that burrowed its way deeper and deeper into his soul, as the days passed. His thoughts turned to the future and where he might go and what he might do after this fiasco was over. Sailing would be good for his spirit, he thought, and perhaps dampen the physical pain his heart carried. The solitude and new adventures: another crossing to explore Africa, Central and South America? It really didn't matter where. He would be alone again, as he had been for so many years.

In Tel Aviv, Simon met with his superiors in Mossad to discuss what to do when Dakar arrived in Washington. There were more

271

than a few issues to address. Some required input from the highest levels. The most delicate issue was how to reveal to the US government that Israel was trying to discover the name of the person responsible for the bombings on the East and West coasts. His superiors also wondered about the wisdom of entrusting such a large amount of their gold to a goy.

To date, Simon had been handling the affair solely and his superiors were pleased with the admirable job he was doing under difficult circumstances. Dakar had proven absolutely capable and trustworthy. In the end, they decided to send Simon to Washington to oversee the whole operation. When Simon arrived they would tell him whom to contact with the informant's name and how. Israel was petrified that the US might think Israel had orchestrated the bombings, and wanted to keep as much distance as possible between themselves and that scenario. Talking to the wrong person at the wrong time could do that.

Simon arrived in Washington a week before Dakar and Mick were due to arrive and set about selecting whom to use as Mossad's operative for the physical exchange of money for information. Martin was already involved in the operation and was steady as a rock, but Simon worried he might be under surveillance because of potential traces of the cell phone Teddy had used when he escaped. Besides, Martin was in his seventies and had done his duty; it was time he took it easy.

The informant had become impatient with the length of time it was taking to get the gold and Simon had assured the woman who called that the exchange would take place within ten days. He told her the approval for the expenditure of such a large sum of money took time, and it had taken some days to assemble and weeks to ship the gold to the US. Before leaving Israel he reviewed the personal dossiers of Mossad operatives in the US and using a woman would be a wise move, if a woman was the traitor. He called a young woman, Ariel, in New York and told her to meet him in Washington. Her file showed she was reliable, didn't rattle easily, could handle a pistol and would follow instructions to the letter.

Simon knew virtually nothing about security issues. Dakar would be solely in charge of the location and security of the exchange. He received instructions from his superiors a day after he arrived. He was to contact the head of the FBI. Mossad's information was, he was out of favor with the president. It was the best way to handle the situation. The FBI was the agency responsible for domestic issues. The argument could also be made that such sensitive information could only have come from someone who was part of the president's innermost circle. Therefore, the FBI should not share any information with other agencies. Although Allan Hoffman was Jewish that was purely happenstance. There was no way he was a friend of Israel's. He was an American through and through. Israel also had to convince the director they were sincere. Simon was to be forthright in some of the details of how Israel was first contacted and the unusual circumstances of the payment demanded: pounds of gold, rather than a set dollar amount, and being deliberately obtuse about the rest. He should contact the FBI director in a semi-official way, two days prior to the exchange.

As instructed by Simon, Dakar and Mick docked at a small marina in Colonial Beach. Dakar was very anxious to see Teddy and he called him from a pay phone a few moments after they tied up.

Dakar's first words were, "I'm home, honey. Come and get me."

Teddy laughed and replied, "OK, but you may not like the accommodations much." Annie and Matt had agreed to put Dakar and Mick up for a few days.

Matt arrived at the marina with the large van, and loaded Dakar and Mick into the van for the short trip to the farm. Teddy and Rosie were waiting for Dakar when he stepped out of the van. Immediately he was crushed by the great arms of Teddy wrapped around him. He felt so happy to see his friend again and tears immediately welled up in his eyes. Rosie gave him a kiss and hug also. They marched straight into the house where Annie and Rosie had a hot lunch ready for them all.

Dakar and Teddy spent hours telling each other their adventures. At times Dakar was in tears describing the loss of Jennet at sea. Dakar's heart was heavy with worry for Teddy who had almost been captured and killed. Teddy didn't tell Dakar, Jenn had e-mailed him because she had asked him not to and it wasn't the time to burden his friend with the information. Perhaps later when things were closer to normal.

Rosie watched the two of them laughing, talking and marveled at the depth of the friendship the two had. Teddy was overjoyed seeing his friend. It was not jealousy or envy. She knew Teddy loved her deeply. She was touched by the capacity for love Teddy had. It was, she realized, what had attracted her to him and him to her.

Matt had managed to dig out a bottle of scotch, which he and Mick were busy enjoying. Later that evening the three of them retired to the barn to discuss tomorrow's activities. Teddy was to stay put at the farm. It was too dangerous to risk him leaving. Simon had arranged for a panel van to be picked up by Dakar in nearby Fredericksburg the next day. It contained the weapons they would use and would be the means to transport the gold to the exchange. The UZIs were great and Dakar loved the submachine gun as a toy, but they lacked punch. Dakar had asked for and gotten some different fire power and the grenades for good measure.

Tomorrow they would scout out the three locations Dakar had chosen for the exchange and decide on one. The last thing they would do tomorrow is unbolt the stanchion from the deck of the Jenn, unscrew the plug from the bottom and load the gold into the van. They would return directly to the farm—no cruising the streets armed to the teeth with five hundred pounds of gold in the back.

The sleeping accommodations were in the barn on a couple of cots in the back of Matt's office. It was warm. The wood stove chugged away efficiently and Dakar had not forgotten how to keep the stove stoked. Dakar usually slept soundly, but Mick lay on his back. The scotch made him snore loudly, great snorts punctuated by a short period of silence and then the snorts again. Dakar had to wake him and tell him to roll over on his side. Mick told him to fuck off for waking him up.

The next day, while Dakar and Mick scouted locations, the Israeli ambassador contacted the director of the FBI, requesting a meeting with him ASAP regarding a domestic matter of great importance to the United States. The director called the ambassador and was given instructions to meet Simon in the Great Hall, at the Library of Congress at 2:00 PM. Simon knew the director would be accompanied by half a dozen or more FBI agents, and he would be under surveillance the entire time. He would never get to talk with the director one-on-one without surveillance.

Simon recognized the director the moment he entered. He looked like a FBI agent, complete with the long overcoat. He approached him, stuck out his hand, which the director refused to take and said, "Hello, Director Hoffman. I am Simon. We must talk in private. Please, sit with me on the bench." As Simon pointed to an austere wooden thing against the wall. Hoffman surveyed the area quickly for potential threats and motioned his personal body guard to step away. The recording microphone he wore would remain turned on.

Simon launched into his spiel immediately, when the director was seated. "Some weeks ago, my government was contacted by…" The enormity of what Simon told him shocked and excited the director. He understood immediately what it meant and also knew it might be his ticket to keep his job. A terrorist and spy within the president's innermost circle of advisors would spell the end for the president politically.

Director Hoffman was blunt. "What do you want from me?"

Simon said, "This is not good for our country or yours. We want nothing, sir, absolutely nothing. You give me your personal cell phone number and I will send to you the name and the proof. This will happen within one week. I am sure this person would find out if you do not keep this secret. It is best to be cautious, but I think you know this."

Hoffman pondered for a moment and printed his cell phone number on a slip of paper he handed to Simon. The director rose and exited the building without looking back at Simon. When he reached his personal bodyguard, his orders were swift: "Abandon the operation to follow or trace this man. Bring all the information and personnel involved in monitoring, or with knowledge of this meeting, to my office immediately."

When the agents were assembled in his office, his orders were clear. "We have a direct threat to our national security and it is probable it originated in the White House. You are all forbidden to speak of my meeting today or anything leading up to it, until further instructed. This operation will be in-house and under no circumstances are you to contact any other federal agency about the events that took place today. This is very serious business. Keep your mouths shut. Treason at the highest levels is likely." As the agents left his office, his thoughts raced. *How stupid this person must have been to precipitate such a crisis and dangerous if they were that stupid.*

The FBI was one of the tightest knit, loyal agencies in the country, but not leak proof. The agent in charge of FBI liaison with Homeland Security picked up the phone and called his counterpart at Homeland Security with a single sentence. "The director had a secret meeting with someone from the Israeli embassy today."

CHAPTER 34

Treason

Lincoln Lancaster was delighted to hear that Hoffman had a meeting with the Israelis. He would be able to use this to his advantage. Lancaster would orchestrate the information to make it look like the Jews had set off the bombs and then attempted to attribute it to white supremacists or hired them directly. The blame would fall on Israel, Hoffman, and the Jewish bankers, who controlled everything.

There were only a few more tasks to complete and he could be on his way safely out of the country. He would resign in a week, a national hero for having uncovered the Jewish conspiracy against the Free World. With the type of high profile he would have nationally, he could run for president in the near future. Maybe not next term, but perhaps the one after. He would cite health reasons for his decision. Some of the gold would remain hidden for a rainy day. He would spend a few years somewhere warm and white. Argentina was his first choice. They spoke Spanish, unfortunately, but many

Argentineans were very light skinned. Then return to the States after things calmed down in a few years and live in luxury, telling everyone he made his fortune in Argentina buying and selling gold to wealthy Argentineans. It was all working out very well and now he had a Jewish scapegoat. He would tell President Haines, after he had the gold, that Hoffman knew about the leak and did not inform the president, the CIA or Homeland Security about this information and his meeting with the man from the Israeli embassy. It all fit perfectly. If Hoffman's actions didn't implicate him directly, they would cast a pallor over his reputation, at the least. He wouldn't last long at the director's job, in any event.

First things first—get the gold. Then erase any ties to himself by blaming the Jews. Lastly push the price of gold to even greater heights. In three days his gold would be delivered. He could get rid of his scapegoat at the exchange and tie her in as the Jew's mole, in the White House. He would say he suspected her and had her followed. He had three teams of men he had personally hired and could trust to follow all of his instructions implicitly. One team was in Montana now, firing multiple mortar rounds into the Malmstrom military base, an attack he would make sure was blamed on the Montana militia. Lancaster would then urge the president to use the threat of force against the renegade National Guard in Montana, by surrounding their base with the troops that had returned from Iraq and move other army units into Helena, the state capital. The argument that Governor Maier had lost control of the Montana militia and the safety of America's nuclear weapons was paramount to all other considerations. Hell, he could write that speech himself. It would be very convincing to the American people. His other two teams would accompany him to the gold exchange; a small amount of the gold would be left with the dead and incriminating secret information from the White House.

Matt dropped Dakar and Mick in Fredericksburg to pick up the small panel van that was decorated with the name Sure-way Plumbing and contained assorted plumbing tools and materials. A couple of dirty work jackets completed their cover. The weapons were stored in a large cardboard box that used to hold a bathtub. They scouted the three spots that they had selected from Google Earth as candidates for the exchange to take place. Under a chilly gray sky punctuated with periods of light rain, they drove from place to place, looking at access routes, proximity to major roads, the best place for the exchange to happen, concealment locations and how close to other buildings the exchange location would be.

Dakar decided, and Mick agreed, that Caledon Natural Area State Park was the best choice. It was some distance from the main road, offered a single access point (road in) and good cover for Teddy, Mick and Dakar. There were some buildings fairly close and it would be noisy if a firefight erupted, but the dense woods would absorb all the errant rounds. Their fallback exit would be "Jenn" tied up just off Somerset Beach, fifteen miles from where she was now berthed. The dinghy would be waiting on the beach to take them out to the Jenn, if need be.

Another question occurred to Dakar—whether to show force or remain concealed. Three heavily armed men would be a mighty big deterrent to the use of violence. On the other hand if the informant came alone, he or she might be frightened by their presence. They opted for concealment to start with and a show of force if more than one person showed up at the exchange.

Dakar phoned Simon with the location for the exchange. Simon would call the woman and tell her to be ready in two days at 15:00 to leave Washington. He would call her with directions to the exchange location while she was en route. She was to come alone with the information. When she got close Simon would call Dakar on another phone and the two could direct her to the exchange location.

Finally, they drove to the Jenn. No one was out and about in the dreary weather. Simon had thought ahead and there were four empty metal tool boxes to store the gold in and a small dolly to move the boxes with. Dakar and Mick set about unbolting the stanchion from the deck, tipped it slightly, and removed the threaded plug in the bottom. Out spilled the gold pieces onto the deck. There were eight thousand of them and it took some time to transfer all of them to the boxes.

Mick started up, "Lad, it is fucking cold enough for this sort of work. Do ya think we deserve a small bonus?"

Dakar answered, "Greedy fucker. How much money do you need?" An hour later they were on their way.

Dakar and Mick parked the panel van in the yard at Annie and Matt's. They took the weapons into the barn to check their condition. Matt was busy turning furniture legs on the lathe. Wood shavings blanketed the floor as he expertly worked the chisel up and down the length of the leg. Teddy was mesmerized by the process of turning a block of wood into something so beautiful. Matt walked over to Dakar and Mick. He was shaken and blunt. "You can't bring guns into our home or on our property."

Dakar turned to Matt and said, "I'm so sorry, Matt. We'll take them somewhere else." He was embarrassed at having upset his host and thought, *What an idiot. I should have known.* Mick and Dakar drove back to the sailboat, and stowed them below deck. Jenn was going to the party, too, and it would be safer transporting the weapons by boat than in the van. The gold would remain safely in their possession. The next day Dakar and Mick returned to the boat and checked the weapons. Teddy would have to be shown on the day of the exchange what weapon he would be using.

Two days later, Simon called the woman at 15:00, telling her to head south on I-95. He was careful to remove his battery after each use and change locations for each call. Lancaster let Colonel Bernice Guay in on the whole plan he had devised in the gold for information Israel deal, except for the fact that he was the real informant. He told her the traitor had already been arrested. The Bitch was proud to think she was part of the operation to expose Israel for spying on America and being behind the terrorist attacks. She was shocked to learn that the Jewish director of the FBI had met with someone from the Israeli embassy and might be involved. Lincoln Lancaster had been profuse in his praise for her, for a job well done. Lancaster let her know he was stepping down soon and recommending her for his job to the president. It was to be a Homeland Security operation solely, no air cover, no other agencies involved. She had in her possession a small thumb drive containing information on all proposed US foreign policy initiatives in the Middle East that she was to exchange for gold.

Thirty minutes into the trip her phone rang again. She was to turn east at the Warrenton Road exit into Fredericksburg and then east again on 218. One three man team was with her in the blacked out SUV. Another team in a non-descript SUV followed a mile back, tracking her.

Lincoln Lancaster traveled with them, telling both teams that Colonel Guay was a suspected traitor, with links to Israel, who was going to pick up her payoff for sensitive government information. The trap was set and within a few hours he would have five hundred pounds of gold in his possession, less the small amount he would leave on the scene as evidence of her guilt. No telling where the price of gold would wind up, with the situation in Montana being so volatile and the Jews being implicated in the terror attacks. Maybe the US would nuke the motherfuckers. That would be sweet.

Lincoln Lancaster was now in control. The president was deferring to his opinion and judgment almost to the exclusion of anyone else. The secretary of state had lost touch with reality and was getting more rabid in his assertions that the president attack immediately in the west, before the Western Coalition had a chance to arm themselves even more. Against that backdrop Lancaster's suggestions appeared reasoned and reasonable.

President Haines's address to the nation about the attack on the Malmstrom Air Force base was very presidential. Haines thought his ability to handle these tough situations for the good of the nation would be seen by all, in the near future, as an act of courage and faith in the American way. He was saving the country from itself.

The President started, "The evidence is now clear that radical elements in the Montana militia were responsible for the recent attack on Malmstrom Air Force Base. America's nuclear deterrent is under threat and the threat to the American people is too great to allow further attacks to take place. Therefore, I am asking Governor Maier of Montana to assist his country in tracking down the individuals responsible for these attacks, order the National Guard in Montana to follow federal orders to aid in this effort, and order the Montana militia to stand down and disband. This cannot wait. Too much is at stake. At noon in three days time I will order units of our military forces to enter Helena, restore the rule of law and find those members of the Montana militia that were responsible for the attack..." There was more, all of it ominous and threatening. There was also the suggestion that the governor should resign for letting the situation deteriorate to this point.

Ariel, the young Mossad agent, who would conduct the exchange for Israel, had arrived two hours early. She met up with Mick and Teddy in Fredericksburg and joined them in the van. She was a tall, raven haired beauty, with a shapely figure that Mick could not resist ogling, until Teddy told him to put his tongue back in his mouth. Ariel, Dakar, Mick and Teddy had been in position for thirty minutes prior to Simon placing the original call to the woman. Dakar had taken the sailboat under power to the beach at the park and gone ashore in the dinghy with the weapons. The dinghy was pulled up into the bush and covered with some brush. They all had their very own UZI and three grenades each. Mick was given the light tripod mounted machine gun; Teddy opted for his favorite weapon—a pump, twelve gauge shotgun. Dakar had his rifle with scope, the weapon he knew so well for so many years. Ariel carried a small pistol in her pocket; otherwise, she looked completely harmless.

Their tactical position was great. The beach was fifty yards behind them, making it difficult for anyone to get in back of them. Their fields of fire overlapped so that one could cover any of the others. The trees on either side of the meeting place made it a natural funnel. For effect the gold would be placed on the ground in front of the back doors of the van. A camouflaged video camera to the left was focused and would be recording the who, what, when and how, of the whole thing. Mick would be set up inside the van with the light machine gun for effect, if any heavies showed up at the exchange.

Ariel was to dive to the ground in the event any shooting started. Dakar hoped that if Ariel opened, or Mick pushed open, the back doors of the van the sight of the machine gun would be enough to deter anyone. Teddy was situated about thirty yards to the right side of the van in the woods. The heavy artillery with the twelve gauge shotgun. Even with body armor on, a shotgun blast at close range would knock any man down. Dakar was on the left perched a small rise about forty yards from Ariel. This was supposed to be a peaceful exchange, but his intuition told him that was not fucking likely. *Damn, too late to back out now,* he thought. All wore small radio transmitters and ear pieces.

Simon and Dakar directed the first SUV with The Bitch in it down the isolated road to the park. Through his scope Dakar could see there were three other people in the vehicle and told Simon. Simon asked the woman why she did not come alone. Her reply was the men would stay at the SUV provided there were no problems. He ordered her to stop one hundred yards from the van and proceed on foot to meet Ariel, who was standing at the back of the van. Dakar had Ariel open the back door of the van to show Mick's position and his toy. The men who were at the SUV immediately focused their attention and weapons on Mick. The Bitch walked forward to meet Ariel. Teddy could plainly see who it was and asked Dakar if he could kill her now, knowing full well that was not possible.

The usual pleasantries were exchanged, Ariel pointed out to her that men were also located to her left and right. She showed The Bitch the gold in the tool boxes, and the colonel passed the memory stick to Ariel, who plugged it into her netbook for a quick look at the goods. Ariel informed Dakar that the goods appeared to be genuine and he relayed that to Simon.

The colonel motioned two of the three men to come forward and help with moving the gold using the dolly next to the tool boxes. As the two men loaded the boxes onto the hand cart the other SUV pulled up behind the first. Everyone saw the second one arrive. What they did not expect was the sudden gunfire from the four men who poured out of the vehicle. Bernice Guay recognized Lancaster, but could not figure out why everyone was firing, especially given the fact she was in the line of fire. She dove to the ground and Ariel did the same. Ariel pulled her small sidearm and returned fire in the direction of the just arrived SUV. Mick wasted no time in cutting down the two men, coming to load the gold, who had raised their weapons to shoot at him. Then he shot at the five men clustered around the SUV. One was trying to run to the right to outflank their position and Mick managed to mow him down before being hit himself by the fusillade from the men at the second van.

Dakar's attention was on the four men left at the second SUV. The Bitch had pulled her weapon and shot Ariel in the head. Ariel never saw it coming. Teddy rushed at her in a rage, covering the one hundred or so feet screaming at her and shooting his shotgun until one blast tore into her body and she lay limp. Crazy with rage he picked up her lifeless body and smashed her down across his knee breaking her in two so that her body was now like a rag doll. Then he was cut down in a hail of gunfire from the SUV.

Dakar had managed to take out one of the shooters at the SUV. He was the only threat left and they started shooting in his direction, forcing him to keep his head down for a moment. During that time two of the men snuck away to the left and into the bush to outflank him. The other asshole in the SUV would have to wait while he took care of the two who had slipped into the bush. He desperately wanted to go to Teddy, Mick and Ariel to check on their condition. He thought he saw Teddy moving as he lay on the ground.

Dakar backed away down the small rise and deeper into the tangle of leafless brush and trees in the exact opposite direction from all the action. He ran for sixty yards before he halted. He turned back towards the direction of the SUV and slowly crept forward, looking for the two men. He hoped they were at that moment approaching his former position. He could hear Teddy's raspy breathing and moaning in his earpiece, and his desire to get to his friend, made him for the first time frantic and off his game.

Dakar succeeded in outflanking the men who were creeping up on his previous position and opened fire with the UZI dropping one with the first burst before a bullet caught him in the stomach. It hurt like hell. If this was what it felt like to be seriously wounded, he would just as soon pass on the whole experience. His second burst tore the shooter's face apart. With only one man left, he hoped the asshole had enough sense to clear out as he struggled back to Teddy.

As he cleared the rise, he saw the last man raise his Glock and put a single bullet into Teddy. Dakar fired the remains of his clip into the man and he fell over on top of Teddy.

He walked over and dragged the man off Teddy, noting that it was Lincoln Lancaster, the head of Homeland Security. Teddy was dead. He knew it, but could not believe it. He set about checking on the condition of Ariel. She was dead from a head shot and Mick had died from multiple wounds. In an increasing state of rage and grief, he took out his 45 and killed The Bitch and Lancaster again.

His mission was almost complete. He took a picture on his cell phone of the dead Lincoln Lancaster and sent it to Simon along with the message, "They are dead. They are all dead." The light was fading fast and he could hear the sirens that were headed in his direction. What would he tell Rosie? What would he do? They were gone, all gone: his Dad, Jenn, Jennet, Teddy, everyone he had ever loved or had loved him was gone. He hurt, he hurt a lot, and there was blood everywhere from the wound in his stomach.

It was time. Dakar put the barrel of his handgun in his mouth.

CHAPTER 35

Salvation

The world held its breath, as the United States edged to the brink of a civil war. That surely would be the downfall of everyone, plunging the globe into decades of economic ruin. The declaration from President Haines that the National Guard in Montana stand down and once again take direction from the federal government, that the army was to move into Helena, and the suggestion the governor resign within two days, put fear into the hearts of many all over the globe.

Simon forwarded the picture of the dead Lincoln Lancaster and his location to the FBI director. A team of FBI agents arrived on the scene, displaced the local police and secured the evidence, including the digital video record of the whole mess. There were a lot of dead bodies to clean up: two of Lancaster's men survived. Both were seriously injured. The FBI would use their stories to fill in the blanks. Hoffman had the information in the hands of the Freedom America Committee within an hour.

The members of the Freedom America Committee reckoned that it was now or never. The evidence was clear. Lincoln Lancaster had orchestrated the bombings on the East and West coasts. The president would sooner or later be ousted for his part in appointing Lancaster to the job. The problem was, later was too late; if the president ordered the army to confront the National Guard and Montana Militia, there would be a blood bath which would plunge the country into civil war. Their pleas and evidence of complicity would fall on deaf ears. Minds would be occupied with war, not peace. Congress and the Senate would fragment, and the support they now had would evaporate. Freedom America had to act now. The vice president offered to issue a televised appeal to the American people—their last and only option, and a gamble of the greatest magnitude.

Her address to the nation started thus, "To the citizens of this great country, for all of you watching a national tragedy about to unfold. I ask you to join with me and stop this needless violence, which is tearing the nation apart. Only we can stop this madness. We have all been victims of a terrible crime. Lincoln Lancaster, the secretary of Homeland Security, orchestrated the terrorist bombings that precipitated the economic ruin we face. I am asking all of you to stop what you are doing and join with me in two days, at noon on Thursday, and march to your town halls, federal buildings, state capitol buildings, wherever governments do business and let the president know we will not tolerate any more violence against the citizens of our nation. President Haines has lost touch with the American people and cannot continue to govern this country as if he were a king."

She paused for a moment to let the scope of what she said sink in and continued. "I and the majority of representatives in Congress and the Senate have joined together to demand the president take the following actions immediately. Remove the army from Montana and all other affected states to their barracks and homes where they belong. Repeal martial law immediately. Release the thousands of men and women being held in federal concentration camps unjustly under martial law or held under mental health laws. Lift censorship completely. Disband the Presidential Patriotic Force. Lastly we call upon the president to resign, or face impeachment and criminal charges."

She paused again. "We offer the American people hope. We have a plan, a comprehensive economic plan, to put America back on its feet again, to get our economy moving again. It is not perfect, but it will work with your support. The time for apathy will only end when the American people demand it. Thursday at noon we march for our freedom." With the short video there was a longer news release that included an overview of Marguerite's Economic Renewal Plan in detail as endorsed by the majority of the House and Senate.

The short clip containing Vice President Emily Johnson's words was remarkable, electrifying and broadcast to the nation over all the major networks, except Fox whose editors had deemed it too inflammatory to be aired, opting instead to edit the clip. This distorted the vice president's words and made it appear as if she were inciting violence and promoting some sort of socialist economic agenda. The other networks carried the message verbatim, and repeated it over and over again throughout the evening. No American was unaware of what she said. Discussions of the pros and cons of The Economic Renewal Plan were presented in depth. Corporate America set about getting their "neutral experts" to comment on how ill advised, unworkable and unnecessary the Plan was, and how President Haines was standing up for the country and liberty.

President Haines was angry that he had been betrayed by his running mate. He had no knowledge of Lincoln Lancaster's death. Lancaster was missing—that was true—but he suspected he was the victim of some sort of plot to overthrow the government and his presidency. When FBI Director Allan Hoffman had asked to see the president he had turned him down. Hoffman would obviously present some sort of outrageous lie about Lancaster. A coup was underway and he would not allow America's democracy to be subverted by it. He would preempt the vice president and her coconspirators. He ordered the Joint Chiefs to proceed with the deployment of military units to Helena a day early, before the planned protest was to begin. He was absolutely sure the National Guard and Montana Militia would stand down when faced with an overwhelming number of battle-hardened, professional soldiers. When they did, he would be proved right in the eyes of the American people. Congress and the Senate would shift their support back to a victorious president. He would deal with that bitch Johnson in a few days and demand she resign.

Even if fighting did break out, it would be over very quickly and he could claim victory again. He was positive it was a win-win situation for him. The country would be too preoccupied with the fighting, if it started, to take part in any sort of protest. He would issue a plea to the American people to remain calm, go about their daily lives and stay home for the next forty-eight hours.

The president's and vice president's speeches were repeated back to back many times on all the major networks over the next day. The vice president was in hiding along with her family. Members of the Congress and Senate worked feverishly to cobble together some sort of compromise that would delay any military action. It was to no avail. The president had his mind made up. The majority of the Joint Chiefs were against any military action, but would do as their commander in chief ordered. The secretary of state was still pushing for coordinated military action across the western states.

Captain Michael Murphy received orders at 22:00 that he, his soldiers and transport units were to be combat ready at 08:00 the next morning. Murph had twenty MRAPs at his disposal. The rest of the troops would travel in un-armored Humvees and trucks to where ever they were ordered. It looked like that would be Helena. He was not looking forward to a trip into downtown Helena, and neither were the women and men he commanded. The people in Montana were Americans. They would fight; he knew he would if he were in their position and many would die on both sides. This was wrong, so wrong.

News of the preemptive military action took the vice president, Uncle Billy and the rest of committee by surprise. The day and time of protest could not be changed. They were powerless in the face of this new tactic by President Haines. However, the strength of the response to the march was a pleasant surprise. Facebook, Twitter and e-mails were filled with positive comments. "I'll be there with my kids," wrote one mother. "Time to stand and be seen." "This cannot be allowed to happen." And like comments filled the Internet. No one was sure what would happen on Thursday, if there were war.

Montana and the Western Coalition states prepared to do battle. The original four states of the Western Coalition had grown to twelve. Granted, population-wise, they were all small in comparison to the country as a whole, but the area they encompassed was most of the western United States with the notable exception of California. The militias had grown in size, to number almost two million men and women. Fighting would doubtless double that number. They were in agreement. An attack against one would be an attack against all. Once again the president had seriously underestimated the strength of the Americans he faced.

At 08:00, Murph stood ready with his company of one hundred and five soldiers along with four thousand others, ready to seize control of Helena and put an end, as the president was saying, to the terrorist attacks against America's nuclear forces.

Lt. General Imhoff, the overall commander of the assault on Helena, faced a difficult choice. She could do as she was ordered and send Americans to battle their countrymen, or disobey her orders and face a court martial for doing so. She chose the time to end her military career wisely. Perhaps she could delay the civil war by a day. She waited until the last moment to issue the order to stand down and return to barracks. The troops were relieved and wasted no time getting away from the assembly point and to their temporary quarters. It was half an hour before the news that she had ordered the stand-down reached Washington. She was under no illusions. She would be arrested shortly, relieved of command, court-martialed and one of her more ambitious subordinates would take over and be ordered to continue the operation.

Because of the delay, the marine division surrounding the National Guard base was ordered to hold position. It was crucial that all the units act in a coordinated manner. It was 13:00 before Murph and the rest of the troops were assembled again and ready to move. They hit the road at 13:20. The attacking force was to be separated into different columns and enter the city at four points.

It was a bitterly cold, clear, windy day in Helena and not unusual for the time of year. Many of the men and women of Montana, young and old, sat huddled behind whatever shelter they could find to block the roads into the capital. Many armed with hunting rifles and shotguns. Heavy machinery and any materials at hand were pulled onto the highways for roadblocks. They stood shoulder to shoulder with members of the National Guard. They had little in the way of heavy weapons to stop the heavily armored vehicles they would soon be facing. Rumor had it that a large force of tanks, MRAPS and Strykers would lead the assault. The governor issued a last message to the people of Montana to remain firm in their commitment and faith.

Helena was awash with media also. Live feeds to all the major networks showed the major highways and barricades at the main entrances to the city. At 1:30 the nation and good folks of Helena were told the army was on its way. One young man and woman with their two young children were being interviewed by a reporter, as they walked towards the barricades on the outskirts of the city.

The reporter asked, "Where are you going? You know the army is coming."

The woman answered first, "We will all be in danger, if this isn't stopped and stopped now. We are not going to stand by and watch so many people die for nothing. My family and I are determined that we will stand between the army and our friends and neighbors." The man turned to the reporter and added as they left, "My family and I chose life and freedom. We are prepared to pay the price demanded to stand." The defenders behind the barricades were stunned by the words of the couple and parted to let them through to face the oncoming storm. The citizens of Helena witnessed the simple act of courage on television the family made. The army would arrive in a few hours at most. The people of Helena left their homes in the thousands for the barricades.

Captain Michael Murphy approached the outskirts of Helena and was met by the sight of three thousand unarmed men, women and children standing on the highway in the freezing cold. Everywhere in America, TV sets were on and tuned in to the drama of a nation about to consume itself in violence. Murph pulled his lead MRAP to a stop one hundred feet in front of the people who shouted at them. The scene looked surreal, as four of the giant MRAPS stood lined up abreast of each other in front of the people whose arms were locked and who now stood defiantly looking death in the eye. The radio crackled with commanders at the other assault points. They all faced thousands of people blocking the road.

Murph looked out at the group and said simply, "Fuck this" into his headset. He exited the vehicle and walked unarmed toward the group congregated on the highway. When he reached the front of the group he took off his helmet, turned around and sat on the ground facing his troops. A roar went up from the crowd as another American joined them. This time, one that was in uniform. Soon he was joined by others. Staff Sergeant Simmons, Laskins and Sanchez. In ten minutes, there were two hundred unarmed soldiers sitting in the front row. Even if they wanted to, the vehicles in the back could not get through. Most of the MRAPS in the front had been abandoned by their crews. The radio buzzed with orders to move forward; the orders were all disobeyed as Americans refused to fire on their countrymen. For an hour they sat with the freezing wind biting into the exposed skin of soldier and civilian alike, before Murph got up and said, "Let's go home." The nation breathed a sigh of relief, as the army turned around and headed back to their base.

The Joint Chiefs abandoned any thought that military force was going to work. They reported to the president that he better find another way out of the mess the county was in because the military forces of the United States were not going to fire upon their own citizens. The president was shaken and asked about the possibility of using the Marines or other units who would be more likely to carry out his orders. At that point, several of the Joint Chiefs let it be known that they would refuse to give such an order. Haines reluctantly agreed to have the troops stand down and return to base. He now thought he might be able to appear as a conciliatory president if he offered to delay military action and hold talks with the rebel states about lifting martial law. Tomorrow afternoon he would address the nation and propose exactly that.

That evening the nation and news were filled with the images of what had transpired in Helena, Montana. Americans were eager to be part of the movement. At noon the next day, they left their homes in droves, in the millions. One hundred million Americans took part in the marches. Every city, town or village was filled with people on the street, marching towards town halls, federal buildings, any place the government was. Police officers and federal employees joined their colleagues, friends and neighbors in many communities. Those who couldn't march stopped what they were doing, in silent support of those who marched. A few acts of violence occurred, but largely the crowds were peaceful. The Presidential Patriotic Force stayed home that day.

Vice President Emily Johnson and Uncle Billy, along with hundreds of members of Congress and the Senate, marched to the White House together in a group that exceeded one million people. President Haines resigned that afternoon and President Johnson took the oath of office with a pledge to the American people to devote the next three years of her term to the American people and not to seek reelection.

A unity government of Democrats and Republicans took over the job of piecing the country back together. Using The Coutts Plan and the Braxton Predictive, as they came to be known, the economy recovered over the span of three years. The Plan had to be modified and changed as the months went by. Regulations governing corporate conduct and executive remuneration brought fairness to the stock market and restored a great deal of confidence to the American people and the world as a whole. Several corporate officers of pharmaceutical companies were tried and imprisoned for withholding wonder drugs that cured some types of cancers as were ten oil company executives for suppressing the release and development of new fuel saving and battery technologies. America joined the rest of the free world with a public health care system. The work Teddy and Marguerite did should have won them a Nobel Prize in economics had they not died. The Coutts Plan and Braxton Predictive were talked about for years to come by economists and the common man the world over. Dakar received no international acclaim or awards. He was remembered by the few people whose lives he had touched.

* * *

It was June before the snow was gone in the high mountains. June before Rosie and Jenn could take Dakar and Teddy home. The ice had barely gone from the lake; the air was fresh with the smell of new growth and the aroma of pine. The snowy tips of the peaks reflected the late afternoon sun, in brilliant contrast to the lengthening shadows in the valley. The cabin was still in need of repair and exactly the way Dakar and Teddy liked it. The wood stove still worked and the bench on the porch was always inviting after a long day of hiking or fishing together.

And so it was, Rosie and Jenn brought their love for Teddy and Dakar, along with their ashes to rest in their place of wonder and beauty. Beside the lake, Rosie and Jenn emptied their ashes and they mingled together, some drifting into the air, some floating on the lake or blanketing the reeds at the water's edge.

They turned and walked back to the cabin. Rosie thought about the rack and ruin that had been brought into their lives, taken away Teddy and all the promise of a life well lived together. Brought the country and world so much pain and years of hardship to come and for what—greed and the lust for power of a few men? Rosie and Jenn cried and sobbed their tears of sorrow and love once again.

Clinging to each other was all they had left; that and the memory of their lost loves.

Jenn never got to see or talk with Dakar again, never got to tell him that she knew he always loved her, or that from deep within she had always loved him. It was late and the sun was setting fast. Jenn turned to look at her son, who was still at the water's edge peering out into the lake in the hopes of seeing a fish or frog and wondering what the ashes were about.

Jenn called to him, "Come on, Dakar. It's time to go home."

Made in the USA
Middletown, DE
25 August 2019